IMAGE
OF
EVIL

Also by William Beechcroft:

POSITION OF ULTIMATE TRUST

IMAGE
OF
EVIL

William Beechcroft

DODD, MEAD & COMPANY   NEW YORK

Published by Dodd, Mead & Company, Inc.
79 Madison Avenue, New York, N.Y. 10016

Distributed in Canada by
McClelland and Stewart Limited, Toronto

Manufactured in the United States of America

First Edition

LIBRARY OF CONGRESS CATALOGING IN PUBLICATION DATA

Beechcroft, William.
  Image of evil.

  I. Title.
PS3552.E32I4   1985   813'.54   84-18650
ISBN 0-396-08558-X

CHAPTER

1

THREE INITIALLY UNRELATED incidents took place in September and October. One involved Canadian apes. Another concerned the rapidly deteriorating health of a renegade Argentinian. The third incident took place in Marty Horn's backyard, so to speak.

He was unaware of that. He was unaware of all three incidents, though they were to have the potential of ending his life at age thirty-seven. He was thirty-seven now.

On September 18, a Friday blessed with a warm Maryland wind but cursed with the drizzle it carried, Marty poured himself the fifth cup of coffee in his eight-hour shift. From its continuous reheating on the coffee maker in the corner of his ground-level office, it tasted like swamp water. Coffee was a brief diversion from boredom, maybe even an addiction. Certainly not a pleasure coming out of this overused, undercleaned, impersonal brewing machine.

He dragged back to his mastic-topped, gray steel desk in front of the battery of seven-inch TV monitor screens and settled into his government-issue swivel chair. It squeaked. Chief of CIAS security, and he couldn't even get his damned

1

chair oiled without a half-ream of requisitions, all requiring approval by Carlisle.

Here it was again: end of the week melancholia. Friday was the final daytime escape from home, the last day of the weekly pretense that he was accomplishing something. Now would come two days back-to-back for Celia to strip him of whatever sense of worth he had left. Reveal him to himself as the ineffective ex-cop he was. Use the weekend to prove herself superior. How she loved to prove herself superior.

She didn't have to prove it to him. She was superior. No black viper coiled in her still pretty blond head.

That was how he had come to think of it. A snake. It feigned dormancy, but its flickering tongue gave it away. It waited for him to give up the effort to hold it back there; waited to spring loose and squirm madness through his brain. Sometimes he thought he could hear it, even feel it. A stirring of bloated, venomous horror.

His hand shook when he lifted the mug. Its printed-on cartoon of a droopy-winged bird was faded by daily washings, but the black lettering was still legible. *It's hard to fly like an eagle when you work with turkeys.* Abner Dortman, the night supervisor, had given him the mug three years ago, the Christmas after Marty had gotten here. It was meant to be a morale booster, but it cut the other way, too.

The snake was already in place by then, and Marty didn't know why. He didn't know then and he didn't know now. He wasn't sure he wanted to know. Would the knowledge kill the thing? Or would it be let loose to kill him? He was terrified of finding out. "Retrograde amnesia," the departmental psychiatrist had called it. "You're an interesting case, Horn. In the classic occurrence, we find the memory erased by something in the nature of a blow to the head. That is, the victim fails to recall the blow itself. In postincidental self-defense, the mind has obliterated recall of the trauma. In your own case, we do find evidence of a blow, but the CAT-scan has failed to reveal signs of deep-seated physical disturbance. It appears to be an incident of retrograde amnesia over a remarkably extended post-incident period."

Medical monga-monga, Marty had thought at the hearing. He knew only that from the moment he scrambled up the rotting steps of that South Chicago house to the instant of his coming back to consciousness in the howling ambulance, there was nothing. Twelve to fifteen minutes of his life had been obliterated. In their place was the black viper, the embodiment of something apparently so overwhelming that his brain would not allow it to be remembered.

The Chicago Police Department thought the ferret-faced, overconfident psychiatrist's singsong was more than textbook jargon. The blank faces of the review board called it duty-incurred disability. Disability! A small pension came with it, but so did getting fired.

If Precinct Captain Herman Ott hadn't had a friend, God knew what would have happened to Marty Horn. Ott knew people in medium-level federal places, and one aspect of Marty's difficulty turned out to be fortuitous: its timing. An obscure government-funded think tank in Maryland's Catoctin Mountains needed a chief of security quickly. Red tape was sundered, and Marty informed Celia that they were moving East. That was about the last assertive action she let him get away with. After their establishment in a rented house near Thurmont, she assumed command. He hated himself for letting her do it, but he was powerless against her newfound organizational abilities and assertiveness. "The front door needs weather-stripping, Marty. . . . We're going to Frederick tonight because I need a warmer sweater. . . . Get back outside and wipe your feet. . . . Yes, I do have to be on top; you know I can't come any other way. . . ."

Marty sighed, heaved to his feet and carried his half-full mug to the security office's single window. It looked out on the lawn of the rambling, two-story former private mansion that now was CIAS. Catoctin Institute for Advanced Sciences. Drizzle beaded the lawn's autumn-burnt zoysia, a soggy tan carpet for a hundred feet between the gracious stone mansion and the jarring functional brick of the lab building. Beyond the lab, the triple run of chain link gleamed in the fading afternoon. The fencing enclosed the entire seven-acre site, a devilish arrangement of parallel eight-foot-high runs, spaced ten feet apart. The outer fence was surmounted by four strands of military barbed wire on outward-facing struts at a forty-five degree angle. Similar barbed strands topped the inner fence, these on inward-tilted arms above each vertical pipe. Between these armored runs stood an innocent-looking barrier of chain link with no barbed strands.

Shortly after the fence had been put in place, an inquisitive raccoon had scaled the outer run, somehow worked through its barbed topping—thereby setting off the silent alarm system—then brushed the center fence. The raccoon's fur exploded like a flashbulb in the night. When the first security guard rushed to the site of the puzzling flash, he found only a little mound of black char between the center and outer fences. Marty had been chilled by the fact that no animal of any sort had ever again ventured near the compound. The encircling fences and the fact that every phone call in or out was recorded and filed were the two most depressing aspects of Marty's CIAS assignment.

He glanced at the big clock above the TV screen console. Dortman would be checking through the gate now. He walked back to his desk and stood behind the chair to watch on monitor 5 the night supervisor of security present his ID to the gate guard.

"Sergeant Dortman verified," the speaker over the monitor bank rattled. "Access permitted."

Marty reached across the desk to press the blue button in the row of buttons beneath the monitor display. The reinforced steel gate at the guard's booth swung open. Abner Dortman's little gray Honda rolled through. Marty took a last swallow of rank coffee, cold now, and walked across the hall to a small pantry to wash the mug. As he returned, he

4

heard the front entrance security officer greet Dortman, then he watched on monitor 6 as the green button beneath his thumb released the front door lock. It always shook Marty a little to hear Lydia Whimple's almost tender tone trying hard to make pompous securityese sound crisp.

"Take off, Chief," Abner sang out as he took the two foyer steps in one and strode down the hall. "It's the donut man!" He was one of those slender, whiplike guys who could eat and drink you under any table and not put on a pound doing it. "Home to your blonde, Marty. TGIF, right?"

He was a local who had put in his military years as a National Guard weekend warrior while he helped keep Thurmont cars running up and down the western Maryland mountains. He stayed at the garage part time even after the arrival of CIAS brought him the night supervisor's position. They wanted locals for permanent cadre if they could find enough who were qualified. Abner fitted in like a Marine in a parade. A 982 out of 1,000 on the Fort Meade rifle range. Only a little less in pistol—not with the hopelessly inaccurate Colt .45 automatic, but with a CIAS issue handcrafted version of the Smith & Wesson .44 Magnum Model 29.

"You still farting around with that crazy Cuban's Toyota?" Marty asked Dortman.

"Turned out some bigoted asshole poured a couple cups of sugar in the gas. Take me a week to clean the caramel out. He rented a Hertz in Hagerstown. Take care, it's pneumonia weather out there."

In the hall, Marty slowed deferentially to let Reifsnyder, the tallest and most human of the four current resident wizards cross in front of him with the briefest of nods. The residents were a remote lot, focused on their own worlds of electronics, light wave transmission, and God knew what other high-tech gobbledegook. Marty understood none of it.

He was glad he'd worn his jacket. The evening looked cold through the leaded glass panes of the ponderous entrance door. He nodded a good night at Officer Whimple. Hell of a name for a cop. He knew the guys inevitably called her

"Wimp." Not to that little round face, though, with its hard blue eyes and close-cropped straw hair.

"Good night, Chief." Her soft voice reached hard for officiousness. No love lost here. Marty paused until back in the security room Dortman pressed the front door release. He pulled the heavy door inward when the electronic lock buzzed. The place was tight as a prison.

In the blacktopped parking area west of the entrance, his Reliant started grouchily, then seemed as eager as he to get out of here. While he waited for Crawford, the main gate sentry, to signal Dortman back there in the security center to open the remote-controlled barrier, Marty adjusted the rearview mirror. He caught a glimpse of his eyes: sunken, tired, watery blue. The eyes of a washed-up cop marking time. At thirty-seven, you knew about how far you were going, and he'd already gotten here. Not far at all. Nowhere near the dream he'd had in the grime and slime along the Mekong. Nothing close to the supercop dreams of a gung-ho infantry lieutenant just out of stateside training. A volunteer like most of them over there.

Those had been some days. Race forward. Kill. Rush back high on adrenalin, then do it all over again. And over and over again, all the time thinking you were winning the war when back in some strategic planning center, just about everybody who wasn't ducking shrapnel knew you weren't. A cockamamie war in a cockamamie life. He'd thought he was winning a war in Chicago, too, but the cops with gold braid knew they were barely holding their own. Up the steps of that house he had run, winning the war with his .38. A laugh. He came out of there a broken man with a snake in his head.

At the end of the two-mile-long macadam entrance drive—with three pole-mounted security cameras monitoring its length—he waved at Joe Blanchard, the plainclothes guard in his little "Catoctin Tour Information" booth. Joe had maps and pamphlets, and he could lay out a nice auto tour for anyone who stopped to ask. He also had, beneath

6

his bulletproof glassed-in counter, a CIAS issue S & W .44 and an MBA Gyrojet pistol that fired five rocket-propelled armor-piercing projectiles capable of stopping any vehicle up to and including an armored truck. Joe was the first link in a security chain that stretched two miles from Route 550, then branched into the ring of electronics and steel around the CIAS compound.

Marty headed north and reached his little A-frame in eleven minutes. Half hidden in scrub pines a hundred feet back from the mountain road, the house had been built four years ago as a weekend hideaway for a Baltimore stockbroker. The broker had sold it when he moved his family to Florida after trying to cope with just one unpredictable western Maryland winter. CIAS had picked it up cheap. Marty and Celia hadn't chosen to live here; it was required. Going flat out, he could reach CIAS in less than seven minutes, even in the docile four-cylinder K-car.

He parked beside Celia's yellow Datsun in the port beneath the tentlike structure and clumped up the open steps to the porch. The front door squeaked as he swung it open. "I asked you to keep this door locked," he grumbled.

Celia looked up from the littered card table. She was off on another of her short-lived kicks, this one an attempt to compile some sort of cookbook.

"Who's going to bother anybody way out here?" Her voice was high-pitched and querulous. It matched her angular body. She was as tall as he, but he outweighed her by a good fifty-five pounds; too damned many pounds. That came of camping on your ass in front of a battery of TV screens and killing the hours with coffee and the donuts Dortman and the other night man left him. They were only a little stale by morning, a token offering from subordinates who honored him with leftover pastry instead of respect.

"You can't tell who might be driving along that road out there," he said as a matter of rote. They had this conversation a lot.

"Maybe a bushy-haired stranger would break the monotony." She rolled a file card out of her portable typewriter and sank back in her chair, her fingers drumming on the card table's plastic top.

He sniffed and smelled only the woodsy stuffiness of the house.

"There's nothing on the stove." She didn't miss much. "We're eating out. There's a new mall opening in Waynesboro. We'll eat there."

He cursed himself for it, but he said, "Okay. Sure."

They were back by eleven. The fast food had left him with a leaden feeling. Or was it the weather? The drizzle had thickened, and fog crept out of the woods. Ragged trails of it flared in the headlights as he turned into their gravel drive.

They hadn't talked much. They never did. When he came out of the bathroom after his shower, she was in bed, blankets to her chin, watching him. She said, "It's still early." That had become her code phrase. Not "let's make love," or "Honey, let's do it." They never used words of endearment. He might even have preferred a harsh but purposeful "let's screw, buster." But her bland "it's still early" somehow reduced it all to bloodless routine.

She left the light on. He slid in his side of the double bed and lay on his back. She was already naked under the blankets and sheet. With the confidence of long practice, Celia mounted him in an effortless sideways wriggle. Her small breasts flattened in his chest hair.

He wanted her but dreaded the instant of release. It was then that he felt he was powerless against the coiled serpent. It was then that he feared the suppressed memory of the hideous event so carefully closeted in a distant corner of his brain could burst forth and overwhelm him.

Yet he felt himself begin to swell against her. She was good at this. She could always bring him up, no matter how acute his fear.

"You're doing fine," she whispered, her long, white-blond hair framing her slim face above him. Her peculiar, pale gray eyes focused on his for only a moment, then they rolled

8

upward. The eyes closed, cornsilk lashes moist. No way out now. He always thought that. He could have rejected her and suffered through a weekend of silence, but that wasn't escape. He was irrevocably caught the instant she decided she wanted it.

He began to concentrate fiercely on the apex of the planked ceiling, the seam where the two sloping walls joined to form the ridge line of the A-frame. The room was tentlike. He'd lived in plenty of tents, on Alabama maneuvers then along the Mekong where his unit officially wasn't supposed to be. There were no records anywhere of the long sweats on that spongy bank, the destruction of infiltrating native dugouts riding low under ammo loads. Marty's team had used bazookas. Swish. . . . Bam! Debris pocked the sluggish river.

He twitched himself back to the bedroom, alarmed that she had made his mind drift. "Don't you dare, before me," she warned, misinterpreting.

His fingers splayed across her back. His body was responding, mechanism A-okay, reflexes all go. Only the mind did not compute, and somebody had assured him that the best part of this was in the mind.

She was happy in her work. A little hum; not a moaner, she hummed. Like a cook with things coming out right. Humming, for God's sake. She was a hummer, all right. She really had been one when he'd married her. Celia Gunnarsen, sweet Swede from Milwaukee. Swee—, mind drifting again, dammit! Her head dropped beside his. Breath raggedy. She flattened on him, shuddered, held her breath. Then: "Oh!" As if it was always a surprise.

He riveted his eyes on the fourth board from the ridge joint, right side. Now would come the terror. The board was shades paler than the rest of the dark ceiling planking. What in hell would possess a carpenter in his right mind to pick a mismatched board like that one and lift it in place up there?

Damn, woman. Oh, damn.

9

The board. One-by-four. Tongue-and-groove. Pine? No doubt.

His body was all hers now, sliding away from him fast. But the mind. Could he hold it to the pale board? Was he going to be able to—

"There!" Celia said victoriously. Bitch. Bitch!

He raced for the steps. His heavy cop's shoe crushed the first termite-riddled riser. He stumbled. His hand slammed the third step up, jolted him back in balance. He scrambled across the narrow porch. The door splintered away from his shoulder. Inside—

Where was it! His frantic eyes found the bleached-out plank again, fixed on it unblinking. Held it. Damned if it would get away again. But that didn't matter now. It was over. She was pulling off, crouching over him, forehead shiny. Mona Lisa smile. Did she know? Was this her dumb way of trying to tear him open, to let the serpent escape? Bed therapy?

He sat up, wrapped his arms around his knees. She looked as satisfied as a millionaire's mistress, but he knew this would hold her for three, four days at most. Then he'd have to fixate on the pale plank all over again.

"It's only eleven-twenty," she said from the bathroom. "I'm going down to watch TV."

Five minutes before, at the moment Celia had brought Marty to the jagged edge of sanity, the first of the three September-October incidents had taken place in Montreal.

CHAPTER
2

SWEETSTUFF STUDIED THE keyboard for fifty-eight seconds. Then precisely at 11:15 P.M., she reached with her right hand to tap, in rapid succession, the four coded buttons for "PLEASE I WANT KIWI."

Dr. Bela Csorna, his oversized, liquid coal eyes riveted on the female orangutan, felt electricity flash up his spine and burst across his shoulders. "My God," he said to the empty lab. "My God!"

There could be no mistake. He had selected the gangly uncoordinated animal specifically for her slowness to comprehend. "The dumbest ape I've ever seen mangle a banana," the lab animals' gangling custodian had marveled. "Why in hell do you want that idiot to replace a near-genius ape like Kong?"

Csorna had disregarded the mop-haired technician's bafflement. One did not explain to minions. And to be considered a bit irrational was even an asset: Csorna, the Hungarian emigré with—how would you say?—not all his paddles in the creek. A little bonkers, maybe. Interesting language, English. Flying out of Kapuvár eight years ago under the radar and barely over the barbed wire would make anybody a little—"Well, he's a nice enough chap," Csorna had overheard the laboratory facilities director say, "even if he's a bit out of it."

Perfect. The precise image Csorna had worked to achieve. Smart enough but bumping harmlessly along in his own skewed world. He knew, there were rumors that he'd had "something to do with surgery" back in Budapest. There was no need for McKenzie University Administration to know they had made lab facilities available to one of Hungary's most skilled neurosurgeons. He had come to Montreal with a $175,000 grant from the Hergenroeder Fund. That was credential enough for them.

No one, Csorna had reflected more than once, had ever worked harder for a grant than had he with dumpy affection-starved Emily Hergenroeder. He had sweat like a—how would you say?—son of a dog to find a foundation with money to burn, preferably in medical pursuits; a foundation headed by a frustrated middle-aged woman who thirsted for the kind of attention Csorna was prepared to lavish on her. After an embarrassing and abortive misalliance with an appealing but, as it turned out, sadly underfunded Philadelphia heiress named Krenchlow, he had found Emily Hergenroeder.

He had found her first in the annual Directory of Family-Held Foundations then in the files of the New York Public Library. Next came a face-to-face meeting at a reception he managed adroitly to crash in the Waldorf Astoria ballroom. Followed by a casual lunch at the Russian Tea Room, a lavish dinner at Lutéce, a less caloric but more intimate dinner at Roma di Notte. Then, sooner than he had planned, a flesh-to-ample-flesh exchange in her own Louis-something-or-other bed. The bed creaked. For what he was after, it could have played the Hungarian Rhapsody in ragtime, and he still could have delivered. He delivered a lot over the next several months, then Emily delivered the so lovely grant. "For neurological experimentation in the area of behavior

12

analysis." That was how he asked her to word the transmittal letter. Impressively vague. They liked it at McKenzie. Eternally overshadowed by prestigious McGill, they probably would have liked anything that arrived unbidden with a six-figure check attached.

The transmittal letter said nothing about mouse brains, but those were what Csorna started with. He would have preferred rats, but there was a waiting list. His slender fingers were nimble enough, but even a tiny tremor was magnified to devastating proportions in basal ganglia that would have fit inside a lentil. The early failures made him wonder whether his unique theory was no more than intellectual meringue.

Of the fourteen brown field mice, one was an IQ standout. He named it Magyar. The mouse learned the maze in one quarter of the time it took the next best performer to find her way without hesitation to the food pellets. Magyar mastered the more complex string-and-ladder climb in one third of the time of his closest competitor.

At the nether end of the intelligence scale was Breshnev, a chunky little bumbler who couldn't find his way through the maze even by unlimited trial and error.

With a touch of regret, Csorna conducted the twin operations at the beginning of the third week. Magyar died on the tray. Breshnev recovered, but the inserts—or some tiny nick or scratch—had affected his equilibrium. Or maybe the thesis was wildly improbable, after all. Yet before he, too, died, Breshnev did wobble through the maze for the first time in his brief life-span. Csorna was left with two dead mice, a highly suspect, enhanced performance by one of them, and more questions than answers.

The next transplant, from Mouse 2 to Mouse 13—he had discovered that naming them was psychologically undesirable—was equally inconclusive: 1) Because Mouse 2 was intelligent but capriciously so, thus was not really a priority donor; 2) Because Mouse 13 was several degrees more adept than Breshnev had been. He had learned the maze though

13

not the string-ladder climb. Therefore when Mouse 13 recovered sufficiently to scuttle up the ladder then tug the string until the balsa ladder was raised to the next platform for the climb to the subsequent level, Csorna couldn't decide whether he had on his hands a scientific breakthrough or a caprice of rodential exuberance. Could Mouse 13 have been as intellectually capable as Mouse 2 all along but perhaps simply depressed by lack of attention?

Mouse 2, the donor, died promptly. Csorna was undismayed. He was concerned with the donee. Mouse 13 lived and mastered the string-ladder climb, though he was never really good at it. That was disturbing, but it was overshadowed by a startling realization. Though Csorna had prepared anti-immunosystem medication, there was no need for it. No rejection!

Mouse 13 lasted unmedicated for two months then abruptly died of what appeared to be a virus infection unrelated to the experiment.

Had the sequence been a success? Csorna wasn't sure. There were two positives. Mouse 13 had not been able to work out the string-ladder climb before the transplant, but had laboriously mastered it afterward. And the donees had not rejected, even without countermedication.

Csorna was irresistibly impelled to move ahead, but not with mice. He needed something larger than a lima bean to work with. He selected beagles. Rather, he ran into a good beagle deal. A Montreal dog food processor had acquired a half dozen of them as a taste panel. The beagles loved his new product, but test sales in eastern Quebec proved disastrous. When the returns passed the fifty percent level, the manufacturer made a couple of panicky phone calls and learned something he should have known had he not been new to the business. "Any mutt but a beagle," a Pennsylvania packing-house VP told him. "They got no discrimination. They'll eat anything."

The dog food processor had a heart. He offered his daughter her pick of the six. She unerringly chose the most forlorn and hopeless specimen, one Csorna could well have used. The other five were given to McKenzie U as lab animals.

"What do I want with five beagles?" the lab animal custodian had grumped to Csorna.

"I'll take them," the spidery little doctor said without hesitation. Providence had smiled.

The beagle with the all-brown face was a remarkably fast learner. None of the five dogs was stupid. Csorna decided on ignorance where previously he had depended on differentials in learning abilities. He isolated the brown-faced animal, Dog 1, from the other four and taught it to sit, lie down, heel, beg, even roll over on command. Smart animal. Csorna barely resisted naming him.

Of the other four, a predominately white bitch seemed the most unwilling to cooperate in anything but eating. Dog 5, he called her.

The dual operation took place on a wind-tossed Friday evening, tough going because Dog 1 hemorrhaged before Csorna was through. He had to let it go. This time he involved not only the basal but also portions of the parietal, upper temporal, and occipital lobes.

In three days, the bitch was able to stand on wobbly legs. "Sit!" Csorna ordered. The dog stared at him, her big eyes wet. But a week later when Csorna snapped, "Sit!" she tucked her rump and sat like a statue.

He felt a hot wave of excitement. "Down!" The bitch settled her muzzle on her forelegs. "Roll over!" She did.

Csorna was so elated that he managed to sound warm and human (her favorite phrase) when Emily Hergenroeder called from Boston to hint that she could use some warmth and humanness herself. He flew to Logan, caught a limo that somehow evaded the evening traffic crush, and he was naked in her Ritz-Carlton suite before the traffic noise in Newbury Street had diminished.

He felt absurd standing there unclad while she, also stripped, filled his champagne glass. But whatever—how would you say?—turned her up?

"I'm afraid I've been naughty, Bela. Look at me! Eleven more pounds. Oh, dear."

What difference did it make? He needed monkeys now.

"In my country," he said, coasting his eyes over her naked acreage, "you would be considered an irresistible confection."

Her skin prickled with gooseflesh. "Oh, *God*! You've made me feel so uncontrollably erotic! Finish your champagne, you wicked, wicked man!"

He left on the 9:47 A.M. flight to Montreal with a supplemental grant for $45,000.

The pair of orangs arrived with names: Sweetstuff, the dense female, and Kong, a much larger male with a passion for kiwi fruit and abilities that were excitingly close to human. He understood and responded to dozens of orders, ranging from "roll over" to "bring me the ball."

He was more impressive than that. The Hanssons had trained him to punch sequences of keys on an electric keyboard that was set to gong when the sequences were correct. Their ma-and-pa Animal Study Center, a poorly funded lash-up in the basement of the young couple's suburban Laval home, claimed that Kong had learned to "speak" through his keyboard. That had been disputed, as had similar experiments with chimpanzees in the States, in too many scientific papers, professional journals, and in the popular press. Disillusioned, storklike Franklin and sparrowlike Susan Hansson were easy enough to approach, particularly since Kong, with maturity, had developed into a real bastard of an ape. He was tranquil only when he was rewarded with his beloved and expensive kiwi fruit upon punching out his favorite request. "Mean as a wounded weasel," the animal attendant had promptly informed Csorna.

For the outsized check Csorna gave them, the Hanssons threw in the electric board and an intellectually hopeless little female they had named Sweetstuff. "A lovely animal," Susan Hansson had told Csorna, "but worthless to us. No discernable mental development past childhood, as best we can judge." Perfect.

"I should have joined the circus," the acne-pocked attendant groused. "Mice, dogs we've always had. Now it's apes."

Csorna made a point of isolating Kong from Sweetstuff as the little doctor labored to teach the aggressive male new sentence sequences. The ape was better at it than Csorna was. Despite the big, red-haired animal's obvious dislike of everyone around him, Csorna did feel a touch of regret when the three-hour operation took place.

Sweetstuff recovered rapidly, and again, remarkably, there was no evidence of tissue rejection. Could the brain be an organ that assimilated foreign tissue without trauma? Csorna felt he was probing the limits of knowledge.

Kong appeared to regain strength for fourteen days, but he was listless. He stared at the wall like a senile old man for another week and showed little interest in food. On a dreary Tuesday morning, the attendant slouched into the lab to announce with unconcealed satisfaction that the male ape had died.

Csorna's interest now lay with the female, of course. When she seemed sufficiently recovered, he chained her on a pad in the corner of the lab and faced her with the electric sentence board. For two frustrating weeks, the delicate little orang chirped and chattered and became, to Csorna's growing concern, her old inane self.

"Damned ape." But he kept watching. He offered her a kiwi fruit several times a day, first intact in its suede skin, then peeled to expose its slippery, emerald sweetness. The ape refused to accept it either way.

On the nineteenth day, now wearing only a light bandage over the immediate area of the incision, Sweetstuff touched the electric keyboard for the first time. She tapped two keys: the orange painted disc indicating "I" and the square blue button for "PLEASE."

"I PLEASE"? Gibberish. Or was something happening? She had never before even indicated that she knew the board

17

was there. Then at quarter after eleven the evening of that same day—Csorna was recording his observations minute by minute now—the gentle little ape reached out a delicate forefinger and in deliberate sequence tapped "PLEASE . . . I . . . WANT . . . KIWI."

She ripped the small fruit open and scooped out the bright green pulp. She also threw the empty skin at Csorna. Sweet-stuff had not until now shown any sign of aggressiveness.

Emily Hergenroeder had insisted that Csorna publish whatever he might accomplish and do it with prominent credit to her foundation. He began to condense his notes into a sequential narrative. He had thought that recognition in itself would be enough for a once-penniless refugee. Now that it was at hand, he realized he had only opened a door-way. His thesis and its corroboration would be just a beginning. Mouse, dog, ape. An evolution. The needed next step was obvious.

CHAPTER
3

THE SECOND OF the three September-October events that were ultimately to focus their combined impact on an ill-prepared Marty Horn occurred in New York City. September 16 was a day of unremitting sunshine, hardly the kind of a day in which Raphael Kooven expected finally to face the inevitable.

At 11:45 A.M., in a surprisingly sumptuous, seventh-floor office in lower Manhattan, he was clamped in a huge pliers of pain. A fiery tentacle probed down his left arm. In that moment, his knowledge of biomechanics confirmed what he had feared since the first hard twist four months ago. Fingers of death thrust deep into his chest, not ice but molten lead.

His Latin heritage rebelled, but the blood of his Dutch father enabled him to set his teeth against agony, remain upright in the ornate rattan chair and hold his chocolate eyes on Lefroid's. The other man's gaze was as impersonal as glass, his pale eyes seeming to let through the light from the window behind him.

"Your report," Lefroid prompted. He was blade-nosed

with the slicked-back ebony hair of a man who cared only to get it efficiently out of the way. As likable as a jaguar, Kooven had learned, and as dangerous. But he paid well.

Kooven struggled silently against the pain. "I have made contact at CIAS. A security guard."

The glass chip eyes blinked once.

"A dolt of a guard. He is also a part-time mechanic in the nearby town. We are on good terms. It will cost me several hundreds of dollars, I believe." He couldn't control a sudden grimace.

Lefroid misinterpreted the facial twitch. "You will be reimbursed."

Kooven was grateful for the response. He knew that Lefroid, frail himself, had no patience with frailty. Kooven fought the dance of black speckles that began to cloud his vision.

"This mechanic-guard of yours." Lefroid's voice was as dry as winter leaves. Kooven could read his irritation in the tightening of the too-wide mouth and the thin, bloodless lips. Lefroid had curiously irregular teeth for such a precise man; shark's teeth. "He suspects nothing, of course."

"Nothing. To him, I am an unfortunate anti-Castro visitor victimized by a local vandal. He is in sympathy." His voice caught. The pain was excruciating. Perspiration beaded his forehead. His fingers dug the yielding rattan of the chair arms.

He knew Lefroid saw it now, and that knowledge was as terrifying as the physical agony. The slender man leaned forward, palms flat on his teak desk. "What in hell is the matter with you?"

"*Nada*—it is nothing," Kooven lied. "It has happened before." But not like this. He swallowed against a drying throat. "The next stage is . . . is to . . ."

Lefroid had risen. His head hung over Kooven like a threatening hammer. "Can you or can you not proceed with this assignment?"

Kooven felt like a wounded fish who faced a larger hun-

20

gry fish. But now pain exceeded fear. All he wanted was sur-
cease, a loosening of the terrible pliers.

". . . sick. Useless to me." Lefroid's voice echoed down a
lengthening tunnel. Fingers grasped Kooven's shoulder,
shook him. Kooven found a dwindling shred of coherence.
"I believe," he said almost calmly, "that I am having a heart
attack."

That son of a bitch! Lefroid raged silently. After all the
planning, the expense, the high-level risk Rapier had in-
vested in getting Kooven into the country, the little half-
breed bastard had fallen apart.

Lefroid forced himself to think. Think. Take it in steps.
First had come the skinny man in the outdated Chesterfield
coat. Middle European. Lefroid didn't care; business was
business. "We don't know what it is precisely," the skinny
man had said, "but it is important. We understand that Rapier is in a position to act as . . . ah, intermediary." He
licked dry, blue lips. His English was slightly accented, but
New England A's were more dominant than the Balkan undertone.

"We are importers." Lefroid was stalling for the required
four minutes. The man had automatically been photo-
graphed as he entered the Rapier Imports outer office.
While they talked, Gerta telexed the Polaroid to a Rapier
payrollee who had illegal full-scan compuvideo access to international embassy files at State. The autosort was completed in 106 seconds. Lefroid's phone buzzed.

"Excuse me," he said to the thin man. "Yes?"

"Draja Zagora, third undersecretary for cultural affairs,
Bulgarian Embassy in Washington," Gerta's impersonal
voice reported. "Born Sofia, nineteen fifty-five. B.S. Har-
vard, nineteen seventy-six. Major in English. Masters degree
in advanced studies, Wharton School of Business. Returned
to Sofia, nineteen eighty. Details to be mailed."

"Thank you." Lefroid replaced the phone with a smile.
"Precisely what is it that we might do for you, Mr. Zagora?"

The visitor started at Lefroid's use of his name. Lefroid knew he hadn't given it at Gerta's desk. Zagora recovered his composure with effort. "Unfortunately we don't know precisely what we are trying to purchase through you. In fact, it may be no more than a concept at this stage. But if such a concept is developed into practical application, we will be perfectly amenable to paying generously for its delivery."

"How generously?" Lefroid was pleased with verbal waltzing when he knew he was in control.

"Three million dollars, American."

"For something you're not sure even exists?"

"Five hundred thousand for information on R and D, I believe you call it. The balance on delivery of specifications and working drawings. A bonus, of course, should you be able to deliver a working prototype."

Lefroid tipped his chair back and regarded his visitor across tented fingers. "I assume you can give us some particulars."

The skinny man, still in his ill-fitting European overcoat, snapped open his briefcase and extracted a blue folder. He flipped the cover and scanned the contents. "There is an American government research installation in the mountains of Maryland," he said, "called the Catoctin Institute for Advanced Sciences. CIAS. Scientists from various disciplines are invited—paid well, in fact—to develop freely their ideas and theories. Particularly in the fields of offensive and defensive weaponry."

"You can get that out of any American science magazine," Lefroid said. The man's confident manner had begun to irritate him.

"Precisely," Zagora said smugly. "The American urge to publish has saved us time, personnel, and money."

"Might you get to the point?"

"The point is that one of the scientists at this CIAS became more than a little intoxicated some weeks ago while he was

22

on a brief vacation in Florida. He was in the company of a particularly attractive woman—"

"One of yours."

"One of ours, Mr. Lefroid, yes. Unfortunately, she was unable to obtain details, but he is involved in developing an entirely new concept in, her report states, 'bioelectronic propagation.' "

"I don't know what that means."

"Neither do we. But it frightens us nonetheless. We are ready to pay you well to alleviate that fear. The world does not need further development of offensive weaponry at this—"

Lefroid waved an impatient hand. "Spare me the false justification, Zagora. I don't need it. You don't need it. What talks in here is money."

Zagora shrugged. He lay the blue folder on the corner of Lefroid's desk and snapped shut his briefcase. "How would you like the initial payment, Mr. Lefroid? Currency, precious metal, or untraceable computer transfer?"

Kooven was to have been the key to the operation. His contact with a CIAS security guard hadn't seemed potentially fruitful to Lefroid, but he had known Kooven at work before. The little bastard was like a termite infestation. You didn't notice what was underway, but after a while, the whole structure fell open. Not only that; the little Argentinian had a mind like a mainframe memory bank. Rapier needed him, but now he was lost to the operation. Horger Clinic had reported that Kooven was now in intensive care. Prognosis: doubtful. He could be a wheelchair liability for months. Or he might not survive without continuous life support.

In his empty office, Lefroid slapped the desktop, stinging his palm. *Damn!*

Rapier was a thin organization. Only Lefroid and Gerta Heissen knew how thin. The others—the field network of corruptible men and women he had so carefully enrolled—

had an impression, he was certain, of a powerful, far-flung enterprise whose demands were to be heeded, whose payments were prompt and generous, and whose vengeance for botched assignments was swiftly administered and brutal.

Rapier, in fact, was a clearinghouse, a prime contractor with subcontractors available in industry, business, government, organized crime—wherever essential services could be bought profitably. And Lefroid was not in the practice of bidding. He paid promptly and well.

Sometimes he was able to compromise an entire organization. Such had been the fortunate case with the Horger Clinic in upstate New York. It now was a Rapier facility, in effect, because Dr. Elmo Stanhope Horger depended more than a little on Rapier contractual work than on the not inconsiderable income from the clinic's activities as a "health enhancing facility"—a fat farm with a schedule of cosmetic techniques also offered with considerable sales enthusiasm.

For Rapier, the Horger Clinic handled certain problems of medical natures, such as the matter of Kooven's heart attack that now faced Lefroid. The clinic also provided Rapier with medical intelligence that Lefroid found valuable. From Horger, for example, he had learned of the discontinuation of the birth control product, Ovanorm, because it was suspected of causing cervical cancer. When the FDA rejected the manufacturer's appeal, all existing supplies of Ovanorm were reportedly destroyed. Interestingly, the identical quantity of a newly labeled birth-control drug turned up in Indonesia within three months. Rapier received a seven-figure fee for its ingenuity and efficiency in salvaging a chaotic corporate situation.

At a wholesalers' conference that Lefroid had attended to enhance his legitimate business cover, another merchant had heard of Lefroid's refusal to accept a return of a $50,000 shipment of beetle-infested bamboo goods. Rapier Imports maintained that the infestation had taken place in the customer's warehouse. "Bamboo beetles in Minneapolis?" the other wholesaler had scoffed. "You got the conscience of a handgun manufacturer." Lefroid had considered that a compliment.

With Kooven out of it, the CIAS operation was going nowhere. Zagora was unaware of that, nor was he to be told. Lefroid was satisfied that Zagora had supplied all the information he had available. There was no further benefit to be gained from additional contacts, only the risk of discernment by Zagora of Rapier's impending failure.

There could be no failure. Other specialists were available, of course, but none had proved nearly so resourceful as Kooven. Moreover, Kooven had the bioengineering background that Lefroid felt was necessary to interpret what had begun as no more than a sketchy lead.

Lefroid slapped his desktop again. The $3,000,000 fee for this operation should be enough for him to find a way to raise Kooven even from the dead.

A lot of cops Marty Horn had known would have been happy to turn in their shields for a cushy spot like this. "Congratulations, *amigo!* You got it *el mado!*" Sergeant Pepe Ruiz had said when he'd handed Marty confirmation of the CIAS appointment. Congratulations for a declaration of psychological unfitness and relegation to the Appalachian outback? Get the psycho out of here. Put him in the woods where he won't hurt anybody.

That was one way to look at it, the Chicago departmental counselor had agreed. "On the other hand, it's a job, Horn. The title sounds good, even if the pay isn't braggable. And you're still young enough to earn a nice federal pension out of it." That was another way to look at it.

"You got to see it from the department's viewpoint," the counselor said. He was ten years Marty's junior, burdened with over-education and the face of a kid trying too hard to believe in the book. "A: You were found standing in that place with your gun in your hand. B: Two shots fired. C: Both the male subject and and the female subject dead. D: Neither of them armed. That's pretty conclusive, isn't it?"

25

"It may have looked that way, but I couldn't have . . . I can't remember one damned second of what went on in there."

"That's what's saved you, Horn. The retrograde amnesia."

"Some save."

The counselor had hitched his chair closer. "Accept it, Sergeant. Life can be simple enough for you from here on out. Remember what Teddy Roosevelt said: 'Walk fast and carry a big clipboard.' " He waited for the laugh, but Marty wasn't having any.

The guy had been right, though. Work hard at looking like you're working hard, and you can fool everybody except the one who's always with you. Yourself.

He checked his watch. Two hours and forty minutes until Abner Dortman was to come on shift. He stepped toward the coffee maker then stopped. Enough already, Horn. He returned to his chair, sat down hard, propped his feet on the desk and pulled a tattered copy of *Penthouse* out of the drawer. This time he really would read the articles.

Neither he nor anyone else in effective range had any way of knowing that the third portentious September-October incident was about to take place.

Three of the scientists in the cherry-paneled CIAS living room were here at the invitation of the fourth. Dr. Albert Reifsnyder, taller and heavier than the others and a potential shambler of a man had he not kept at least a loose check on his weight, darted a green-eyed gaze from face to face and wondered why they were here.

"I'm going to give each of you a yellow pad," Dr. Strakhan said in that Munchkin voice of his. Roland Strakhan looked like a frantic little owl, hair frazzled from his endlessly running fingers through it. Maybe bioelectronics did that to you, Reifsnyder thought. Two disciplines that didn't seem to mesh.

"I'd like you to jot down whatever comes into your mind

for the next several minutes," Strakhan said as he trotted to the sofa to hand pads to Moyle and Natali. Ed Moyle raised his big paw to accept his ruled yellow pad unenthusiastically. He had eyebrows thick as mink tails on a face like a wrestling ref's. Deceptive, Reifsnyder thought. Dr. Edmund Moyle was one of the most knowledgeable fluid force experts in the world.

Next to him on the deep sofa, almost dwarfed by Moyle's chunky bulk, Dr. Amerigo Natali took his writing pad with delicate fingers. Natty Natali always wore a coat and tie, Reifsnyder realized, maybe even to bed.

"Just write down whatever thoughts come into our heads?" Reifsnyder repeated as Strakhan scurried to the fireplace to hand him the third ruled pad.

"Yes, beginning precisely at three ten."

"I fail to see why you feel I can be of any use to you," Natali said petulantly. "After all, the study of plasma propulsion—"

Strakhan waved an impatient hand. "That's of no consequence, no consequence for this. Reifsnyder here is a doctor of mass communications, not even a hard science. It doesn't matter." He checked his watch. "Remember. Your impressions, beginning precisely at ten after three." He departed abruptly.

Natali cleared his throat and stood up, a compact man, proportioned like a TV actor. They always turned out to be smaller than you expected, Reifsnyder reflected, thinking of his study project at NBC last spring.

"Is he pulling our leg?" Natali's speech pattern had a slight Milanese lilt, though he had been naturalized three decades ago. "Impressions is what he asks? Impressions of what? Has Carlisle approved this?"

"Do as the man says," Moyle rumbled. "Carlisle's in Washington, anyway. It's obviously just an experiment, though I'd expect this kind of thing to be more your line, Reifsnyder, than Strakhan's. Wonder what he's up to?"

"I'm as intrigued as you are."

"You're sure you're not in cahoots with him?" Moyle's tone was impish. "I wouldn't put that past you."

Reifsnyder chuckled. He'd been wondering the same thing about Moyle and Natali. What kind of human reaction experiment was conducted without an observer?

An oak log snapped. Reifsnyder became conscious of the fire's warmth against his brown twill trousers. More casual than the others, he favored earth tones in his dress. Natali was a Brooks Brothers fashion plate. Moyle wore outdated tweeds. Reifsnyder took flyers into turtlenecks, even an occasional sports shirt-ascot combination. He suspected the others at CIAS considered him a bit on the undisciplined side. His masscom specialty itself was a not-so-subtle albatross in this federally funded den of hard sciences.

Reifsnyder eased along the mantel out of the fire's direct heat and tapped his ballpoint on the blank pad. What was Strakhan up to? He checked his watch. "Three minutes to go, gentlemen."

Moyle grunted impatiently from the sofa. Natali had wandered to the bay window, and he gazed at the frost-burned lawn and its triple security fencing.

Strakhan was a little bonkers, as the BBC people Reifsnyder knew would put it. A bonkers boffin. Wasn't "boffin" what the Brits had called their World War II research scientists? They'd secluded those people, put up with their whims and wants, and hoped they would come up with better ways to kill. Here we were fifty years later doing the same thing.

"The witching hour." Moyle tapped his watch.

Reifsnyder forced humor, realizing too late that his voice sounded tense. "I wonder whether we should expect a bang or a whimper?"

A log popped. At the window, Natali jumped then smiled in embarrassment. "A wonderful discovery! How to explode pitch pockets by remote control."

"He wants us to make notes," Reifsnyder reminded them.

"You suggest I put that down?"

"How do I know what you should put down?" Sometimes

28

Natali could be disturbingly obtuse. *They don't understand directions*, Reifsnyder scrawled on his pad. Then he rubbed the back of his neck. He wondered what Moyle was up to, scratching away over there.

They were silent. The fire sizzled and settled. What in hell was Strakhan trying to do? *Stupid exercise*, Reifsnyder wrote. He was sorry Elizabeth Carlisle had been called back to Washington for the day. She would have had a grand time pooh-poohing this nuttiness with him.

Moyle looked up like an uneasy gorilla sunk in the soft cushions. What made CIAS think *he* had anything to offer?

"You superior bastard," Moyle growled. "What are you staring at?"

"I'll stare at what I want!" Reifsnyder threw back at him. On his pad, he wrote, *Moyle acting like an ass.* The ball-point dug in.

"You two think you're so damned smart!" Natali burst out. "Shut up! Shut up! I can't think."

"You aren't supposed to think," Reifsnyder shot back. "You're supposed to write down impressions. Can't anybody follow instructions?"

They both were insufferable. How had he put up with assholes like Moyle and Natali for the past seven months?

Jerks, he wrote. *Both of them.*

"What did you put down?" Natali demanded. He dropped his pad to the carpet and strode toward Reifsnyder, fists balled at his sides. "Just what in hell did you write down?" His voice had climbed to a screech.

"You dumb little foreign fruit! I can take you with my hands tied together!" Reifsnyder roared. He threw his pad at the fireplace screen and stepped out to meet the oncoming space propulsion expert.

"Kill the little bastard!" Moyle shouted. "Then I'll take you on, you big tub of lard!" He leaped off the sofa and hunched into a fighter's crouch.

The room tingled with unbearable tension. Reifsnyder

could feel it, actually feel it up the nape of his neck and along his arms.

Moyle lumbered in, head tucked, fists cocked. Natali came on like a bantam rooster in an uncoordinated strut that was . . . absurd! Ridiculous!

Reifsnyder couldn't restrain himself. He threw his head back and howled. Moyle stopped dead, straightened then burst into laughter with him. Natali's sudden whinny joined in.

It had been ludicrous. Three sober scientists about to come to blows over . . . over what? Reifsnyder couldn't recall.

Nor could he stop his booming laughter. Tears rolled down his cheeks. He seized the mantel for support. Pathetic. Just plain pathetic. An incredibly sorry sight, all three of them.

Now he was infused with a wave of melancholia. The afternoon was dismal, the fire dying. They were brutally isolated from humanity by a triple fence and armed guards. And they were behaving like idiots. How in God's name could a man live like this? How long could you go on? Reifsnyder found himself fighting tears. Could there be only one sure way to end it?

Natali stood in the center of the room, arms limp, face collapsed. Moyle turned away. The odd tingle in Reifsnyder's neck and arms seemed to have spread through him, thinning but pervasive.

Then it was gone.

Unaccountably, he felt like a man who had just awakened. Slightly confused, a little stiff; but the world had fallen back in place.

He twitched his head in confusion. Had it really happened? Had they all been ready to kill each other, next grotesquely hysterical, then finally depressed almost to contemplating suicide? Astounding.

He cleared his throat. "I don't—" His voice caught in a

dry mouth. "I don't know what you gentlemen experienced, but—"

"Some sort of mass hypnotism?" Moyle offered without conviction. He sank back to the sofa, perplexed.

Natali stood where he was, slowly moving his head from side to side. "I do not understand. Do not understand."

The paneled French doors to the hall opened. Strakhan looked like a devil's gnome. "Your note pads please?"

Reifsnyder retrieved his from the flagstone hearth and stared at his disorganized scratchings. "I wasn't much help."

"None of us was," Moyle admitted. "Damndest thing I ever witnessed. Don't know what the hell came over us."

"Whatever you wanted us to do," Natali said, "we did not do it. Somehow we argued. Then a laughing fit, then . . . sorry, but the experiment, whatever it was meant to be, was a failure."

"No, gentlemen," Strakhan said, still standing dramatically in the doorway, "it seems to have been something of a success. Unfocused, but yes, something of a success."

His curious pixie face was blank, but Reifsnyder sensed an aura of elation about the little doctor of bioelectronics. An icicle slid along Reifsnyder's spine.

Marty Horn had been slumped before the bank of luminous television screens leafing through the office's single tattered magazine when the wave of anger hit him. Who in hell did these naked sluts think they were, flashing tits and ass around like this! Flaunting it like it was some kind of gift to mankind! He'd like to get his hands on their airbrushed throats, by God. He'd show them a thing or two.

He seized the magazine in both hands and ripped it down the middle. Then he stared at the tatter. Ridiculous! He'd gotten infuriated over a *magazine,* for God's sake! Laughter bubbled deep in his chest. Then it burst forth. He was further convulsed at its unexpected sound, a high-pitched giggle.

He dashed to the door, slammed it shut, and leaned against it, weak from uncontrollable mirth.

Was this funny? What in hell was he laughing at, he wondered as his mood changed abruptly. He was one sad apple, a discredited detective sergeant whose life had funneled down to this stark security center, making a buck by watching a row of eavesdropping TV screens.

He barely fought off a gush of tears. His eyes burned with them. And he noticed that a weird tingle had invaded his body. Like a little shiver that took a long time to go away. When it did, he fell back in the chair and wondered if you reported something like this.

At the front entrance, Officer Lydia Whimple experienced the same rapid changes of mood. First she was swept with sudden anger focused on the inequity of her endless hours standing out here while Chief Marty Horn spent most of his time in Security Center with his feet up on the desk. The son of a bitch didn't deserve it. He was a psycho! Everybody knew that. A bomb waiting to go off. Even if he did, she'd never get a crack at anything better than this. Security was still a macho business. Full of dumb macho bastards.

She fumed impotently in her little vestibule post and rubbed the odd discomfort along the nape of her neck. Then to her surprise, she began to laugh at herself. What was her problem? This whole thing was an Alice-in-Wonderland comedy, anyway. If they wanted to pay her to stand here eight hours a day and guard a bunch of weirdos who seemed as effective as her Uncle Delbert, fine with her! It sure beat the airplane factory in Germantown.

Of course, she did miss the girls she'd worked with in the A-10 airframe assembly section. Those had been the days, and they would never come again. Never. Where did time go? She'd be a middle-aged woman in a few years. An old maid. Men were happy enough to use you, but when it came to— The rush of tears horrified her. Her mascara ran before she could grab a tissue from her shoulder purse.

* * *

At the compound's main gate, Corporal Crawford experienced an identical sequence of abrupt mood changes. But at his booth at the intersection of the entrance drive with Maryland 550, Officer Joe Blanchard found the afternoon no different from many others. The weather was fall crisp with a hint of cold rain or even snow by tomorrow. At 3:10 P.M., Blanchard passed time by writing a letter to his mother. At 3:18, he had completed another page and felt as unperturbed at his lonely lot as he did any other day out here. He loved solitude, pine, hemlock, and every bird that visited the feeder he'd hung in a tall spruce across the road. While Crawford's front entrance post was in an almost direct line extended from the laboratory building through the center line of the residence hall, Blanchard's booth was a good twenty-five degrees south of that line.

The Wallista family, though, was carried straight across the invisible line precisely at 3:12. Frank and Marcy, both in their mid-thirties, had been enroute from Washington to Gettysburg on U.S. 15 for less than twenty minutes after a late stop at a McDonald's in Frederick, but suddenly their two sons in the back seat of the station wagon showed all the signs of travel weariness.

"Get back on your own side!" eight-year-old Donny Wallista screeched at his younger brother.

"I will not! I will not!" Joey shouted. "I *hate* you!" He flailed out with a twiglike arm and caught Donny square in the eye.

The older boy howled in pain and swarmed over his brother. Marcy twisted around, her face crimson with anger, and smacked the side of Donny's head with her open hand.

"Stop it!" she screamed. "I can't stand it. I just can't stand it!"

Driving with one hand, Frank shook Marcy with his free arm. "What's the matter with you! You've never hit them before. Never." He shook her again, hard. Damned woman. She needed to be shown what it was to be hurt.

33

Then Donny let out another howl, not anger this time but a shriek of laughter. It *was* funny, all of them exploding like that over nothing. Joey's shrill giggle joined in. Marcy released her son's arm and was seized with such violent giggles that she was afraid she wouldn't be able to control herself. Frank's craggy face was screwed up in near-hysteria of his own.

What was she laughing at, Marcy wondered. It was all so futile, this frantic search for the honeymoon magic of a decade ago. Washington had been a glorious city then. Now it wasn't safe to walk outside at night. And Gettysburg probably would be no more than another tourist trap. What was she hoping for with two shouting kids in the back of a seven-year-old car and a husband who'd turned into a rock?

But the kids weren't shouting now. They were sobbing. And tears ran down Frank Wallista's rough cheeks as he brought the car to a jittering stop on the road's shoulder.

"God, Marcy. . . ." He buried his head in her neck, his warmth accentuating the strange tingle she had become conscious of there.

Then that little vibration was gone. The overwhelming depression lifted too. Just like that. Frank straightened up and stared at her. She was as puzzled as he. He put the car in gear and guided it with exaggerated care back to the travel lane.

In the back, Donny said, "What was it, Momma? What happened?"

Marcy cleared her throat. "Why don't you and Joey look for animals? There are raccoons here, aren't there, Frank? Maybe even a bear."

Frank nodded without looking at her. She was thankful that the kids were so easily diverted, but when she reached in her purse for a cigarette, her hand shook.

No one outside a narrow wedge thirteen degrees wide and six miles long experienced any of the reaction sequence. The potency of the effect faded in the unpopulated wooded area between Thurmont and the Pennsylvania border.

CHAPTER
4

THE FIRST ANNOUNCEMENT of Dr. Bela Csorna's personality element transplants was made by Csorna himself at a January medical convention in Miami Beach. He had expected stunned silence before thunderous applause; had even allowed for perhaps a murmur of disbelief. He would have settled for formal congratulations from the chair.

To his dismay, he was rewarded with none of these. Perhaps if he had been granted any agenda position other than 8 A.M. on the convention's fourth morning, he would have enjoyed at least a modicum of the recognition he was certain he deserved. What he got was a three-quarters empty hotel ballroom, a smattering of applause from an agenda-surfeited audience of general practitioners who promptly drifted out the door in search of coffee while at the podium an acutely disappointed Csorna crammed his notes back in his briefcase. This had been the wrong place at the wrong time.

"Dr. Csorna?" The voice was female and youthful. Csorna shaded his eyes against the spotlights that still speared the speaker's platform from the rear of the almost empty room.

"I found your talk fascinating." She was a bookish type, half-lensed glasses, horizon blue suit, straight body, prematurely graying at perhaps thirty.

"Let me get out of these damn lights."

The woman's grip on his arm was enthusiastic. "I represent *Medical Peripheries*, a biweekly newsletter for the profession?" Her thinly pencilled eyebrows rose in a question.

"No, I am sorry, I do not know it. It has not reached Montreal."

"It has reached McGill, Doctor. A dozen subscriptions."

"I am with McKenzie, not McGill. But I need no subscriptions." He turned away in impatience.

Behind him, the young woman laughed. "I'm not selling subscriptions, Dr. Csorna. I'm the field editor. I want to file a feature story on your work."

Csorna stopped. "You would print what I tell you?"

"As quotes, certainly. We are very careful with our reporting."

"Then, perhaps," Csorna said as she fell in step beside him, "you will allow me to buy you a breakfast."

Dr. Elmo Horger's reports were terse, as Lefroid demanded. This one was even more laconic than usual, but it set Lefroid's mind racing.

Word out of Montreal in "Medical Peripheries" newsletter claims transfer of character traits, abilities has been effected by Dr. Bela Csorna in McKenzie University lab mice, beagle dogs, pair of orangutans. No human experimentation, though Csorna believes technique should be effective and of value in treating certain cases of mental disorder.

Lefroid stood at the broad window of his eighteenth-floor apartment, Horger's report in his hand. Manhattan was a channel of glittering light between the black voids of the Hudson and East Rivers. Three million dollars, he told himself, should be enough to impel him to raise Kooven from the dead. A joke?

Was it possible? Surely it could be tried. He doubted that

the cost would be more than moderate. In point of fact, it could be attempted for virtually no cost at all.

He lifted the cordless phone on the rosewood desk at the window and punched the number. Almost no cost and no risk to Rapier. Worth a try.

"Horger?"

"Yes, Mr. Lefroid?"

Lefroid had never thought his own voice distinctive, but it obviously was, because he always seemed to be instantly recognized on the phone.

"I asked that you not call me at home." Horger's tone was low, but failed to conceal his apparent irritation. In the background, Lefroid heard conversation and music. TV or a party?

He disregarded Horger's rebuff. He owned the man. "I have a project you will find interesting. Meet me at noon tomorrow, location four."

"But I have facial surgery scheduled at ten." Horger's whine was unpleasant.

"Assign it or cancel it." Lefroid clicked off. He had no reason to believe that his phone line had been compromised, but a prudent man took as few chances as possible. It was wise to hold traffic to his office to a minimum; lunch with Horger in the crowded dining room of the Grand Hyatt would be convenient and seemingly innocuous.

Lefroid, Horger knew well, didn't believe in circling his target. "About this brain thing."

"Brain thing?"

"The piece in your report, Horger. That doctor in Montreal."

"The Hungarian? Csorna, I think his name is."

Lefroid took a cigar from his platinum case and replaced the case in his breast pocket without offering it to Horger. "Would it work?"

His cheeks sucked in as he lit the slender panatela with a

37

Dunhill lighter, snapped the lighter closed and replaced it in his pocket. "With a person, I mean."

Horger stared at him. Then he diverted his stunned gaze to his Waldorf salad. "God!"

"Would it?" Lefroid persisted, his pale stare as penetrating as a cold draft.

"How would I know?"

"You go ask him."

"He won't know either. He can assume, I suppose, that certain effects would carry through, but he can't know without conducting . . ." Horger's mouth dried. He reached for his water glass, swallowed hurriedly and cleared his throat. "He can't know without conducting a further experiment and observing the results over a period of—"

"Ask him."

Horger snatched up his napkin and wiped his peculiarly feminine lips. "I'll call him in the next few days."

"No, I want you to go up there tomorrow. Evaluate him, his work. If a human application appears at all feasible, convince him."

The doctor's fleshy face was impassive, but he was afraid Lefroid could read resentment implanted there.

"It's worth a lot to me," Lefroid said in a less abrasive tone. Horger flicked his eyes up to the lean face with its peculiarly wide, bloodless lips and ill-aligned teeth. Lefroid frequently used this technique of demands interspersed with appeals. Despite Horger's awareness of that, it inevitably worked. But anything would have worked. The occasional but major business Lefroid generated controlled the clinic, not the uncertain trickle of overcharged, legitimate patients. They were for show.

"I'm expecting a positive reaction from this Sarna."

"Csorna." Horger took passing satisfaction in correcting him.

"I'm not requesting a favor, Doctor. You are authorized to offer this . . . Csorna fifty thousand initially, but to go as

38

high as a hundred—no, a hundred fifty thousand if he resists."

The pudgy doctor blanched. "But you're talking about something that's never been done before in medicine, so far as I know. You're talking about an incredibly risky experimentation."

"Oh? How risky, Doctor?" Lefroid's smile was positively sharklike.

Horger frowned. "I assume . . . I don't actually know, of course. The . . . donor is at obvious risk."

"The donor I have in mind," Lefroid said, "is already at hopeless risk."

Horger finally grasped a substantial part of what Lefroid planned to have him do. "My God!"

"The operation would be conducted at the clinic, of course," Lefroid said smoothly. "I realize there will be certain expenses."

"The OR team. Whatever additional equipment will be needed. Overhead. Overhead?" He looked at Lefroid with expectation.

"It could be a tidy sum," Lefroid agreed. "Including your own consultancy fee, Doctor."

Horger could almost hear the heady chime of an old-fashioned cash register. "Tonight, you said."

"Correct." Lefroid reached in his breast pocket again, this time withdrawing an airline ticket folder. "I've taken the liberty. There is also a car rental reservation, and overnight accomodations in Montreal have been arranged. I trust you can make this flight?"

Dr. Horger pocketed the EAL ticket without looking at it. "Certainly."

The weather was abominable: lashing rain, cold as liquid ice. Montreal's Dorval International had been jammed with weekend travelers fuming over late flights. Horger had gotten confused not five minutes out of the airport and had lunged his rented Ford helplessly through side streets before he found a service station still open and was given heavily accented directions by a giant of a man in a hooded slicker.

"*Merci,*" Horger had muttered, and shoved off into the storm again. When he finally found the rain-blackened towers of McKenzie, the campus navigation instructions Csorna had given him on the phone proved accurate. There was the promised parking space. Horger snapped off the car's lights and sat for a moment in darkness. Then he opened the door and hunkered into the downfall.

Csorna was smaller than he had expected, a little scuttler of a man with more hair than he deserved, a pair of arched brows over deep-set eyes, and a facial bone structure so prominent it made his cheeks look sunken.

In fact, with his comic-operetta accent and his crablike walk, the Hungarian doctor seemed a joke. Until Horger had toured the lab with him and listened closely, making an effort to form no preemptory conclusions. The monkey, Sweetstuff, performed beautifully at her odd keyboard, but Horger had to take Csorna's word that she had been mentally inept before the operation.

Was the whole thing an elaborate con? Horger had no way of knowing. But it struck him that he wasn't at risk. Success in whatever incredible enterprise Lefroid had in mind would be Csorna's, but so would the consequences of failure. Horger was only an agent here. He began to breathe easier for the first time since he'd left the Grand Hyatt.

They returned to Csorna's little glassed-in office off the spacious laboratory. Csorna indicated a molded plastic chair for Horger, then sat behind his steel desk and swiveled his own chair sideways to face his visitor.

"You seem to have accomplished something of a research miracle here, Doctor," Horger offered. "Single-handedly?"

Csorna didn't hide his pleasure at that. "I have used several students to assist—as technicians. I do not think they understood the implications, even in a—how would you say?—in a general sense. Why," he added carefully, "are you so interested in what I have done?"

In the lab, Sweetstuff fretted, apparently upset by the late evening attention they had just given her.

"I'm interested as a fellow doctor." The orang snorted again. Horger nodded toward the lab. "She seems disturbed." He wasn't sure he liked being here with a wild-eyed ape secured nearby only with what looked to him like a none-too-reliable neck chain.

"She has seemed resentful of attention these past few weeks," Csorna said. He turned his full attention back to Horger. "You also are a neurosurgeon?"

"A plastic surgeon."

The delicate eyebrows lifted a trifle. "Why should a plastic surgeon—" Horger noted that he managed to place a deprecating emphasis on the words—"be interested in my experiments?"

Horger tried to keep his voice free of resentment at Csorna's reaction. "You could say that I represent an interested party."

"So."

"So," Horger said a trifle irritably, mistaking Csorna's European "so" of encouragement for an American "so" of impatience, "that party would very much like to help you continue your fascinating line of experimentation."

"It is still in a primitive state. I do not see that money could be made from what I have done up to now. And," he added waspishly, "why else would an American be interested?"

"We would like to help, nonetheless."

"Nonetheless?" Csorna appeared not to have heard the expression before. "Nonetheless?"

Horger shifted in the uncomfortably hard chair. "Quite obviously, from what you have told me, the next step is upward in the primate order."

"Upward," Csorna repeated tonelessly, seeming not sure where Horger was going with this.

"Well, certainly. None of your experimentation means much, does it, unless it has practical application?"

"Practical? It is practical! You saw the ape yourself. She was a slow-witted—a . . . a nothing until I—"

"Sorry," Horger relented hastily. A film of perspiration had materialized on his broad forehead despite the air conditioning. It had just struck him that the failure he himself could be accountable for would be the failure to convince Csorna to cooperate. "You misunderstand me. I refer to human application."

Csorna didn't change expression, but his jaw muscles pulsed.

"Surely that has been your intention all along, Dr. Csorna?"

"I had thought . . . of course. But the actual possibility, no, I hadn't dared to hope."

"I bring you that hope, Doctor. Even more than that. I bring you the next logical step in your work."

Csorna put thumb and middle finger to his temples and shook his head. "I do not follow, Dr. . . ."

"Horger."

"Horger. Do you say that you want me to somehow find a . . . human subject?"

"I am saying that we want you to work with a human subject, yes. But we will provide that subject for you."

Csorna paled. "God in heaven!" he whispered. "Do you know what you say?"

"I know precisely what I'm saying. Naturally we don't expect you to work without compensation for the risk."

"Compensation? Ah, you refer to money."

"Indeed." Horger fixed his surprisingly lustrous mahogany eyes on Csorna's deep-set gaze. "Fifty thousand dollars."

Did the Hungarian's pupils suddenly dilate? Horger had heard that this was what physiologically aware salesmen looked for. The visible sign that the hook was set.

"But my research is not done to sell like a vase at an auction."

Had he appeared too eager with his offer, Horger wondered. "You understand, Doctor, we don't want the rights to your research. We only want to participate in one experiment. Perhaps I've underestimated the complexities involved. Would seventy-five thousand be more equitable?" Now, he thought, we'll see whether it's morals or money.

Csorna leaned back in his chair. They both were out of the desk lamp's glare now, both in shadow, eyes obscured by deeper shadow. Csorna folded his arms. A body signal lacking openness.

"We will provide the facilities," Horger said by way of offering additional incentive and implying reduced risk.

"Facilities?" Csorna echoed. He had an irritating habit of repeating key words, apparently a tactic to elicit further information without revealing the degree of his interest.

"A clinic in New York State; in something of a remote area. Medical technology for a moneyed clientele. Additional equipment as you require. All at your disposal. There would be a distinct advantage to you in conducting, shall we say, advanced work in a private facility of that kind. Away from here. In fact, I am certain you would be unable to carry it out here at all. The authorities certainly would never permit it. I suspect your current experiments are dead-ended because of that."

Csorna, arms still folded, nodded.

"Your expenses would be in addition to the fee, naturally."

"The risk to be the subject's. It would be considerable."

"Every great physician-pioneer has faced risk. Else we would still be letting blood and prescribing pouches of garlic."

"That I do realize. I was wondering why you want to share that risk. Why do you want to be involved at all?"

"I have a benefactor," Horger said carefully. "A layman with means who wants to share in the advance of medical science. Not for gain, you understand, but for the benefit of mankind." How easy it was to pour it on, he thought, when

43

you had powerful enough motivation. "There are such people, thank heavens."

Csorna flicked his mobile eyebrows upward. But he said nothing. Horger shifted his feet and frowned. Then he said into the uneasy silence, "I believe my backer would permit me to guarantee you a fee of one hundred thousand dollars. In cash."

In the lab, Sweetstuff growled and shook her chain. A wind gust rattled rain against the black rectangle of the office's single window.

Csorna's sunken eyes met Horger's stare, held it. His voice, when he finally spoke, sounded parched.

"American dollars," he said. "Not Canadian."

CHAPTER

5

"LET ME MAKE it crystal clear." Lefroid enjoyed his use of the cliché on Horger as a subtle put-down. "The obvious subject would be Strakhan, himself. The work in which we are interested is his." That much Kooven had told him.

In fact, Kooven had been surprisingly effective in his limited activity prior to his heart seizure. From Dortman, the naive security guard-mechanic, Kooven had acquired a roster of current CIAS scientists-in-residence: Edmund Moyle, a specialist in fluid force, whatever that was; Amerigo Natali, a naturalized, Italian expert in deep space propulsion; a mass communications specialist named Albert Reifsnyder, and Dr. Roland Strakhan himself, a leading figure in what Kooven said was a new science of bioelectronics.

Also at the facility, Kooven had managed to report, was a three-shift security unit at a strength of twelve, headed by a discredited ex-Chicago detective sergeant named Martin Hearn or Horn—Kooven had not been positive on the name—plus various part-time kitchen and household staff numbering no more than eight. The facility was directed, to Lefroid's surprise, by a woman: one Elizabeth Carlisle, the holder of a doctorate in psychology. All of this information had been acquired by Kooven through his cover as a victimized foreign tourist. Lefroid was going to miss that man.

"I would estimate that the physical risk of using Strakhan is considerable," Horger said abruptly. "It's one hell of a risk for whoever you use."

Should he have brought the pudgy doctor so deeply into this? Then Lefroid realized the degree of Horger's essential involvement didn't matter. He controlled Horger.

"That risk obviously forces us to use another subject."

Horger's face regained some of its color as he considered possibilities aloud. "An alternate choice would best be a subject who has close contact with Strakhan but few intimate contacts otherwise. A wife, for example, could complicate the matter considerably. The extent of the personality change—if it takes place at all—will be conjectural. Animal research is only one aspect of any medical study. A human subject can be—"

"We're going ahead with this."

"I didn't mean to imply—"

"But you do have an obvious point."

Thunder rumbled in the Adirondack foothills to the west. Lefroid cocked his head at the sound. "I have to get back to New York tonight."

He did not, but the thought of spending the night in the clinic's overfurnished guest quarters was repellent. He would stop overnight in Kingston if heavy weather threatened.

With the back of his hand, he slapped the sheaf of data Kooven had managed to extract from that idiot guard, Dortman, in such a remarkably short time. Gerta's own research had added to Kooven's initial reports. A labored conversation upstairs in Kooven's equipment-jammed intensive care room not an hour ago had amplified certain additional points.

Had Lefroid noted in Kooven's hoarse responses the first signs of fear he had ever detected in the man? Impossible

46

that Kooven could have guessed why Lefroid had pressed him so hard for previously omitted details on the four CIAS scientists-in-residence. The apprehension in Kooven's voice and his sunken stare had to be the realization of the death that Horger had warned Lefroid was now only weeks away at best.

Lefroid flipped open the file. "Moyle is married," he recited to himself as if Horger had suddenly evaporated. "Two children, one still at home."

He riffled through several pages, including the pink sheets recently added by Gerta. "Natali lives with his father, a retired editor. Evident risk there, too. That leaves Reifsnyder." He scanned the information on "Reifsnyder, Albert." Stringless, apparently. "A much better possibility."

"Not married?"

Lefroid looked up as if he'd just realized Horger was still present. "Divorced eight years ago. No children. Both parents deceased. No siblings. He's the only one who stays at the research center most weekends. The others get out of there Friday afternoons and return Mondays to stay through the week. Sign of a loner."

"How old is this potential subject?" Horger's expression seemed that of a consulting physician called in on a difficult but fascinating case. The son of a bitch had a lot of ice water in his veins, too. Lefroid could almost appreciate him for that.

"Forty-eight." Gerta's stat, right out of *Who's Who.*

"Mass communications, you said. Is that background going to be of use?"

Lefroid's tone was condescending. "Does it matter, Horger, if that Hungarian's technique is effective?"

The plastic surgeon gazed at the beige carpeting. "I suppose not. But if it isn't?"

Lefroid shrugged. "One less doctor of mass communications. We start over."

Sheet lightning flared in horizontal strips beyond the half-closed slats of the venetian blind behind Horger's desk. Its thunder rumbled closer.

"It does seem worth the risk." Horger's voice was a touch ingratiating.

"We will minimize that risk as much as possible."

"I mean the risk to Reifsnyder."

Lefroid's expression was one of mild surprise. "In the long view, Horger, I don't care about the risk to Reifsnyder. The problem is to acquire him in a manner that will protect us in the event that the procedure proves ineffective after he's released and before we can nullify him. *That* is the risk. But steps are already underway to minimize it. You will tell your Hungarian to get himself down here by the twenty-fifth—and in a manner that leaves no stupid trail."

"Obviously."

That was a questionable response, Lefroid thought. Nothing ever seemed obvious to the flabby doctor.

In her infrequent appearances among the resident scientists, CIAS Executive Director Elizabeth Carlisle came across as an efficient fussbudget. She was interested in proper paper work and whether there were sufficient logs in the living room woodbox and snowy linen for all meals in the dining salon.

She wore her ebony hair in a hawser-tight coiled braid. Her glasses were no-nonsense horn-rims that hardened her violet eyes. Her on-duty clothes were solid-color business suits. Her boxy shoes never had more than one-inch heels.

Only in Elizabeth Carlisle's voice was there a hint of what had led Albert Reifsnyder to make a gesture of friendliness beyond the impersonal courtesy required in their working relationship. "The Virgin Queen," Ed Moyle called her. Reifsnyder was certain he was the only person at CIAS who knew how unwarranted that disparaging nickname was.

Certain weekends began with what he delighted in thinking of as "The Transformation." One such weekend was beginning now, a late autumn Friday evening with a breeze

48

soft enough to be welcome through her half-open bedroom window.

Reifsnyder sprawled across the bed in khaki wash pants, plaid wool shirt, and stockinged feet, propped his head on an elbow, sipped a scotch and water, and watched. The matronly brogans were untied and kicked into the closet. The suit jacket was hung carefully, the skirt clipped neatly on its special hanger. In a peach slip, she flicked him a quick smile then sat at her Duncan Phyfe dresser. She placed the heavy glasses in a drawer and slowly slid it shut. Next the bobby pins came out to release the foot-long braid. She unknotted it with strong, fast fingers, shook the raven sheen free to her shoulders. Not a gray hair in it at forty-one, and he knew she didn't touch it up.

Her back to him, she opened the middle drawer and worked deftly. In the mirror, he watched the quick touches of eyebrow pencil, soft dusting of brush on slavic cheekbones, subtle accenting of mascara. Then the precise brushing on of subdued yet erotic lip rouge.

She turned gracefully. "You like?"

The effect was understated radiance. She still was not a beautiful woman, but this contrast with her contrived workday image never failed to ignite a beguiling warmth in his groin. It invaded him now.

"I do like, indeed."

This was one hell of a setup. He, divorced so long ago that he now had trouble remembering what Annelspeth had looked like; she, separated from a foreign service husband who'd been a career-driven bastard. All they had to do to preserve this compelling weekend dalliance was establish and maintain an appearance of mild antipathy between them. They had done it with a staged argument over the bedroom he had been assigned. Thereafter they had made a point of dining at separate tables even when they were the only two in the dining room. Chance encounters were acknowledged with cold nods.

Then on these weekends, and they were satisfyingly fre-

49

quent, when the other residents hurried out of the fenced compound and the housekeeping staff, there just until 7:30 P.M., departed leaving only the Security Center guard on the premises, Riefsnyder and Elizabeth Carlisle pursued their continuing discoveries of each other. This absorbing activity called for separately retiring up the broad staircase. Reifsnyder sat the library fire out, then reported its demise to the guard by way of saying goodnight—and establishing the fact that he was still up and about. Then he mounted the stairs long after Elizabeth had presumably retired.

But she would wait, fully clothed, for him to open then shut his own door noisily from the outside, slip down the east hall, and enter her room through a linen storage area that was accessed from both the hall and her bedroom. This bit of clandestine traipsing added piquancy, he discovered, though it wasn't done for added fun. The fact was that the proper entrance to her room could be seen from one portion of the downstairs hall.

Reifsnyder sipped his scotch again and watched. Elizabeth stood, crossed her arms behind her head, and slowly drew her slip upward. She had surprisingly good legs. Slender ankles rose to firmly fleshed calves. Knees with little cherub faces. Thighs a bit substantial but satin to the touch.

She sat again and slipped off her pantyhose. Stood, unhooked her bra, peeled it away with thumb and forefinger. Substantial breasts too, but not yet in middle-aged sag. The aureoles were dusky rose.

She lowered her head coquettishly and smiled. He had to shift position and adjust.

"Albert, patience. And remember, tonight it's your turn."

"So it is." He set the glass on the night table.

Elizabeth slid her utilitarian white panties over her thighs and flicked them aside with a playful toss. He shucked off his shirt and undershirt; unbuckled his belt.

"Albert," she admonished gently. "Remember the importance of pacing."

The soft night air was pleasant on his skin. Hands at his

50

sides, he moved to her. She stood statue-still. This was their game. This was her turn to remain passive, and he was allowed to employ only the gentlest of kisses.

He looked down into her moist eyes. Then, arms at his sides, he twisted and his mouth brushed her dimpled navel.

Elizabeth shuddered. "Oh, you *rat!* You know what that does to me!"

Downstairs, Abner Dortman glanced at the clock over the panel of TV screens. They ought to be going at it by now. He wished to hell there was a monitor in her room. It drove him nuts having to put it together by sounds. Dortman had the ears of a jungle animal. His CO in the Guard had noticed that and had used him way out front during night maneuvers. He could hear a twig crunch that a dog might miss. He could hear Reifsnyder sneak through the linen closet, and he could hear murmurs of conversation through Elizabeth Carlisle's solid oak door. And he could hear her make other noises, too. Little muffled animal squeaks. That wasn't backgammon they were playing in there.

There was no percentage in telling anybody. Marty Horn would yap at him to mind his own business. Might even get him fired. So Dortman listened and let his imagination race. When he heard Reifsnyder pussyfoot back to his own room, Dortman chewed his lip and tried to concentrate on the new magazine he'd brought in to replace the one that had been unaccountably ripped in half and tossed in the trash basket.

On the second Saturday in November, Reifsnyder sat at his desk in a cherry-paneled den off the main hall. Since he required no laboratory facilities for his study of the Behavioral Control Potentials of Subliminal Implants in English Language Television, he had been assigned this small office in the main building. His VCR and monitor crammed the little room where there was no real space for his desk, files, and chair. But he liked clutter; there was a feeling of security about it.

He liked Saturday work too. The phone was silent. The reduced staff stayed out of the way. Most of the time the CIAS residents found diversion off campus, so to speak. Reifsnyder reserved Saturdays for refinement of his growing body of notes and leisurely perusal of his mail. He was in the midst of the week's accumulation of mail now, and he turned the engraved cream-colored card over as if its blank back held some sort of clue to its appearance in the yield of field reports, the anticipated hardcover copy of Addison's *Subliminal Techniques in Consumer Product Advertising, 1974–1984,* and general junk.

He had never heard of the National Federation of Broadcast Sciences. That wasn't remarkable. The world was full of broadcasting groups and splinter organizations he wasn't necessarily aware of. What made this one interesting was the neatly penned message along the bottom edge of the printed invitation: "We would appreciate your joining us as a featured speaker. Will call to arrange honorarium."

Reifsnyder was not above supplementing his current CIAS salary with lecture fees. He was a better than average speaker and had discovered that audiences generally wanted form, not substance. Hence the secrecy of his CIAS work was not jeopardized. In his lectures, he didn't say much at all, but he said it well. Broadcasters were particularly easy audiences, hardly any of them sure of what they were doing in a business so dependent on audience whim. Most of them grasped for straws of wisdom that might do no more than indicate the direction of the public wind. For an equitable fee, he could provide a fair number of straws.

The invitation named the time: December 4, a Tuesday; and the place: Ames, New York. Not on the world's most traveled airlanes, by a long shot. Well, he'd see what they had to say when they called.

They—a sweet-voiced woman—called the following Wednesday, a day of cold sunlight that bounced off the triple security fences in frigid glints. His eyes ran along the fencing as he stood, receiver to ear, and scrabbled for a note pad. She had caught him on his way to the hallway coffee station.

"You will come, of course, Dr. Reifsnyder. It is to be a twenty-minute talk on your choice of subject. I'm afraid the honorarium isn't princely, but we can afford fifteen hundred dollars."

Fifteen hundred wasn't half-bad. He'd done more for less. Often. Her voice was unusually compelling: "And, of course, we will pay your expenses. Air fare to Albany and the rental of a car from there. And if there is any . . ." She seemed to search for words. ". . . Any amenity you might require, all you have to do is ask me."

She had managed to sound suggestive without saying anything specific. His groin tightened. Good God! Over the phone.

"Very generous of you, Ms. . . ."

"Lovell. Heather Lovell."

Was she kidding?

"My calendar is clear," he said without looking at it. "I thank you, and I'll be there."

"Oh, that's wonderful, Dr. Reifsnyder. I'll surely look forward to meeting you. Now don't you do a thing. Let me do it all for you. You'll want to arrive on the third and stay the night because we have you scheduled to speak at ten on the fourth. I assume you will want to leave from Baltimore-Washington International?"

"That will be fine."

"Wonderful, Doctor. Now you just put yourself in my hands. Let me do it all for you. I'll be back in touch when I've made the reservations."

Hands. Touch. Do it for you. She was a little devil, that girl. He hung up grinning. And he'd thought he was the expert at subliminals.

At Rapier Imports, Gerta Heissen replaced her phone with a smile of her own. She was a lean, well-muscled woman, a half inch taller than Lefroid. There wasn't a soft fiber in her copper-blond body. But she had the flexible

53

voice of an actress. The image she had just projected to Albert Reifsnyder was one of suggestive pliability. That was as far removed from her true personality as a pet Persian is from a panther.

Twelve minutes after takeoff from BWI Airport, the US Air DC-9 climbed above the thin altostratus overcast. Sunlight streamed through the oval windows on the right side of the slim cabin. Glorious, Reifsnyder thought, after nearly a week of winter rain. Elizabeth would love this. He hunched forward to gaze across the gold-touched cloud layer below the jet. He had discovered that she was unusually responsive to weather. On drizzly, oppressive nights, it took her a long time. When the evening was still, and they could hear katydids in the distant woods, she was almost too fast. In bright sunlight? They hadn't had an opportunity to try that.

A surprisingly short time later, the sun was swallowed in cloud again as the aircraft knifed downward, broke through four thousand feet over Albany, then trembled as the wing flaps and landing gear were extended. The *No Smoking* and *Fasten Seat Belts* signs flashed on.

His bag came to the roundel quickly. He strode to the car rental desks. A Buick, the yellow-uniformed brunette told him. To be charged to one Heather Lovell, credit already cleared and paper work accomplished. All she needed was his driver's license.

Well, how about that? He picked up his keys and bag, brushed past a woman with a cat carrier and a man in an olive green trench coat, wove through slowly moving arrivals, and emerged in the winter damp of upper New York State.

The car was blue, new, and, curiously, lacked seatbelts. Reifsnyder was in the ninety percent of drivers who didn't use them anyway. On the right front seat, he smoothed the map Ms. Lovell had mailed him with his ticket. Route 155 for about a mile to Interstate 87, then south on 87 to NY 30. West on 30 nearly fifty miles to the northbound turnoff to

Ames. The conference center, she'd said, was just beyond Ames. The engine purred. Reifsnyder drove unhurriedly out the airport access road.

In the terminal, the man in the green trench coat completed a phone call. He could have made the call from his car, but vehicle phones were open broadcast. His pale moon of a face wore the blankness of a none-too-confident janitorial employee on his first day. But Rollo Stark had worked efficiently for Rapier for nearly four years.

"Light blue Buick Skylark," he said and gave its license number. "Departed Albany airport at—" He exposed his watch with a stab of his left arm. "—twelve-oh-six. . . . Certainly he's in our control. He has been since he boarded at BWI."

By one o'clock, Reifsnyder had penetrated the Appalachians past Howe Caverns. The overcast had melted away, but sunlight failed to brighten the bleak, winter-stripped hills.

He almost missed the Ames turnoff, hit the brakes, and swung hard right amid an embarrassing tire squeal.

He glanced around, abashed. He needn't have felt self-conscious about his sloppy driving. The highway he had departed from was deserted save for a single car a half-mile behind.

In that car, a brown Ford that would not excite a second glance, the trench-coated man, named Stark, depressed the button on his CB mike. "Turned on 'final' at one-oh-three." He didn't expect a response. The less said, the better the security. The car was equipped with both CB and telephone; the CB had a very short range.

The two-lane blacktop rolled through naked woods and rock-strewn fields. Four minutes after he had turned off US 30 and still a mile out of Ames, Reifsnyder approached a side road that met his route at right angles. A gray van waited at a stop sign, blue exhaust curling under its blunt rear.

Reifsnyder felt no need to slacken speed. The van obviously waited for him to pass. He settled back in the cushioned red velour. Then the van leaped onto the main road.

Was the driver drunk?

Reifsnyder wrenched the wheel hard left. The sensitive power steering danced the Buick sideways. The van's solid nose slammed its right rear-quarter panel with an explosive crump. Glass fountained in a red-amber fan.

The impact jolted the car's skid forty-five degrees to the right. That kept it from plunging headlong into a swampy cutover just to the left of the roadway. Reifsnyder was conscious of the swift passage of stumps startlingly close to his vehicle as he jammed the brake and fought the yield of the road's shoulder.

The front end bounced back on the pavement. The rear skidded sideways along the shoulder, then whacked a suddenly materializing power pole. The Buick began to spin left, dug deep in the shoulder, and stopped as it hit a culvert headwall.

At that instant, Reifsnyder heard a sharp detonation. He was smacked in the face and chest by a solid mass, not unlike a huge piece of bread dough; blinded by its luminous elasticity.

Just as suddenly, it lost its mushy bulk and fell away. In his lap lay what looked like a big collapsed balloon. In the aftershock, he failed to realize he had just experienced the deployment of an automatic restraining device built into the steering column.

His legs began to tremble. He reached for the door handle but couldn't seem to find it. The door was yanked open from the outside.

"Not hurt, are you? Let me give you a hand." The man's face was out of view above the Buick's roof, but his arm reached into the car. Reifsnyder slid sideways toward the open door. Then he felt a sharp jab of pain in his lower back. Just above the belt. One quick stab, then it was gone. Peculiar. Otherwise he seemed all right.

Until he tried to step out of the car. The roadside swamp

whirled. He would have pitched onto his face if the man beside the car hadn't caught him. Reifsnyder sagged, his cheek distorted upwards against the hard fabric of the man's coat. As the early afternoon dissolved into black eclipse, Reifsnyder thought inanely, that's the second green trench coat I've seen today.

The two men from the van hustled Reifsnyder through its rear doors, one supporting his shoulders, the other hefting his slack knees. Stark unscrewed the heavy gauge steel needle from his syringe, shook out the remaining drops, and replaced needle and barrel in the black plastic case from his coat pocket. All the while, he threw nervous glances north and southward along the road. This was a necessarily speculative part of the tightly structured plan. He didn't need witnesses, though he did have a contingency precedure to deal with them.

He needn't have worried. The two men trotted back to Stark as he inspected the flattened front bumper of the van.

"No problem," the taller one, a blue-jacketed black man, said. "These things are built on a truck chassis."

His partner, a short man with a bush of gray hair and a drooping Hispanic mustache, stuffed a cigarette in his mouth and struck a match with his thumbnail. "Let's move it."

Stark nodded. They were utility goons, on Rapier retainer to do whatever they were asked. The two men climbed back into the van. The engine balked, ground over again, then howled.

"Easy," Stark warned beside the van. The driver threw him a sour look and rolled up his window. Stark returned to the shattered Buick, took Reifsnyder's overnight bag and briefcase from the floor of the front seat, and walked back to his car fifty feet down the shoulder. He got in, pulled past the side road and followed the van northward.

A dark oil stain crept from beneath the battered rental car and threaded its way around a clod of displaced earth. It bloomed into a rainbow in the roadside ditch. In a few minutes, the distant rattle of a poorly maintained pickup grew into a mechanical shout.

"Holy Hannah!" its aged, overall-clad driver said to the collie on the seat beside him. He stomped on screeching brakes, stalled the truck, and ran stiff-legged to the crumpled Buick. He found himself disappointed to discover there was no one inside.

CHAPTER

6

CSORNA ENJOYED THE nasal bite of antiseptic through his surgical mask. And the equipment here! Who could imagine that in the grottolike basement of this stone pile of a building such an operating room could exist. It had been a long time since he'd had facilities like this and a team of assistants who responded instantly and with deference. In Budapest, a doctor was just another technician, no better paid than a master mechanic and not much more highly regarded.

With fingers he could barely restrain from trembling in excitement, he gentled the flap of scalp and bone back in place. Then he deftly sutured it. The other four green-gowned members of the OR team were silent. Only Csorna and the anesthesiologist had spoken during the past three hours and twenty-seven minutes. Their words had been limited to essentials. Otherwise, the procedure had been accomplished in silence, broken only by the *hiss-poc* of the respiration equipment and the occasional clink of instruments on the steel tray overhanging the operating table.

At Csorna's side, Elmo Horger had been quite useless, a silent presence capable of attending to only the most routine aspects of the dual operation. Worse than no one at all. Csorna could better have used another nurse.

When he had begun the procedure and the initial whine of the craniotome filled the little OR, he had thought the ensuing total silence was the product of awe. Who wouldn't be impressed by the magnitude of what he was attempting here? Then more than three hours later, when the transfers were complete and the furrow-browed anesthesiologist and the two nurses realized the import of his subsequent neglect of Kooven and full attention to Reifsnyder, he knew the silence was the sweaty muffle of fear.

He had done the best he could for the already weakened donor, but seepage through the dura was too copious to control without a lengthy commitment of time and a diversion of the team from the already prepared recipient. There simply had not been such time to spare. Kooven had died at three-seventeen. Nothing dramatic. He just stopped breathing. By then, all of them were working on Reifsnyder, anyway. The only outward acknowledgement of Kooven's passing had been offered by the dark-haired nurse: a quick roll of her amber eyes toward the gurney to which Kooven had been relegated, face gray as an oyster, mouth now gaping, but eyes decently closed.

He had been brought to the OR already comatose, as much from his disintegrating heart as from the injected sedation Csorna had prescribed. The man was perhaps—how would you say?—legally dead already, barely sustained by portable and clanking life-support equipment.

Csorna, too, heard the stuttered last breath of his passing, but he did not look up from his work until the large *V* of neat little stitches was completed and tied off.

"So," he said loudly. "It is done."

He had followed the technique that had worked so well with Sweetstuff: less attention to the basil ganglia, more concentration on inserts in the parietal, upper temporal, and occipital lobes, with the last receiving additional implantation.

It was most regrettable that earlier today Horger had insisted on his returning to Montreal this very evening.

"But following the implants, I should observe at least the condition of the patient's—"

"I will handle all that," the fat doctor had interrupted as if he were instructing an unruly patient. "You are paid for the operation only. Post-operative care will be the responsibility of the clinic. You will be sent periodic reports, of course."

"But the value to science, to understand the processes of—"

Horger's pudgy face reddened. "Cut the bullshit, Doctor. You know and I know that you are being paid one hell of a fee for having conducted a dangerous and illegal operation. That's the sum of it. Any other interpretation is so much crap."

Until that moment, Csorna had deadened his conscience with the illusion that he was about to expand the periphery of medical knowledge, and that he was in control of the current project. But earlier this morning in Horger's ice-green office with its dated metal venetian blind, the Hungarian surgeon realized he'd never had any control of this. He had been bought.

Yet was this any less moral than his manipulation of Emily Hergenroeder through her pathetic needs? One could rationalize anything if the motivation was sufficient.

In the wash-up area, a converted storage space adjoining the basement OR, Csorna stripped off his latex gloves. When Horger entered, Csorna didn't look up.

"Fine work, Doctor." Horger stripped off his own gloves with loud snaps.

Csorna concentrated on his soapy fingers. "That is to be seen. You have transportation for me?"

"As soon as you are ready."

"I am ready now." He felt like a man who had created a

work of art and was being sent away before its unveiling. But he did not like these people, even feared them. There was something here to be well away from. "I am ready now," he repeated.

He was driven to Albany County Airport by a moon-faced man who hardly spoke. Night had fallen by the time he hailed a taxi outside Montreal's Dorval International. The cab left him in front of his St. Leonard apartment building, chilled as much by the events of the morning as by the eddy of snow grains whipped across his cheek by a capricious wind.

He had killed a man. Was there any other way to look at it? He now had a Zurich bank account with its credentials securely tucked in his suit jacket pocket, but he had killed a man to get it. Mice, beagles, apes, and now that pathetic form on the gurney against the green-painted OR wall.

But the man had been dying anyway, had he not? Csorna's ministrations had not cost him more than a few more minutes of unconsciousness. Did that matter? He reached for his outer door key.

"Doctor?"

Where had the tall man in the black raincoat come from? That car ten yards along the curb? Another man was visible in its driver's seat. The back of Csorna's head prickled.

"Dr. Csorna?"

The little surgeon edged across the sidewalk toward the apartment's brick walkway. "I have not time." His voice was hoarse with sudden apprehension.

"I have a message for you," the tall man said. Csorna could not make out his face under the hat brim. A homburg. Did muggers wear homburgs? Perhaps this concerned the newly established Swiss bank account. A complication? Some of his apprehension ebbed. Then it surged back. Wouldn't perhaps a plainclothes police officer wear a homburg?

"I said, I have a message for you, Doctor." The voice was oddly soft, almost a murmur.

Certainly not a mugging, Csorna decided. The man knew

his name. He stopped his slow sideways retreat and faced the man who was now no more than a yard distant.

"What message?" Csorna asked.

"Good-bye, Doctor," the voice said gently. But there was nothing gentle about the boot that clubbed Csorna's groin. He was struck so suddenly that he couldn't cry out. He doubled over, gagging at the incredible agony.

The man's double-handed fist crashed into the nape of Csorna's neck. The little doctor's head flew up. His eyes rolled back until only the whites showed. Then he pitched forward, face smacking the concrete walk.

The tall man bent over him, tested for pulse, then rifled his pockets. He stood up, stuffed the Zurich bank credentials and Csorna's wallet into his coat pocket. This had to look like a fatal street robbery. He ran on his toes, lightly for such a tall man, to the little Ford Escort. "No lights until we reach the corner."

"He dead?" The driver's voice was a rasp.

"Isn't that what we got paid for?"

"Jeez, a doctor!"

"I don't ask questions. I get paid. I do my job. Do yours and get us out of here."

The Ford eased away without lights, almost without sound, until it reached the cross street. Then the brake lights flared, the tail and headlights flicked on. The car turned south. The fluttery sound of its exhaust faded. Dr. Bela Csorna would never know that the impressive Swiss bank account folder and its gold embossed confidential account number were frauds. He had performed for no money at all, but he didn't live to be disappointed. Rapier had spared him that.

Lefroid's tone was detached. "So we lost Kooven. To be expected in his condition, was it not? No complications about his disposal, I trust?"

"Cremation. We have the facilities."

"And the OR team?"

63

"Secure."

"Oh, are they?" Lefroid's detachment ended abruptly. "Obviously, Horger, they must be sent elsewhere." Lefroid picked at his steak, a far cry from the medium-rare he had ordered. He didn't like this restaurant, but its advantage of out-of-the-way obscurity on the state highway south of Kingston outweighed the unimpressive fare. When he'd arranged for this meeting, he had found Horger exceedingly nervous. Lefroid had made a concession to the fat idiot. He would not insist that Horger come to Manhattan; he would meet the plastic surgeon part way. He had driven eighty miles up the Hudson. Horger had come one hundred forty from the clinic.

"But these people are part of my permanent staff," Elmo Horger protested. "They're totally trustworthy."

"No one is totally trustworthy, I have arranged—"

"You have arranged?"

Lefroid dismissed Horger's blurt with an upward flick of his cold eyes. "I have arranged for the one nurse, Felkirk, to be employed by Memorial Hospital in Kahalui, Maui."

Horger's fork stopped halfway to his mouth.

"The other nurse, also unmarried, I believe, will be offered a substantial staff position in a private clinic in Juneau, Alaska."

"Alaska! She'll never accept that."

"The salary is to be generous, and I have learned that she is in considerable debt. She will go. As to the anesthetist—"

"Charlie Fritz? I need him."

Lefroid did not like interruptions, particularly those that interjected useless commentary. "I am aware of his name, Horger, and his utilitarian value. But Dr. Fritz is about to find himself in demand in Mexico City. Also at a private clinic, one that caters to an overmoneyed clientele similar to your own. Again, the salary will be impressive."

"That would seem to wrap it all up nicely." Horger's tone edged on the sarcastic. Would the man never learn to control his tongue? "One nurse in Hawaii, another in Alaska.

Charlie Fritz in Mexico. Csorna in Montreal." He speared a broccoli flower. "Montreal, though, isn't all that far away, is it?"

Lefroid's bland expression didn't change. "Dr. Csorna is no longer a concern."

He enjoyed watching the blood drain from Horger's face.

"In that case," the plastic surgeon managed with effort, "there's no one to worry about. The entire attending group will be scattered to the winds."

"Except, of course, for you."

The fat doctor's color did not improve.

Lefroid chewed slowly, swallowed. "The status of the project?"

Horger blinked rapidly. "Still in post-op when I left." He dabbed his mouth with his blue napkin and ran his eyes around the crowded, Bavarian-styled dining room. "I should be there. I really should be there."

"If he is in trouble, there seems to me to be very little your particular specialty could do for him. If he's in serious trouble, we will have to dispose of him. For routine post-op, your resident assistant is no doubt as qualified as you."

Horger let the jab pass. "But Harris has been told it was accident trauma."

"I'm delighted that you have followed instructions." Lefroid's face was expressionless. "Now continue to follow them. You may return to your patient."

He remained after the insufferable doctor had left, outwardly impassive, a bored transient businessman finishing his luncheon sirloin. But Lefroid's bland face masked an excitement that he seldom experienced. *Reifsnyder had survived the operation.*

Lefroid was not an excitable man, a trait inherited from his mother. A New England Trent, she had been processed through Miss Hall's School and Smith. Then at twenty-one, Rosalind Trent had rebelled at the precast inevitability of it all. She wheedled a Paris trip out of her preoccupied bondbroker father, ditched her former college roommate the first week, easily blended into the Bohemian fringe of American art colony emigrees and refused to return. She saw Hemingway at a distance, actually spoke—once—with a disinterested Scotty Fitzgerald, was never quite sober and wandered resolutely from bed to bed until she was brought up short by an acute case of pregnancy.

Remarkably, she was able to name the father because she had been ill with influenza during the identified month, except for the one significant week. He was a Frenchman named Bayoux, a forty-year-old sales representative for a Bordeaux vintner in town on business. The affair had begun as a joke, a drunken discussion of the worth of the three women at the crowded table in the Montmartre bistro were they rated in francs. Rosalind won hands down, and the talk wandered on to less intriguing but fully as boisterous subjects.

In the din of wine-sharpened voices, the sales representative's oddly pale eyes held hers.

"Mam'selle?"

Her reddish eyebrows rose.

"Je sais—I know it was a game. But I would be willing to make you a gift of the amount. Twice that amount, *chéri.* You are *magnifique!"*

Blood rushed to her delicate ears, surely tinting them crimson beneath her helmet of bobbed russet hair, a rush not of indignation, but of excitement—this in the days before she learned to mask emotion with a calmness that was often mistaken for intelligence. The idea of playing whore just once was incredibly stimulating.

There was another factor that led to her impending disaster; could this hard-looking Frenchie with his steel stare possibly know how badly she needed money? Her blue-nosed father had long since cut her off. She was living on the sufferance of these unpredictable acquaintances.

"Twice that amount," she said, taking his slender hand.

In the light of the garret room's single bulb, he was as thin as a stick, his nearly hairless body as pale as his face.

66

She slipped off her peasant skirt and blouse, discarded her lace-edged step-ins. Without warning, he introduced her to a style of stimulation with which she'd had no prior experience. Her fingers twisted his sparse hair, and she lost control in an instant.

Sometime in the early morning, he tossed a blanket over her and left the agreed number of franc notes on her rumpled pillow. He also left her pregnant.

In the throes of morning nausea, she found him again, a simple matter of questioning café owners until she turned up one whom Bayoux regularly supplied. She took up a queasy vigil until he appeared.

"M'sieur Bayoux, you do remember me?"

He looked even colder than she recalled, and now she noticed that he had strangely pointed teeth.

"*Pardon, mam'selle, mais je ne—*"

"Oh you remember, all right, you son of a bitch. You made me pregnant!"

"Shh! *Mon Dieu*, shh, you bitch." He propelled her to a deserted corner booth and crouched across the table toward her. "For God's sake, you whore! I'm a respectable businessman."

"Are you married?"

"No, praise God." His hand shook. He got up.

"Don't you leave, you bastard!"

"Give me a chance, will you?" He returned with wine for her, a large cognac for himself.

"*Ecoutez moi.* Listen, I'll give you money to take care of it, then be more careful in the future. It is no big thing, you understand? Girls are in trouble all the time. They take care of it."

"In some alley butcher's back room? Not for me, Mr. Bayoux."

His face grew pastier. "You don't mean to have the child!"

"I don't mean to have a bastard, thank you. It will have a name, your name, else your name will not be worth having."

67

"Mais mam'selle . . ." He shrugged helplessly. "That is blackmail."

The agreement was simple. They were married in a civil ceremony. He left her in the street outside the building. The checks arrived at the turn of the month and at midmonth with never more than a two-day delay.

Rosalind's sparse circle of friends at first teased her for such carelessness, but when her pregnancy turned troublesome they became concerned. She spotted often and once had to be rushed to the neighborhood doctor when she began to hemorrhage. But she managed to hold the child to term, was careened in a battered Citroen through rain-blackened streets, and delivered in agony in a charity ward.

The birth certificate read "André Bayoux." She thought it just deserts that she name the scrawny, long-faced issue after her father, Andrew. And the shrunken waif was put up for immediate adoption. By prearrangement, the checks stopped coming exactly a year from the day of the distressing marriage. By then, Rosalind had learned a lot more about accident prevention. In another year, she was able to move to almost grandiose quarters across the Seine. Her price trebled. She saw René Bayoux only once again. For him, she charged a truly exorbitant fee, and he failed to recognize her throughout the lightning-fast encounter. He was stunned at its brevity; she had learned a lot.

The child was adopted within seventeen days. Rosalind Trent Bayoux's insistence on providing him with a legitimate name was a hollow effort after all. The boy promptly became André Lefroid. Charles Lefroid, his adoptive father, was the sole owner of Lefroid et Fils, a Le Havre-based fabricator of small boats. He was a taciturn man, married to a domineering American brunette whose lean frame was as tightly disciplined as her survival-trained mind.

She had clawed her way out of South Scranton through a name change from Emma Matusak to Eileen Madison and through a degree of judicious sleeping around with a pair of middle-aged coal barons who were quite happy to be let off their respective hooks by separately financing her through Baltimore's Goucher College. Neither benefactor knew of the other. Emma-Eileen was able to work a remunerative financial parlay. André never discovered that there were similarities in the sexual careers of his biological and his adoptive mothers. He remained ignorant of the history of his birth and assumed that the Lefroids were his true parents. They never disabused him of that assumption.

Eileen Madison met stone-faced Charles Lefroid at a sales convention in New York where she had been sent as a representative of a Baltimore supplier of marine paints. In the late 1920s, women sales reps were a distinct novelty. Charles Lefroid, exotically pronounced "Sharl Lefwa" (she ultimately Americanized the last name to rhyme with Freud, eliminating the French "r," which she never could master), was captivated more by rarity than by Eileen's severe smartness and clipped efficiency. Her efficacy in the vast bed of his Plaza suite also was provocative. He bought a lot of paint and convinced her in heavily accented English to marry him before the convention closed.

In less than a year, he discovered that her physical exuberance in New York had not been typical of her standard sexual proclivities. She permitted him to service her infrequently, and he turned out to be sterile. She also allowed him whatever extracurricular activities he wished so long as he kept his mouth shut about them—her exact words. And she soon turned her repressed maternal instincts, such as they were, to their adopted son.

André's earliest memories were of the grim parental power struggle with Lefroid *père* most often losing; the increasingly disruptive influence of worldwide depression on the family boat business; then, when he was about to enter school, the bitter and highly vocal fight on the sun porch one otherwise bright June day and his mother's inexcusable—to him—packing them both into a cab, then onto a New York-bound steamer.

From then on, Eileen Lefroid seemed at war with much

69

of the world. The bank drafts from Le Havre weren't enough. She took a job with Best & Company in the buying department. She was a fighter, and she instilled that virtue in her now gangling son. She also imprinted indelibly on his consciousness that reward came only to those who reached out and seized it, that morality was an impediment, and that most people were basically stupid. This credo, forged in desperation in a crumbling world, never left him.

The war swept away Lefroid et Fils. Charles disappeared after an ill-considered harangue of a black-uniformed SS major who was charged with impounding the small company's assets. By then, André was enrolled in a forbidding brick pile of a junior high in Queens, defending his physical ugliness with guile that consisted of planting rumors about his tormentors' sexual deficiencies. It was difficult to maintain supremacy when the class girls twittered about the reported tininess of the stumps between their legs.

He developed into that grim sort of youth whom peers shun because of obviously superior intellect and even more obvious physical limitations. His peculiarly pointed teeth in a wide, near-lipless mouth earned him the behind-the-back nickname, "Barracuda."

Barracuda Lefroid in City College was known in the vernacular of the postwar day as a wheeler-dealer. He knew which co-eds would do what for how much. He pimped. At rates that wouldn't be legitimately equalled for three decades, he loaned the money he made. He collected from deadbeat classmates by threatening to disseminate the same kind of rumors that had served him so well in his hardscrabble high school. He was loathed and feared and known as a son of a bitch without a conscience.

He knew he could never work for anyone but himself. The first major entrepreneurial break came right after graduation in the guise of a classmate in trouble. The sweating young man, fat as a boar and just as obtuse intellectually, needed money to regenerate a small and staggering wholesale gift business he had inherited from an abruptly deceased father. Legitimate sources wouldn't touch the deal. In desperation, he remembered Barracuda Lefroid.

He got his six thousand, an impressive amount for Lefroid to have amassed through CCNY's limited female resources. It would have been more except for an unfortunate setback in which Lefroid had been forced, for the good of the business, to finance an abortion. But only one.

He realized, of course, that his porcine classmate could never relaunch the lurching wholesale operation. Lefroid had written the loan terms so that the business became his before the full six thousand had been blown. Now Lefroid had a base of operations, not impressive to the eye but strategically situated on Sixth Avenue before it became the extravagantly renamed Avenue of the Americas. That same year, his mother conveniently died, even paying her own way out through a burial insurance policy he didn't know she had.

He expanded over the backs of additional small wholesale operators who were desperate enough to accept his quiet offers of instant cash. One of them, a Lebanese merchant named Zahle, flatly balked at the hugely inflated repayment and threatened to visit a friend at Manhattan Precinct concerning usury rates. That was the last threat he ever made. Mr. Zahle was found face down in the New Jersey Meadows, apparently the victim of some obscure mob action. Lefroid hadn't touched him. Lefroid was a manipulator, not an activist. A certain freelance specialist handled the labor. That was Lefroid's first business venture that incurred a fatality. It had gone well.

He had deduced that the standard organization that engaged in sublegal activities—the "organized" crime that was federal law enforcement's stock-in-trade—was a highly inefficient way to conduct business. Its basic problem was one of size, an armylike table of organization that worked its ponderous way through lieutenants in nominal charge of income production down to the lowly soldiers who enforced payments, bent recalcitrant whores back into line, guarded innumerable backs and even chased coffee at staff meetings. Despite their reputations, nurtured by the press and by the law enforcement agencies dependent on them for staff and budget increases, pay raises, and professional longevity, such organizations were, in Lefroid's opinion, payroll-padded, exposure-prone, high-overhead, inefficient anachronisms in the computer age.

He had turned his back on that approach. He had neither the traditional family connections nor the demands of ego that led to the formation of such ponderous organizations. And he perceived that the risks increased geometrically with the addition of supernumeraries to the payroll.

Thus Rapier Imports was a contractual operation sequestered behind a facade that conducted a legitimate wholesale business and employed two dozen people to do it. Of this permanent staff, only Gerta Heissen—and Lefroid himself, of course—were crossovers. Anyone else who worked in the cavernous third-floor warehousing areas or in the import-export office on the seventh floor would have been astounded to discover that he or she was no more than part of an elaborate cover for Rapier's far more lucrative activities.

Lefroid had found Gerta Heissen in the law offices of Sharp & Kidwell, whom he had briefly retained to draw up incorporation papers for Rapier's legitimate screen. She was of Swiss parentage, born in Lausanne, sent by affluent, disinterested parents to secondary school in the U.S. at her own insistence. The Heissens, a family known for the manufacture of plastic furniture, which was passed off as Scandinavian, failed to discern Gerta's analytical sense and her gifts in the areas of mathematics and language. Had she been a victim of the American public school system, her superior IQ would have been detected early, then it would have been largely wasted through pressures to make her conform to class norms. In Lausanne, a reverence of tradition overrode more progressive educational concerns.

At sixteen, Gerta became fascinated with the potentials of the computer. In the U.S., she discovered through voracious reading, it was something of a national cult, even an intellectual substitute for the semieducated masses the U.S. public school system persisted in producing. But American private schools, some of them, had managed to escape the *mano morte* of bureaucratic conformity. She selected Crider Hall, buried in the hills of Connecticut, a little brain tank of a girls' school whose steel-gray headmistress was dedicated to the premise that woman's mind was not equal to man's; it was a hell of a lot better. From there, Gerta Heissen, now a lean coppery blonde of seventeen, raced through four years of advanced computer logic at John Phillips Institute of Technology, a little-publicized northern New Jersey college concentrating on high-tech training, primarily for the six leading corporations that financed the school.

She was headed, at least two professors agreed, toward a career that would make Mary Cunningham Agee look as if she were walking backward. But they were wrong.

Although she was not a classic beauty or even a routine flashy one, Gerta did possess the subtle but irresistible sexual challenge of the coldly intellectual girl. She wore amber-rimmed glasses, the kind preferred by literary types. Her shoulder-length copper hair was drawn back from her angular face and secured at the nape of her neck by a gold clip. The soft brown eyes masked a personality as detached and calculating as the FORTRAN and COBOL languages she had learned so well in the Farmington Valley west of Hartford.

A hulking Phillips junior named Roland "Rolly" Pepp from a town near Hazleton, Pennsylvania, was captivated by those deerlike and seemingly vulnerable eyes behind the oversized glasses. "I'm going to have that, one way or another," he informed his half-listening roommate. That was the first and last time he mentioned her, though he didn't simply drop the subject. In fact, he pursued it avidly until Gerta, wearied by his persistence, allowed herself to be driven to a secluded park just outside Pompton Plains where Rolly attempted an approach that might have been termed amiable rape.

With lots of gruff laughter, he pawed at her. She resisted traditionally at first, prying his chubby hands loose, turning her head away from his urgent mouth. When he dropped his hand to her inner thigh, though, she spat one word. "Stop."

He did hesitate, but then he considered the humiliation of defeat. "Stop, hell. You've got me in a sweat, babes. Where I come from, it's a girl's duty to do something about that."

What he failed to perceive, in addition to her obvious disdain, was that she possessed a monumental temper. Now she fought to channel her boiling rage into effective counteraction.

Her cotton blouse was secured at the throat by a brooch of carved ivory. While Rolly Pepp concerned himself with the barrier of pantyhose, she detached the brooch. In the darkness, he was unaware of that. It is doubtful that he would have noticed in full daylight.

The brooch's pin was a full inch of gleaming gold-plated steel. She held it delicately between the thumb and forefinger of her right hand and grazed his crotch with her left.

"Now you're coming around, babes," Rolly Pepp said.

She wasn't doing any such thing. She was targeting. She slid her right hand along his leg, poised the brooch's extended pin. The motion of her wrist wasn't noticeable in the dark front seat, a forward flick of an inch and a half.

He felt as if he had been hit with a flaming club.

"Holy God!"

His forehead slammed the steering wheel. Both hands clamped his shattered groin. The agony fanned upwards, compressed his stomach into his throat. He twisted sideways and vomited out the open window. "Oh, God!" His head lolled back. "What the hell did you do to me?" His stomach rolled over again and he retched foam.

"Take me back to the dorm, please," she said with no emotion at all.

He struggled with the gears and drove like a drunk. That was as close to sex with a partner as Gerta ever came. She fulfilled her occasional needs herself and with far more advanced techniques than any man—or less informed woman—could have. She was a born researcher and never undertook anything without an expert's knowledge, if not an expert's experience.

Unfortunately for her, Mr. Pepp had a need to assuage his trodden ego. He was in unconcealable pain for several days. His goggle-eyed roommate could not suppress his curiosity. For his benefit, Pepp concocted a story about Gerta's insatiable sexual demands.

"A wild-eyed nympho! She bit me! Would you believe that?"

His roommate, a studious virgin from Atlanta, certainly would. The story became more convincing as he retold it. The vision of Gerta Heissen uncontrollably clamping her even, little teeth on Pepp's balls became campus lore. And it worked its way, in a modified version, into the confidential personality profile that was maintained and continuously updated on each student. The profile was available to potential employers who were willing to pay the considerable fee for its access. In a field where the acquisition of government contracts frequently depended on the impeccable records of the holder's key employees, a blemished personality profile could be costly indeed.

Hers cost Gerta executive-level positions with the first five companies she approached. She couldn't understand what had gone wrong. She had graduated near the head of her class. Could archaic anti-feminist psychology be not yet dead in this advanced year?

Ultimately she faced a choice: home to parents who appeared interested only in sidetracking their troublesome daughter through a marriage to some preferably titled but certainly affluent business type; or buy her independence with whatever suitable work she could find. She found it with the law firm of Sharp & Kidwell, a small organization with Navajo-rugged offices on Central Park West, specializing in business law. Gerta got the job in the most mundane manner. She responded to a *New York Times* want ad.

Charlie Kidwell, a perpetually scarlet-faced man who looked more a Kansas farm equipment salesman than a Harvard-polished attorney, realized almost instantly that his new secretary was not an average college product; not even from an average college. Charlie was in the throes of installing a computer terminal accessing a Boston-based mainframe, and he had advertised for a computer-trained secretary. When she extracted more information than he dreamed existed on the first request he had her process, it was evident that she wouldn't stay with Sharp & Kidwell long. After a few weeks, he had reason to facilitate her departure.

"You noticed that cool number in the office next door?" he confided to Lefroid after he had known him less than ten minutes. "Mind like a steel spring. Computer-trained. I mean *trained*. Went to some special college where they major in that kind of stuff."

Lefroid realized that Kidwell would never make a top corporation lawyer with a free-running mouth like this, but he was interested.

"Computer-trained?" He had just installed his own on-line terminal, ostensibly for Rapier Imports inventory control and customer files, but he had a lot more than that in mind.

"Like an Einstein with a gash," Kidwell said irreverently. "And we can't pay her enough to keep her around long."

"How much, might I ask?"

"Seventeen K and standard fringes."

Lefroid hired her for just over twenty thousand and didn't care whether Kidwell was miffed at having such a bright woman whisked practically from under him. Kidwell wasn't. His problem with Gerta had been that he couldn't get her precisely under him. He'd discovered that she was as cold as an ice water shower.

He had set Lefroid up and felt well rid of the brittle Ms. Heissen. But Lefroid needed her brain. Her slender body was of no interest to him. Nor was any woman's body. He had determined, after a single embarrassing episode with a shallow brunette co-ed (who'd first laughed at his ungenerous equipage, then at its sudden uncontrollable spasm) that he need only sublimate sexual urges into more productive energies. Women seemed to sense this and found it menacing. Gerta Heissen found it not so different from her own attitudes, but she did not deny herself skilled self-release.

What they did together—after Lefroid had determined that she had the same amoral need to succeed as did he— was to build Rapier.

CHAPTER
7

REIFSNYDER STRUGGLED TO gluey consciousness. He forced his eyelids open against white pain. Then the whiteness resolved itself into a plaster ceiling. When he moved his eyes against the throb centered behind them, he found almost luminescent whiteness in the walls, too.

A hospital room? What in hell was he doing in a hospital room?

If he was indeed in a hospital, there must be some sort of patient signaling button. He found it behind his head, a white cord looped over the birch headboard with a brown button at its bulged end.

He slid an arm from under the sheet and pressed the button. The simple effort was exhausting. His hand dropped beside his head. He was astounded to feel the rough texture of gauze with his fingertips.

The door beyond the foot of the bed opened on oiled hinges.

"No, don't move your head just yet." The voice was male, overstuffed. A fat man's voice, though Reifsnyder couldn't yet see its source without raising his head against the voice's professional-sounding admonition. Then the man moved into Reifsnyder's view, a chubby fellow indeed, his jowls and multifold chins accentuated by Reifsnyder's upward angle of vision.

"I am Dr. Elmo Horger." The officious tone did not altogether disguise a thread of underlying apprehension. Reifsnyder was tuned to subtle transmissions by the nature of his work.

"And this place?" His own voice sounded cottony.

"This is the Horger Clinic. A salvation for those in search of more fulfilled life through cosmetic improvement."

"A fat farm."

"We prefer to put it another way. We also offer cosmetic surgery. You, obviously, are uncertain as to why you are here."

"To put it mildly."

"Your name?" Horger cleared his throat with a little explosive grunt.

"I'm sure you know my name through the personal effects I assume I've been relieved of."

"The point, sir, is not whether I know your name, but whether you know it. In cases of severe concussion, it's a routine question."

"My name is Albert P. Reifsnyder. P for Payson. Address: Four-two-oh-two West Classon, Bethesda, Maryland. Want the zip code?"

"No need to be facetious."

"No need to assume I'm suffering from concussion."

"Are you a doctor?"

"As a matter of fact, I am. A doctor of mass communications."

"Obviously I meant physician." Horger sounded miffed.

Reifsnyder had tired of this indefinite supercilious conversation. And his head thudded. "Dammit, Doctor, I want you to tell me where in hell the Horger Clinic is and precisely why I am here!"

"We are in upper New York State, near Sacandaga Lake.

You are here because . . . don't you recall the circumstances of the accident?"

"Accident?" His mind wouldn't focus. There had been an empty road, a truck of some sort. Light gray.

"A collision. You struck a roadside culvert and received a head injury. Fortunately for you, one of our staff vehicles happened on the scene and brought you here. Had you been forced to rely on paramedics from the local volunteer fire department, it is doubtful that we would be enjoying this conversation at this point."

"That bad?"

"A severe scalp laceration which bled profusely." Horger cleared his throat again.

A picture flashed through Reifsnyder's mental muzziness. A huge mound of bread dough. His face sank into its spongy folds. Then it was gone.

"A scalp wound?"

"Yes, a triangular flap of the scalp the size of your palm torn loose on two sides above and behind the right ear. Cleansed, carefully sutured back in place. There will be a scar, but your hair will cover it. The greater fear is the possibility of concussion."

"Brain damage."

"Concussion sounds less threatening."

Reifsnyder thought that over.

"We notified the NFBS," Horger offered.

Reifsnyder scowled. The bandage's adhesive pulled at his forehead.

"The National Federation of Broadcast Sciences."

Reifsnyder began to shake his head, but the motion produced a penetrating throb.

"If you know what I'm talking about," Horger said in a flare of what appeared to be impish nervousness, "signify by saying aye."

"I don't."

"You were to speak there, I believe. The invitation was in the car with your notes."

Memory flooded back. "My God, they're expecting me to-day."

"Yesterday. I told you, we notified the conference of your inability to attend. They no longer expect you and have already arranged for a substitute speaker. We have also notified CIAS of your temporary stay here."

That disturbed Reifsnyder. He had purposely given his home address in Bethesda when Horger had tested him. There seemed no reason for the doctor or his clinic to be privy to Reifsnyder's CIAS connection. He concentrated. His wallet and briefcase, of course. Perfectly understandable for them to seek his ID and whom to notify, was it not?

The really upsetting element was Horger's aura of apprehension. The man transmitted it by so many little signals: The flick of his washed-out eyes away from prolonged contact with Reifsnyder's. The soft drumming of his right forefinger on the left bicep of his defensively folded arms. The frequent clearing of the throat.

"You notified CIAS? What did they say?"

"The director—a Dr. Carlisle? She expects you to remain with us until you are out of danger."

"From concussion." Reifsnyder's tone was waspish.

"From concussion." Horger cleared his throat. "I'll leave you for the moment, Doctor." Did he emphasize the title a shade derisively? "Your need will be attended by Nurse Felkirk."

"My current need, I'm afraid, is an urgent requirement that I take a leak. I assume that other door leads to a bathroom?"

"It does, but you are confined to bed for the moment, I'm afraid. I'll send in the nurse."

Reifsnyder raised his head slightly to watch Horger leave, the exertion popping sweat beneath the bandage.

The door swung open again.

"You're Felkirk?"

The dark-haired nurse was short and low-slung, her light blue uniform skirt taut across her buttocks. She nodded and held up an enameled urinal. "Can you handle this yourself, or shall I join you?"

A real card, this one. He reached for the thick-spouted utensil. The motion shot a bolt of pain straight up the back of his head. For a long moment, he thought he would throw up, but the nausea passed.

She lifted the blanket and sheet, helped him roll on his side, and gazed at him with expressionless coffee bean eyes. "On your back," she commanded when he had finished. "Doctor says you're to stay on your back."

"You're sweet," he said to her departing rump through a haze of cranial pressure.

He tried to recall the details of the accident. The car was not his. He knew that. A borrowed car? Rented, that was it. Rented at a booth. An airport booth. Albany . . .

Then west on a good road that worked into mountains. A turnoff to a secondary road. The gray truck. No, a van. Gray van. It pulled out too soon, too damned soon. Impact!

He remembered hitting the brakes, slewing sideways. Another impact. Then the blanket of bread dough enveloped him, fell away. Hands reached in?

He shook his head in reflex to clear it and was punished by a deep throb. Lights of pain shimmered against his clamped eyelids. He'd remember not to do that again.

Maybe the fat doctor was right. Reifsnyder had never experienced the effects of concussion. Could it produce this floating disorientation? He fixed his mind on facts. My name is Albert Payson Reifsnyder, born forty-eight years ago in Nuala, Downstate Illinois, to Edward and . . . My God! And *Ella*, that was it. Ella Reifsnyder. The brief blockage dismayed him. A lapse of concentration amid post-trauma smog, that was all, wasn't it? He was sharp enough.

Ed and Ella—and Hemp Hill, his father's wry name for the slight rise in the one-hundred-twenty acres he had bought reasonably from the government just after World War II. Marijauna had been raised there, not for its cannabis but for the tough fibers of its stalks that had gone into assault glider tow ropes.

His recalling that little detail, Reifsnyder decided, had to be a positive indication.

At Nuala Consolidated High School, he'd been fascinated by the school's low-power, student-operated radio station. He made it to staff announcer in his senior year, a competent year, but one that was undistinguished except for his work at the mike. He got into Chicago Northwestern easily enough.

He'd majored in communications before it became a national fad. He was good at it, a late bloomer headed for honors until he was sidetracked by a dark-eyed little ball of sparks improbably named Annelspeth Duellen, daughter of an Indianapolis Chrysler dealer. "You Can't Go Wrong Dealin' With Duellen."

If he could recall that, he couldn't be too far disassembled.

He knew he could never forget Annelspeth—the fact of her, if not the details. Piled mahogany hair. Couldn't really picture her face, but he hadn't been able to for quite a while. Wanted to forget it, of course, and did. She'd been a bitch. But not until after he'd married her. A mismatch on the face of it, big lunk Reifsnyder and his little Barbie Doll. True enough; he'd bought himself a living toy he could sleep with. That was the problem. What man in his right mind wouldn't want to cuddle that armful of rich hair, smoky eyes—weren't they a bright emerald? And who wouldn't fall for that dusting of pinhead freckles. Oh, it was coming back to him fine now.

He was "away a lot." She "got bored." Mundane soap operatics, he thought, but they were her excuses for sleeping around while he was on the featureless Illinois, Iowa, and Hoosier highways, trying to sell a packaged "good music" format to radio stations not yet captivated by the formatting concept.

She couldn't even argue creatively, let alone screw

creatively. Maybe that had been her trouble, Reifsnyder reflected, staring straight up at a minor flaw in the ceiling plaster. She couldn't give. A lovely lump, waiting to receive, to drain. He'd discovered that in their senior year, but he'd had the foolish notion that somewhere in that diminutive construction there had been a fuse he could light.

He never lit it, nor did anyone else as far as he knew. She'd married again. An encore nonperformance with a lawyer from Detroit. Reifsnyder had seen him once, just before the divorce, nodding vacantly at him on the sidewalk as Reifsnyder returned home a day early from a grind into Central Iowa. He'd discovered that she hadn't quite gotten the bed back together in time.

Good-bye, little doll bitch. Good-bye to both his parents the same year. Some year. Ed Reifsnyder, too deep into acreage expansion, then broken by the double punch of flood followed by drought, just folded up. His last words, "The hell with it, Ella," prompted her to follow suit within seven months. Her heart, the perplexed doctor told him. "I know," Reifsnyder agreed. "It broke."

He moved out of the Midwest, away from reminders of Annelspeth's juvenile randiness, away from the now-decrepit farm he was able to sell for nearly half its value, away from the bleak blacktop of his sales beat—to the richer rolling greens of Maryland's Montgomery County, where the action was. To Sutter Group, a minor-league think tank in need of someone (anyone?) with a communications degree to fill out the response to an RFP for a government grant to underwrite a study of "The Effect of Daytime Television Drama on the Work Cycle of the American Housewife." A real nothing of a study, but there was money in it, and Reifsnyder's résumé fulfilled the old broadcasting dictum of being in the right place at the right time. He had a flair for writing the kind of reports government agencies devoured because they sounded authoritative without derailing personal applecarts. An envious co-worker at Sutter Group called it the "gift of shitease."

Sutter introduced Reifsnyder to subliminals. He read everything Wilson Bryan Key had produced and took the trouble to seek out that well-publicized Nader of the advertising world at a Washington Hilton conference on broadcasting in the eighties. Anything Key can do, I can do better, Reifsnyder determined. In less than two years, he was the new expert-from-out-of-town. CIAS offered him a "fellowship," which meant that some government somebody, somewhere, thought there were strategic or tactical possibilities in broadcasting subliminal embeds. When Reifsnyder had detected the subliminals Elizabeth Carlisle was transmitting in his direction and had learned their promises were not empty, he knew he had found a home away from home.

If I can recall all that in such *bas-relief*, he asked the ceiling, why am I lying here flat on my ass with Ms. Buchenwald handing me urinals?

Why, indeed?

He inched his elbows back in increments until he was propped six inches off the pillow, head thunking. He lay immobile in that position until the wash of dizziness weakened. Then he slid his elbows further back. Now he half sat. The pain was no worse. He shifted his weight to his left elbow and drew the sheet and blanket aside with his right hand. He wore a white hospital gown that stopped at his knees. They could have at least dressed him in his own pajamas. Like an old man with palsy, he managed to swing his feet to the rust-colored wall-to-wall carpeting.

"Where do you think you're headed?"

Nurse Felkirk's voice hit him like a slap. He hadn't heard the door open.

"Out of here," Reifsnyder said unconvincingly. His voice was like a petulant child's. "I want to get out of here."

She hoisted his legs, made him flatten on the bed and jerked the sheet over him. "Are you going to be a difficult patient? I know exactly how to handle difficult patients." She seemed to hope he would challenge her.

"I'll bet you do," he managed to gasp around solid balls of cranial pain. "Can't you give me something for this?"

"No pain suppressants for a head injury. Now stay put, or I'll have your butt."

"You wouldn't know what to do with it."

His minor exertion had been incredibly exhausting. Despite the thundering in his skull, he slept.

In a small room behind the nurse's station, Dr. Horger watched the central TV screen in a row of five. Reifsnyder's monitor, in sharply defined black-and-white, had shaken him when the big patient had tried to get out of bed. God knew the consequences of that kind of motion so soon after the delicate operation. Csorna had told him the animal transplants had apparently been durable even under early physical stress. Maybe in a monkey, but Horger's superficial experience with surgery left him shaky. He wished Lefroid hadn't been so damned preemptory in getting Csorna away from here—and eliminating him altogether, for God's sake—but the head of Rapier customarily gave an inordinately high priority to covering his tracks.

Horger found himself in a hell of a position. If he lost Reifsnyder through some stupidity like a fall. . . . Beneath his starched green jacket and voluminous T-shirt, a rivulet of sweat tracked down his side like the point of an icicle.

"Let's go back over it," Marty Horn suggested. This was the first time he'd had to fill out a CIAS Accident Report Form ARF-1. It was also the first opportunity he'd had to hold a little authority over the Virgin Queen.

Elizabeth Carlisle scowled. "I've told you everything I know, Lieutenant."

Had she accentuated the title just a shade? Why not? Everybody at CIAS realized his rank of lieutenant was more of a fringe benefit than a real rank. One small step up from the not much more ignominious position of a leader of a squad of watchmen.

He met the violet eyes for a long moment then took refuge in the form on the clipboard in his lap.

"The call came this morning?"

"At precisely ten-oh-four." She consulted a spiral-bound notebook opened flat on her desk. "Yes, ten-oh-four. From a Dr. Horger at the Horger Clinic near Lake Sacandaga in upper New York State."

"And Dr. Reifsnyder was in that area to address some convention?"

"A conference, Lieutenant. There's quite a difference." Always the little jabs. He was the Rodney Dangerfield of federal security.

"Conference, then. And he never made it."

"That's what Dr. Horger told me. You already have it all down there, Lieutenant."

He ignored that.

"Why the frown, Lieutenant?"

She was a fine one to talk. He tapped the clipboard with his ballpoint. "I'm not a big believer in coincidence."

"Where is the coincidence?" She clearly wanted him out of her office so she could get on with her interrupted daily schedule. Maybe the fireplace had run out of logs.

"The coincidence," he said pointedly, "is that here was an injured man—"

"Just shaken up, according to Dr. Horger, though there is a minor scalp wound."

"Scalp wounds bleed a lot, Dr. Carlisle. You can't tell whether they're minor until you check them out. So here's Dr. Reifsnyder bleeding from a head wound, and the first people on the scene are from a nearby clinic. That's the coincidence."

"I prefer to consider it luck. Rare and good luck. Now, if you will excuse me."

It didn't strike Marty until nearly an hour later that Elizabeth Carlisle had seemed to go out of her way to show him that she wasn't overly concerned with the hospitalization of

87

one of her residents in a remote New York State private clinic.

In the meantime, he had cruised into Reifsnyder's compact little office and taken it upon himself to riffle through the papers on the desk. The drawers were locked, of course. Marty wasn't sure what he was looking for. But boredom can be the father of persistence. There wasn't a damned thing of interest among the appointment book, memo pad, unanswered correspondence, and desk trivia. Well, almost nothing. From the appointment book, Marty copied "National Federation of Broadcast Sciences" into his report. Might as well be thorough.

He was still stewing in midafternoon. If one of his own men had been biffed in an accident like this, he'd damned well want a full story. In fact, he told himself, since you're chief of security here, Reifsnyder *is* one of your own men.

He found a detailed map of New York State in the library file and located Ames in Montgomery County.

The woman's voice was clipped but with an underlying softness. "At 13:39, we received a report of a single car accident on State Route 10. The report was telephoned in by a Samuel Crowther, a resident of Canajoharie. A farmer. Wait a sec, Lieutenant. I'll read from the report of the officer at the scene."

Marty heard a riffle of pages. Her voice swung into a singsong of officialese. "Got it. 'Corporal Harvey McManus arrived at accident locale two miles south of Ames on State Route 10 at Canandaigua Road at 14:06 hours, Monday, Three, December. Observed Buick Skylark, New York plate registered to Hertz Company, having impacted power pole, then culvert headwall, said vehicle having sustained damage to front left quarter, and left and right rear quarters. Driver was not at scene. No other persons in vicinity, report having been telephoned from booth on U.S. Route 20, necessitating the caller to leave the scene. Skid marks on road indicated another vehicle involved, possibly emerging from Canandaigua Road in stop sign violation. Radio call received while at scene reported call from Horger Clinic, Sacandaga Lake, New York. Said call stated that an Albert Reifsnyder'—do you want me to spell that?" the county police spokeswoman asked.

"No, I know how to spell it." Marty took a reflex drag at his coffee without tasting it.

"Where was—oh, here. '—Albert Reifsnyder, driver of rented vehicle, had been taken to clinic and was being treated for superficial scalp laceration and held for observation. According to Dr. Elmo Horger, owner of clinic and its chief of medicine, Reifsnyder was unable to describe vehicle that struck his vehicle. Site and circumstances were reported to Hertz office in Albany. Dr. Horger agreed to forward Reifsnyder this department's notification that standard accident report form must be filed within thirty days. No charges were filed.' "

The clipped female voice paused. "Does that help, Lieutenant?"

"The report puts the time of the accident around one P.M., Monday?"

"That is correct."

But Horger hadn't called CIAS until the following morning.

Marty drove home vaguely put out with himself at trying to read drama of some sort into what shaped up as nothing more than an unfortunate fender bender on a country road.

"It's the monotony," Celia decided for him. "The boredom of it all. You need a hobby."

"Like weaving or silversmithing?" The loom and the box of metalworking tools gathered dust in the storage bay beneath the A-frame's first floor. "Or cookbooks?" he couldn't resist throwing in.

She looked up from her littered card table. "The cookbook is going to fly, buster. My guy in Hagerstown has set a deadline."

"What guy?"

"I told you, but you didn't listen. A publisher."

"You're kidding."

"I'm working. The damned silence of the damned Catoctins is not going to get me." She swore only when she was excited. Maybe there would be a cookbook. Something concrete—were her pastry recipes in it?—at last. He'd believe it when he saw it. Past performances had not been inspiring.

He ended up calling the Horger Clinic himself, at his own expense, from the bedroom while Celia bent over her shaky table, her fine ivory hair shading the file cards she revised with disciplined, looping, private-school print.

Horger, he was told, was not available. Could the voice on the line help? Who was she, he asked? Frances Felkirk, Nurse Frances Felkirk.

"How is Dr. Reifsnyder doing?"

"You are . . . ?"

"I am Lieutenant Martin Horn, Nurse Felkirk. Federal Security Police." That ought to rock her a little.

Apparently it didn't. "Dr. Reifsnyder is stable, Lieutenant. Is there something else?"

"When will he be released?" Marty realized she had taken the conversational clout away from him.

"When he shows no further effects."

"He's had some problems?"

"Anyone with a head wound can have problems, Lieutenant."

He could picture her, no doubt overweight with a bovine butt. He hung up with nothing added and clumped back downstairs. Celia was engrossed in her file cards; white, pink, and blue file cards.

"I'm going for a walk. It's still early," he said, unwittingly using her code phrase.

"Not tonight, Marty," she said absently. "I've got too much to do."

He was glad of that, although when he jolted awake just before dawn, he almost reached for her. He and Sergeant Fanella had been crouching in the dripping thicket for hours, waiting for the sampans. The third one, according to field intelligence (what a laugh that was!) carried the rockets. Sweat rolled down Marty's face. Where the hell were they? Around him, he heard night noises. Then they stopped. Fanella turned to stare back at him over the bazooka's pipelike barrel. Under the helmet, Fanella wore Reifsnyder's long face and bony nose.

"Something's wrong," Reifsnyder whispered.

CHAPTER
8

THERE WERE NO clothes in the small closet, nothing but bed linens. He'd learned that when Felkirk had taken a clean pillowcase from the shelf. He watched her, and he had the queasy feeling that he was watched in turn—not just by means of her periodic appearances, but constantly. Why else would she or a night duty nurse appear a few seconds into his attempts to get out of the damned bed? A television camera?

He could sit up almost comfortably now. His eyes swept the walls' white painted paneling. Had it been mellow stained cherry once? The two birch chairs and matching nightstand added to the room's dreary functionalism. The three-drawer birch dresser with its wall-mounted mirror was equally colorless. One skinny window, with its shade pulled until this morning, looked out on a wall of rough brownish stone, evidently an ell of the building. The camera had to be behind the mirror. There was no other place to conceal its lens.

The bathroom was unexplored because they insisted that he return to bed when he attempted to use it. Apparently his sudden—sudden by comparison with his dazed actions up to then—eruption toward the bathroom had caught them napping. Felkirk had not appeared. Another nurse had; a smaller woman, brown hair cut short, with a much trimmer rear.

"No Felkirk?" he'd asked as she led him back to the stale, rumpled sheets. At that point, his endurance had been good for twelve feet and a hard wrench at the bathroom door.

"She's gone." The voice of this little twit wasn't any more expressive than had been that of the heavier nurse.

"Off duty?"

"No, gone. To a new job. She won't be back."

"Was it something I said?" Then nausea hit him.

How many days had he been here? Three? No, four. He was a frigging prisoner, held incommunicado. "I want the doctor," he said to the mirror. "I want him now."

Horger appeared seven minutes later. A decent interval?

"And how are we doing today?" The man's pudgy unctuousness would have been laughable under saner circumstances.

"Better."

"The dizziness?"

"Subsiding."

"And your name?"

"For God's sake, Horger, we've established that every twelve hours. Reifsnyder, Albert P. You want my rank and serial number?"

Dr. Horger made a little moué of exasperation. "Head wounds—"

"I know, I know."

"Home address?"

"Same one in Bethesda," Reifsnyder responded in exasperation. "Look, I want to use a phone."

"I'll be glad to make any calls you wish."

"That I doubt."

Horger's skimpy eyebrows climbed. "Oh? What prompts that sort of statement?"

93

"Because it's obvious I'm being held here, and I want you to be aware that such an action can have extremely serious consequences."

Horger laughed. Forced it, Reifsnyder thought. "You're free to use the bathroom at will."

"Bring me my clothes!" Reifsnyder thundered, then raised an involuntary hand to the lighter bandage that had yesterday replaced the original turbanlike swathing. "Holy Lord!"

"You understand now?" Horger persisted. "You are still in no condition to travel."

"Maybe a wheelchair ride? This is one boring vista, Doctor."

"That can be arranged—if you'll settle down and agree to behave in your own best interests."

"I promise," Reifsnyder said mockingly. Anything other than this seemingly casual but totally effective entrapment would be progress.

The orderly who arrived shortly with the wheelchair and a woolen robe had a peculiarly bland face, moon-round with remarkably small eyes, nose, and mouth added as an apparent afterthought. He was a shade shorter than Reifsnyder, well-muscled and dressed in a gray sweatsuit. When he reached to help Reifsnyder into the chrome-and-blue chair, Reifsnyder had the odd flash that the man should be wearing green.

The son of a bitch wouldn't talk; only grunted. The chair wheeled smoothly out of the room Reifsnyder had grown to hate into a green-painted corridor with a black rubber runner that muted the wheelchair's progress. To the left, the corridor continued around a corner. He assumed the nurses' station was down there somewhere. It had to be nearby since responses to his attempts to get on his feet had been so prompt. There were two doors along this portion of the spartan passageway, in addition to his.

At the other end of the corridor, the orderly forced open a swinging door with the chair's footrest. Reifsnyder gasped.

94

They had emerged on a broad second floor balcony of what had to be, or once was, a Victorian-styled mansion; an architect's midsummer night's dream of mellow dark paneling and a waist-high railing of polished mahogany supported on a curved row of richly turned posts. At the far end of the broad landing, the balustrade curved gracefully downward to form the ornate banister of a staircase wide as a driveway.

Below, several middle-aged women loitered in a parquet-floored entrance hall big enough to accommodate a sizable soirée—which in past life it undoubtedly had. The place made CIAS's own converted residence look like a hovel.

"I take it I've been put up in the maid's quarters," Reifsnyder quipped. Behind him, the orderly grunted. Possibly in agreement. It was hard to tell.

Across the landing, they entered a small elevator of brown-painted, pebble-textured steel and inched to ground level where Reifsnyder discovered the elevator opened backwards onto a flagstone patio as well as frontwards, obviously into the entrance hall, either door actuated by side-by-side buttons.

The blank-faced orderly wheeled him into crisp sunshine, surprisingly pleasant for early December. It hurt to look upward, but Reifsnyder forced it. The converted mansion was huge, a twin-turreted monolith of ochre native stone, no doubt cut and fitted by hand by artisans who had lived at the isolated site until their monumental work was completed. Surely the tourist guidebooks wouldn't pass up a good bet like this, though he doubted that the overfed Dr. Horger would welcome tourists unless they had signed up for his inevitably high-priced regimen.

Damned if they'd stand for the kind of room he'd been given. Surely the regular clientele lounged in the Old World graciousness of carefully preserved family bedrooms and ornate guest quarters—which led him, as they wheeled along a flagstoned walkway between the mansion and the nearby woods, to wonder how much he was being charged for his enforced visit? Was that the clumsy purpose behind Horger's insistence that he stay put? A whopping bill? Reifsnyder grimaced. A ridiculous hypothesis. Then he remembered the mirror. Something was askew here. Despite the unseasonably warm air, he pulled the woolen robe and blanket around his shoulders.

The air smelled of pine and damp fallen leaves. No wonder the fatties in the lobby went for this place. But they certainly weren't in white-walled rooms with concealed cameras.

"Can we go around the building?" he asked his near-mute motor power. "It's one hell of an impressive place. I want to get a real look at it."

Damned right he wanted a look at all of it. Tonight he was going to get the hell out of here.

Reifsnyder, injured and holed up somewhere in the Adirondacks . . . Carlisle seemingly not overly upset about the absence of one of her charges . . . The coincidence of a medical clinic's vehicle arriving first on the scene of Reifsnyder's accident . . . The delay of that clinic in notifying CIAS . . .

"It just doesn't sit right," Marty told Celia over breakfast of coffee, toast, and something she called "eggs russet," with diced pan-fried potatoes, in a cream sauce with too much paprika sprinkled across it. He wasn't big for paprika.

"You think they should stay in?" Her white-lashed eyes showed concern.

"You mean down?"

"No, I mean in the book, Marty."

"Leave them in. They'll add color." He took his coffee from the dining alcove and paced the living room. He hated his propensity to take on worry. It only amplified the fear that never quite left him, the fear that the coiled serpent would unexpectedly be triggered to savage his sanity. The A-frame tucked in Catoctin pines, Celia and her projects, his slow recovery—it was recovery, wasn't it?— from the

96

horror of Chicago: all of it could be blown away by the release of the serpent.

"So do something about it, for heaven's sake," she called from the kitchenette. "Marty, this is a small house. I heard you on the phone last night. If you're so worried about Rifle—what's his name?"

"I don't bring work home."

"You bring it home every night, Marty. Locked in your head. You lock it in and lock me out."

He stood in the kitchenette doorway, glowering at her. "That's not a fair—"

"No, it's not fair," she misquoted, "but I live with it. Marty, you're chief of security out there. If you think something's wrong, do something about it."

He bit down on his flare of anger and said nothing. Then he looked at his watch. Still early. He turned away, then sank to the sofa.

"Marty?" From the tiny kitchen, her voice was high and strained.

"Yeah."

"Well?"

"You could be right," he admitted.

"I am right." She began to sing softly, her thready little voice not so bad, though he didn't recognize the song. Or was she making it up as she worked on the breakfast dishes?

The odd couple, his partner in Chicago had called them. "King Kong and Jessica Lange." It was hard to be pissed at O'Neill for long. He wasn't mean about anything, just over-stuffed with Mick humor. Besides, he wasn't far off the mark. At that point, Marty wore all the hard muscle of a southside boyhood, a three-year Marine enlistment, eighteen months of sweat-fear in Nam (that toned the body in a hurry), then a time—a long time—of "jobs," just about anything honest that scratched up a buck.

His mother had died by then, exhausted by a husband whose life had dwindled to a disorganized amalgam of boozing, screwing, and short-term jobs. Mary and Hank

97

Horn had been two of a kind after Marty had returned from the murderous misery of the Mekong. They existed together in the same barebones apartment Marty had been raised in, the same cracked-plaster four rooms where he'd blocked his ears to his father's drunken Friday night pleas and his mother's gusty little "ahs!" after she gave in.

She died during one of the days his hunter-killer team had been four miles into certified VC territory. By the time he was notified, the funeral was long over, and he wasn't impressed with the opportunity to fly home to console the man who had helped her into her grave. Marty didn't leave Nam for three more months, when his tour was up.

He found he didn't hate the shattered man, now oddly shrunken in his floppy Montgomery Ward work clothes and dusted with a white stubble.

"How was it?" Hank Horn had asked his son, the first words out of his slack mouth.

"Not so good."

"Wasn't so good here either, Marty." The old man had cried then, and there was no more hating him after that.

For the next four years, they lived on the proceeds of the government bonds Marine paymasters had pressured Marty into buying, then on the meager earnings from grocery shelf stocking, store clean-up, dishwashing, the jobs no one else took. They were scavengers, taking nonbinding work that paid quickly. Marty never could remember half the places he'd grubbed for that quick payout. There were too many of them, and he was pleasantly drunk some of the time.

Nor could he remember a single one of the women he'd brought to the apartment. Not a one. He recalled only that they were uniformly compliant and as vapid as was his memory of them. Probably homely as hell, too, he decided later. He did remember his father's comment, popular in World War II when Hank had been a BAR man in Italy. "Turn them upside down, they all look the same." Hank brought home some pretty damned plain women, too.

Marty's alcoholic, cheap-labor-financed rut ended abruptly on a September Sunday, a noon so dark with slanting rain he'd thought it was dawn. The old man was dead on the rump-sprung living room couch. He'd never made it to his bedroom. Heart, the paramedic guessed and later confirmed. They took him out in a green plastic body bag. Marty shuddered at the irony.

What shocked him sober was the insurance. Through all their boozy whoring, Hank had somehow kept up the payments on a term policy Marty didn't even know he had. After the death expenses, there were still forty-two hundred dollars and change.

Marty was cold sober for the first time in four years. A man at the bottom, but sober. And because of the harsh work he'd done, he still looked good. He walked past three bars and bought a Chicago *Tribune*. The want ads were four years beyond him, whole columns pleading for computer people. But an ad for night courses bounced him in a new direction. He had the money. He went up there the next day, to La Salle Street, and signed in for salesmanship with a side order of criminology. Never once in the past four dismal years had he taken a dishonest dollar. Maybe he had a flair for being straight.

He couldn't hack the salesmanship, but he excelled in the other class.

"You going to be a cop?" a wispy female voice asked him in the hallway during a break.

The little voice had to come from a little girl. He looked down as he turned. Then he looked back up. She was nearly eye-to-eye with him, blond as a Norse goddess including the white lashes that gave her eyes a peculiar look of remoteness.

There was nothing remote about Celia Gunnarsen. She awed him with her rifleshot directness.

"A cop?" he echoed.

"You came out of the criminology classroom."

"I might." Until this instant, he hadn't been sure why he was taking the course.

"College?" She sure knew how to bore in.

"This is it."

"They probably prefer college."

"Maybe veterans have a leg up."

She flicked her odd silvery eyes back to his. It was unnerving to stare straight across into that confident gaze. Exciting, too.

"Vietnam," she said.

He nodded. Then he said on impulse, "How about coffee afterward?"

She was taking a creative writing course that kept him shuffling in the hallway ten minutes after his own class ended. He felt like a gawky teenager, but it wasn't a bad feeling. She'd already stripped away much of seven years of horror, futility, and waste.

She was good for him. He knew that. Conservative Minnesota parents with a specialty clothing store in St. Paul. "Quilted parkas, ski clothes, plaid wool shirts—stuff like that," she told him. Celia did most of the talking on their increasingly frequent dates because he didn't want to tell her how inadequate his own life was. He knew he should show more initiative, but she seemed to have enough for both of them. She kissed him first, and she wanted to go to bed with him. He kissed her back in a great flood of released tenderness, but he refused, to his own amazement, to screw her. Not her.

Steven, an Americanization of the original Sven, and Catherine Gunnarsen didn't like him. But he felt they didn't dislike him either. They were discomfited by his generalizing his background, but they admired the Marine part, and, he discerned, felt a mid-American positiveness about his being a rookie cop. By now, he'd graduated from the Police Academy.

The marriage was a controlled affair, none of it his. He had a couple of fairly close cop friends by now, but damned if he'd subject them to this. He drove her away from the country club reception in a wave of relief. The car was already three months paid for and from here on, life was going to be something great, I'll tell you.

At the Alpine Lodge, north of Eau Claire, he saw her naked for the first time, a slender porcelain sculpture, small breasts tipped with blushes of rose, white-gold crest neatly joining slim legs. It was so easy, he doubted she was a virgin, but who was he to ask?

In the first year, he gradually realized she was possessed by imps. Project directed. First it was freelance writing, the result of her night school fling to escape the business offices at Marshall Field. The outpour of short stories produced a flurry of rejections, one or two with "sorry" penned in the margin. She was too impatient to recognize such responses as the first rung on the shaky ladder to ultimate publication.

Next came calligraphy, good enough to give as gifts to neighbors in their westside apartment building but not quite good enough to sell. Then the jewelry making, a tough avocation in an apartment house because the dapping procedure made a hell of a noise. Then acrylic painting; even cornhusk dolls, for Pete's sake. But all of it was an outlet, Marty decided, for her frustration at her barrenness.

They'd tried the thermometer, diets, medications from grim-jawed Dr. Roper in the medical center three blocks over, and such frequent "firing for effect," as Marty called it, that he was both exasperated and relieved when her periods came right on schedule year after year.

He never mentioned any of this to a soul in the Department. His progress out of State Street's fume-filled canyon was rapid because he was recognized early on as one dedicated cop. In year three, he had been the patrol unit officer who noticed a rotating series of cars parked in a certain place in a certain southside block, had recorded and turned in the license numbers, and thus engineered the first crack in a citywide theft ring case that put him in plain clothes ahead of several candidates with more seniority but less smarts.

Marty was not only a good cop. He was a successful one,

and as several medium-sized politicians—caught with their hands in the public till—learned, he was unbribable.

In year seven, he was climbing fast. A sergeant despite his thin academic underpinnings, he began to look into the possibility of cramming for brass. Then came the Day of the Frame House.

He just happened to be three blocks away. The thing appeared to be a domestic setup, but the uniform who'd initially responded already lay dead beside a scraggly evergreen at the foot of the splintery steps, his skull crushed by something heavy. Sirens howled in the near distance. Marty could have waited. Or not responded at all. It wasn't really his. But weren't officer-needs-help calls everybody's?

He screeched the unmarked Chevy close in, bailed out before the dust had caught up, and found himself flying up the steps with the .38 already out. He remembered glancing down at it. A .38? It was supposed to be an M-16. Where was his M-16? He could always recall tripping as the step collapsed. The door was faded lavender, more solid than it looked. His shoulder took a hell of a shot when he hit it. Then. . . . Blank. He drew a blank ever after. What had happened in there was locked in his brain. The coiled snake. He didn't want it loose.

"Marty?" Her voice was a taut cord that pulled him back to the present. The cup of coffee nestled in his crotch was still warm. He looked up at her.

"I said," she repeated pointedly, "you're the security chief. Do something about it."

"By God, I will." He knocked back the rest of the coffee, set the cup on the end table and stood up with a glance at his watch.

She was right again. He'd call as soon as he got to CIAS.

Horger sweated. His palm greased the receiver. The chief of security at CIAS, for God's sake, orally bullying his way right past the receptionist and the floor nurse who'd bucked the call to Horger. The fat doctor wanted to be out of this, away from here for a while; not dancing on the razor edge of a potential disaster Lefroid had forced him to orchestrate. Reifsnyder wasn't reacting. Now the man's alma mater was asking yet more questions.

"As I told Dr. Carlisle, Lieutenant, Dr. Reifsnyder is doing nicely. He's off our guarded list, and if there are no further complications . . ." His voice trailed off because what he did next wasn't up to him. It was Lefroid's decision.

"Doctor," the hard voice rapped, "I'm not sure you understand that this is a federal agency and that Dr. Reifsnyder is one of our associates. That places him under the jurisdiction of the federal government. As that government's security representative in this matter, I don't think we are getting a whole lot of cooperation out of you."

Horger tried to evaluate that and couldn't. "I assure you," he began in a despicable near whine (pull yourself together, man!), then cleared his throat. "I assure you that our only concern is that our patient recovers sufficiently to be released."

"Soon," Lieutenant Horn ordered. Horger breathed again.

"As soon as medically acceptable."

"On second thought," the hard voice persisted, "I think I'll come up there."

"No!" Horger said much too emphatically. "I'm sure you wouldn't want to waste the trip," he continued in a more controlled tone. "He'll be out of here promptly."

"I'll hold you to it." The line clicked dead.

Horger replaced the receiver with numb fingers. If that man did come up here, there was no limit to the mischief he might stir up. Felkirk had left for Hawaii, but the other nurse had pleaded for a couple of extra days. Horger had relented. Now he kicked himself for his ever-troublesome softness under pressure. The curse of his life. Another excellent reason why Lieutenant Horn should not be permitted here.

Horger dry-swallowed, then reached for his mug of tepid tea. Lefroid wasn't going to like this.

He didn't. "But," Horger pleaded, "it's getting entirely too risky. The man has had an excellent recovery. Some dizziness, but no other apparent complications."

"You've forgotten, haven't you, Horger, that complications were the goal."

"If you want complications, leave Reifsnyder here a while longer. The CIAS's head of security just threatened to arrive here personally." Horger listened to the sizzle of an imperfect connection. Then he was compelled to break the distressing silence himself.

"The operation was a failure, Mr. Lefroid. We have to face that. We're superbly fortunate that the man is recovering so beautifully. Let me release him before we all are dragged down to no purpose."

The faulty line fried softly, interminably. Then Lefroid's snake-rattle voice broke the frightening silence. "Don't try to threaten me, Horger. I'll decide when he is to be released."

In his bed, Reifsnyder ticked off his advantages. One: He had talked the orderly into making a complete circuit of the clinic. He had its layout impressed in his memory. Two: They thought he was sicker than he actually was by now, four days after the accident. Three: He wore his own pajamas at last and had been given his woolen robe as well. That wasn't what he would have chosen for outdoor wear in a northern New York December, but this seemed to be an unseasonably warm one. Four: He knew, or thought he knew, about the TV camera.

Pretty damned meager though, in view of the disadvantages. The chances of finding a car with a key in it among the dozen vehicles he noted in the lot on the far side of the mansion were undoubtedly remote. Only in movies were all escape cars equipped with apparently unremovable keys. The Adirondack woodland was going to be damned uncomfortable if he had to make a prolonged walk out of here. He had no idea of whatever security procedures were in effect.

Even if the place were legit, they'd certainly have some form of security, if only to forestall customers' apprehensions at its remoteness. The rich now were the most security conscious of all.

The disadvantages outweighed his advantages. That was clear. But he had to try anyway. There was an undercurrent of something undeniably sinister at Horger Clinic. Though Elmo Horger wasn't outwardly aggressive about it, Reifsnyder had come to realize full well that he was being held here against his will.

The room was dark, shade drawn. Just a ghosting of light crept beneath the close-fitting door. How sensitive was the camera—if there really was a camera?

He peeled back sheet and blanket, swung his legs sideways and down, pausing to lay flat with his feet on the floor. He elevated his torso slowly, using his elbows. The head pain, now an intermittent dull throb, surged as he hunkered on the edge of the rumpled bed. Then it receded. He wore only a light bandage now, taped to the perimeter of the palm-sized area they had shaved.

He'd packed no slippers. They had retained his shoes, but had provided a pair of loose-fitting throwaway hospital slip-ons for his outing yesterday. They were beside the bed. He worked his feet into them.

Could he stand unassisted for a longer time than it had taken him to stumble to the bathroom and back? With a double grip on the foot of the bed, he pulled himself erect. His head throbbed as he'd expected. He waited for the uncomfortable pressure to subside.

The bathrobe was on a chair near the window. He released his hold on the footboard, teetered in the near-total darkness, shuffled toward the chair. He grimaced. The barely remembered collision had made an old man out of him. He pulled on the robe and refused to give in to pulses of vertigo.

Now for the problem of the door. When he opened it, light would flood in from the all-night ceiling flourescents.

The security camera would no doubt be nicely activated. He slid his plastic-clad feet along as silently as he could manage. The camera lens, if there were a camera lens, could be anywhere behind the frameless glass. Somehow he had to cover all of it.

He ran his fingers along the top edge. It didn't fit flush, but the space behind it was only an eighth of an inch wide. Not enough in which to stuff a towel. He stood there weaving slightly in the dark and concentrated. A wedge of some sort? Not available. Horger even took his used tongue depressors with him.

Adhesive tape, of course. He felt the bandage. If he peeled off a couple of strips, they just might be wide enough to retain adhesion. The terrycloth hand towel he took on shaky legs from the tiny bathroom would cover all but the bottom two inches of the mirror. He'd have to take that much of a video risk.

The room's coolness felt icy on his wound when he peeled off the bandage. It took him nearly ten minutes working by touch to loosen several strips of half-inch adhesive and affix them to the top edge of the towel. To his great relief, the makeshift screening device held—or seemed as if it would hold long enough for him to slip through the door.

He replaced the remainder of the bandage as best he could, cracked the door open and peered down the corridor to its bend. Bright silence there. But he sure wasn't heading that way. He eased through the partially open door and shut it silently behind him. His plastic slippers made little padding noises on the rubber hall runner.

The swinging door at the end of the corridor opened noiselessly onto the broad second-floor landing. He moved forward just enough to see most of the entrance hall over the ornate balustrade. It was dimly lighted now; deserted as best he could determine from up here.

The elevator or the broad staircase? Earlier today, he had noted that the elevator was smooth-running. With security as loose as it seemed, could it be possible that the elevator's peculiar outside access was operable? He stayed close to the wall as he crossed the broad landing, praying that one of the three doorways (better rooms for the voluntary guests?) in the paneling would not suddenly open.

His slippers scuffed the polished flooring as he neared the elevator door. He froze. The mansion seemed to breathe around him. But it was the relaxed breath of midnight sleep. He touched the elevator button with a jittering finger. The exertion had drained him already. He sagged against the paneling.

The elevator, apparently raised and lowered by a hydraulic piston, started upward with a muffled sucking sound, then rose in near-silence.

He found himself tensing as it neared the second level, though he had listened for sounds of movement below and heard nothing but the muted fluid pulse of elevator machinery. The car stopped. The door slid open slowly and silently. Reifsnyder stood off to one side, though God knew what he could do were anyone to be in there waiting for him.

The little pebbled steel car was empty. He slipped in and fingered the black "1" button. The door rolled shut. Reifsnyder felt temporarily secure. Falsely secure, he realized through an encroaching haze of dizziness.

The car stopped. Now he had the choice of two doors. In front of him, re-entry to the mansion at lobby level; behind, possible access to the night. He turned to study the outside door in the elevator's dim light. Was it wired for alarm? The exterior call button, he had noted when the orderly had wheeled him back to the outside door, had been activated by the orderly's key. Was there also an alarm system with a sensitized circuit at night?

He checked the entire margin of the sliding door. No wires. But it could be magnetic, built into the door and its frame. Emerging into the lobby would confront him with just as imponderable a situation when he reached the main entrance . . . if he reached it after traversing the exposed length of the entrance hall. Better to take his chance here. He pushed the button marked "PATIO."

As the door cracked open, his ears thundered with strain. Yet he heard nothing save the oiled tracking of the telescoping doorway. Sharp-edged air poured into the elevator car. He realized how thinly he was dressed. No matter now. He was committed.

The door rolled wider.

Then Reifsnyder sagged against the jamb.

"Why, Dr. Reifsnyder," Horger said jovially in the fall of soft luminescence from the elevator's frosted dome light. "Such an effort to avoid paying the bill?"

But something had changed. He was discharged at 10:00 A.M., given his suitcase and speech notes, wallet, keys, change; his Mark Cross ballpoint pen. Everything intact.

"I certainly owe you something," he said to Horger in the doctor's cold little office, relieved that this ordeal was ending. At the same time, he felt like an about-to-be-released prisoner offering to pay his jailers for room and board.

"A nominal bill will be submitted to CIAS," Horger said pleasantly. "We are glad to have been of service, and I'm happy you are sufficiently recovered. . . . Just how do you feel, Dr. Reifsnyder?"

"Weak, but well enough to get out of here, thank you."

"Of course."

Horger kept peering at him with a strange expression of expectation mingled with what Reifsnyder could interpret only as disappointment. Disconcerting, to say the least. Then the fat doctor sighed, pressed his palms flat on his desk and stood up.

"I'll have one of our staff drive you to the Albany airport. We've already changed your flight reservation to a 12:10 flight today."

"That's considerate of you," Reifsnyder admitted. Had he totally misjudged this place and its flabby-faced doctor? Or was Horger going out of his way to head off the possibility of a formal protest? Not that Reifsnyder had a lot to complain about, now that he thought it over unemotionally. They had pulled him out of a wrecked automobile, treated what could have been a serious head wound, and had not released him until he was apparently out of danger. Investigate them? Reifsnyder could almost hear the county or state police saying, "You should be thanking them." Perhaps he should, but he still had an overpowering urge to get out of here.

The moon-faced orderly drove him the fifty miles in a white station wagon. The man was as taciturn as he had been on Reifsnyder's wheelchair tour, responding to occasional conversational sallies with no more than grunts of acknowledgment. Reifsnyder was relieved when the airport came in sight. Mr. Personality dropped him at the terminal entrance, shoved his bag across the seat, letting Reifsnyder reach for it. Then without so much as a nod from its driver, the station wagon pulled into departing traffic.

Reifsnyder watched the car dwindle down the access road. *"Idiota!"* he said. Then he realized that was a most peculiar word for him to use.

CHAPTER
9

EXHAUSTED BY HIS ridiculous midnight attempt at escape from a "prison" that he'd discovered didn't exist and a bit disoriented by the long silent ride, then his rush to the plane, Reifsnyder couldn't concentrate on the in-flight magazine. The stitches had picked his scalp when Horger had flicked them out this morning—a trifle too soon, the doctor had grumbled. But if Reifsnyder would promise to wear the small bandage at least another two weeks. . . .

His mind unfocused. The magazine sank to his lap. His head lolled back against the upholstery of the jetliner's seat. The engines' thrum was soporific. His eyes closed.

Inexplicably, he was on a sun-drenched road. Barefoot, trailing a stick in the dust. The ill-defined roadway was lined with a straggle of moisture-starved palmettos. An angry female voice shouted at him—in Spanish. He understood her. He turned toward the sound. A woman stood on a ramshackle porch, hands on prominent hips. She wore a cheap print dress. His mother?

"Venga aquí!"

He was supposed to be in the backyard killing one of the

scraggly chickens. She'd whip him for this. He ran toward the *casa*, tripped, threw out his arms and jolted awake.

Thank God he had an empty seat beside him. Had he cried out?

"Sir?" The blond flight attendant's cherub face showed concern. "Are you all right?"

He was sweating.

"Fine," he managed, his voice cutting in with a croak. "Getting over a touch of flu."

She eyed the neat bandage across the shaved patch of skull. He knew she hadn't swallowed that. But on this short flight, she didn't want problems, either. She moved up the aisle unsmiling, her wide brown eyes darting back at him just once.

The dream. . . . Was it a memory? No, a dream. But so sharply imprinted. He even knew that the little boy's outstretched hand had struck a jagged piece of glass in the unkempt yard. The cut had been painful and deep. Reifsnyder caught himself turning his right palm upward. No scar. Of course no scar. This was absurd.

His boyhood had been a comfortable one; if not affluent, at least secure in a land of agricultural plenty. Ed had grown barley and wheat, not scraggly chickens. They'd lived in an immaculately scrubbed and manicured white frame house with a broad porch spanning its full frontage. The lawn had been an emerald blanket among sycamores in a prairie of gently waving grain awns. The troubles that put his father under began decades later. A broken discarded bottle on that scrupulously groomed lawn?

He didn't doze again. The sparsely passengered jet landed with a satisfied thunk, taxied to BWI's flat, black painted terminal pier. He joined the shuffle to the plane's forward hatch. The baby-faced attendant eyed him closely.

"Have a nice day, sir." It came out as a question. He nodded and strode up the exit ramp into the long red-carpeted pier. After he'd walked to the main terminal and taken a down escalator for his bag, then boarded the courtesy bus that took him to the small valet parking building, his legs were jelly. He refused to give in, paid his parking tariff and accelerated his Volkswagen Jetta into the exit road. God, he was weak. When he got back to CIAS, he was heading straight for bed. Probably sleep for a week.

As he swung into the Baltimore-Washington Parkway acceleration lane, he drifted left. Instantly, a horn blared. Tires squealed. His eyes leaped to the rearview mirror. Behind him, he thought he glimpsed a yellow-brown army truck, green-clad soldiers packed along its benched sides. But when the vehicle shot past him, it was only a yellow stake body loaded with ranks of upright propane cylinders, its long-haired driver's jaw set in irritation.

For the second time this day, Reifsnyder broke into a sweat.

On the monitor bank, Marty Horn watched Reifsnyder's silver Jetta check through the fence gate and park in its assigned space near the CIAS entrance. When the big communications expert stepped out of the car, Marty thought he looked haggard. No wonder. As he reached back in for his suitcase, the whiteness of a palm-sized bandage above and behind his right ear was exaggerated by the monitor's high-contrast setting.

Marty pushed back his chair, waited for Lydia Whimple's okay, then touched the front door lock release. He walked into the hall to watch Reifsnyder push through the ornate leaded glass door, his bag thumping the jamb. His coordination wasn't all it should have been, Marty noted.

Reifsnyder checked his watch and signed the log. He picked up his suitcase.

"Afternoon, Doctor," Marty offered. "Glad to have you back."

"Glad to be back." The man looked pallid and impatient. Marty knew this wasn't going to be easy.

"Could we have a word or two, Doctor?"

Reifsnyder grimaced. He flicked his bottle-green eyes toward the broad staircase. You're not going up there just yet, Marty determined.

"I thought you were off on Sundays," Reifsnyder parried.

"I wanted to talk with you."

The communications expert set his bag down in resignation. "Why?"

Marty shot a glance at Lydia. "In the library."

It was awkward not having a decent office for this sort of thing, but meeting on what could be considered neutral ground probably would be less inhibiting to Reifsnyder anyway. Why, Marty wondered as he trailed the larger man into the library, am I so damned suspicious? Because of a cop's cockamamie dream? No, it was more than that. It was a cop's instinct. And Dr. Elmo Horger's voice on the phone. Marty could read voices. He'd read a lot of apprehension in Horger's. That had been one scared man.

Reifsnyder sat on the arm of the red leather chair. He seemed to need to sit down. Marty leaned on his elbows on the back of the sofa, glad of their informal positioning.

Reifsnyder scowled. "I've had a hell of a trip. Is this necessary?"

"Regulations, Doctor. You can appreciate that. I've got to fill out a report on unscheduled absences." He'd purposely left the form and his clipboard back in the security office. No need to make this too inhibitive. Reifsnyder seemed on the ragged edge as it was.

"I just want to get to bed, Horn. I'll admit I'm pretty well shot."

"Let's go over the accident one time," Marty suggested. "Just want to see if it jibes with what they told me at that clinic they had you in."

Reifsnyder's head came up. "You called up there?"

"Damn right. I didn't like the sketchy kind of info they were handing out." He felt no need to add that he'd checked with the local police as well.

The big man sighed. "If you must." His monotone description of what he remembered about the accident wasn't much. Nor was his sketchy fill-in of his four days at the Horger Clinic.

Marty listened impassively. It all seemed to check out: what Horger had told him, what the police had been able to offer, and now Reifsnyder's own account. Maybe I'm trying to come up with something—anything—to break the CIAS boredom. His own form of cookbook, Celia would have been quick to point out.

"Is that sufficient?" Reifsnyder's expression was bland, but Marty couldn't shake the feeling that he was hiding something. It was in the subtle hooding of the green eyes, the clenching of the hands on Reifsnyder's knees, the impatience with Marty's not very probing questions.

"What's the National Federation for Broadcast Sciences?" Marty asked. "I haven't been able to find it listed anywhere."

Reifsnyder shrugged. "Beats me. I didn't call them, they called me."

So much for that lead. Marty shoved to his feet. "If you don't want to push any of this, why should I?"

Reifsnyder stood, reached down for his bag. Marty peered at the skull bandage. An injury behind the ear from a head-on slam against a culvert headwall?

"Should have the doc in Thurmont take a look at that."

"Thanks for your concern, Horn." There was a touch of mind-your-own-business in his tone. "I've got to tell Dr. Carlisle that I'm back."

"She's been at DOD since Friday. Due back later today. Go on up, Doctor. I'll tell her when she comes in."

Reifsnyder lay on his back wearing only T-shirt and shorts, his head cradled in interlocking fingers. The ceiling here was more interesting than the bland plaster at the clinic. The former owner had been a ceiling aficionado of sorts, and this bedroom was graced with the sort of plasterwork you didn't see often: multichanneled Italianate molding around the perimeter and a three-foot plaster rosette in the center of the room where an ornate vaseline glass fixture concealed four electric bulbs.

Some contrast to the single wire-enclosed bulb of the Chacabuco Prison cell. . . . What in hell was he thinking about! These sudden flashes were increasingly disturbing. First there had been the vivid dream when he'd fallen and cut his hand. Then the chilling illusion of the army truck. Now the transformation of the ceiling fixture.

Another concern was his attitude change. He wondered if Horn had noticed that? He was becoming defensive, even secretive. Not his nature at all. He hadn't mentioned the mental flashes, of course. Was that the sort of thing you told a security officer after you'd suffered a severe crack on the head? He knew, though, he wasn't going to tell Dr. Thayer either. Thayer, the Thurmont GP cleared for CIAS service, was a good man for the head colds and backaches common to CIAS residents and staff, but sure to be out of his depth on this case.

Case? A few hallucinogenic flashes? Hadn't Dr. Horger pointed out that a stiff rap on the head could produce unpredictable results? So these flashes could be perfectly normal. He smiled ruefully. He'd just thought of a line from an old skin-flick he'd seen years ago. A psychiatrist reassuring his male patient who had a yen for female underwear: "You are perfectly normal, sir, for the abnormality you have."

The fading afternoon had thrown the room into deep shadow when he sensed that the door had been noiselessly opened. He turned with effort. Elizabeth, her shoes in her hand, slid into the room and locked the well-oiled oak panel behind her.

"Albert!" Her voice was an urgent whisper. "I've been so worried. So damned worried. Thank God you're back safely."

She lay her shoes on the rug, sat on the bed, and trailed her fingers down his cheek. "You're so pale." She felt his forehead. "And cold. You're so cold."

115

The chill had crept over him while he'd lain here in the waning afternoon light. He took her hand. "I'm all right." But he knew that he wasn't.

She took up the folded blanket from the foot of the bed and spread it over him. "Sleep, darling." She touched his forehead with warm fingertips. "Close your eyes."

"Don't you want to know—"

"We'll talk all about it later." She bent down to kiss him gently. He gave in to weariness.

. . . She was lithe as a panther, a mountain girl in Linay Mahuida, a Salado River town where he had a *contrato*. An assignment to kill. He'd gotten her drunk on cheap wine, but not so drunk that she'd lost track of why she had been told to meet him in the *taberna's* back room. He'd stayed in that shabby little cubicle for three days while he watched the comings and goings at the district office across the square. Some contrast after two impatient and politically tempestuous years at the University of Buenos Aires.

"You detain him," he told her. "That's all."

"How do I do that?" Her eyes were dark as polished onyx, her skin bronzed by the sun of seventeen Argentine summers.

"Any way you wish."

"And when he steps out there with me, you will kill him?"

He said nothing. She was far smarter than he'd first assumed.

"Kill him the way he had my brother killed." Her voice was low and lethal, a panther growl. "Not in the head or the heart. In the belly."

"I want to be certain."

"In the belly," she insisted, moving into the room. "I want a guarantee that you will." She kicked off her sandals. Then she lifted her bright peasant's dress over her head.

"You will promise." Not a question. A statement. She was bare breasted, pointed, and plum-tipped. She took the drawstring of her homesewn pantlets between thumb and forefinger, arched her heavy black brows in question.

He felt her animal attraction in the back of his throat. "*Si.* In the belly," he agreed.

She smiled coldly, white teeth luminous in her polished butternut face. The pantlets slid down muscled legs to the dust of the floor.

He took her without finesse on the canvas cot. She wanted it that way. Hard stabs until she cried out and he burst like a bomb.

"*Pantera mia!*"

"What?" Elizabeth asked from the chair where she had been watching him. "What did you say?"

What had the strange words been? "I don't know."

She knelt beside the bed. He held her close, hoping she had forgotten his inexplicable outburst. He'd forgotten the words, but he wouldn't forget shouting them.

Downstairs in the security room, taking a Sunday shift for Kellerman, Marty Horn had heard nothing. He didn't have Abner Dortman's watchdog ears.

The dreams were more vivid than the flashbacks, but the flashbacks were more terrifying. The dreams ended when Reifsnyder shuddered awake under the sweat-cold sheet. But the flashbacks overtook him in the midst of work. Only with increasing effort could he wrench his thoughts back to what he had been concerned with when the mental side-tracking, or whatever it was, overtook him.

The dreams were frightening not so much by their inappropriateness as by the consistency of their theme. Dreams with a story line, night after night? He always seemed to be the same Spanish-speaking (that itself was remarkable), wiry, little man. A rebel or even a terrorist type. One dream forced Reifsnyder to endure a massacre of five people in a jungle clearing, five shabbily dressed, terror-stricken peons huddled in an open area among dense palmettos. They apparently had witnessed something he had done. Reifsnyder wasn't clear about what it had been. He and another man, only a shadowy presence in the dream, abruptly raised their smuggled Uzi machine guns. How had he known that name? The sobs of the three men and two women were erased in the stutter of the guns.

They fell like marionettes with their strings abruptly severed. One of the men began to raise a bloody arm, palm outward to ward off the 9-mm Parabellum slugs that had already gouged fatal channels through his body. Reifsnyder and the other man watched him bleed to death. Then Riefsnyder managed to wrench himself out of the nightmare, shuddering and nauseated.

The following night, he was the same repellent killer again, now stalking a man in a light gray suit along the crowded sidewalk of a city. Buenos Aires? Caracas? The street was extraordinarily wide with a row of palms between the sidewalk and the traffic-choked boulevard. His assignment was to kill the man with the briefcase, now twenty paces ahead of him.

He knew by the man's quick glances at angled storefronts that he was aware he was being followed. And he was becoming panic-struck. Every body motion telegraphed his fear: the hunched shoulders, the rapid steps, the jerky motions of the sleek, black-haired, bulletlike head.

At an intersection, the pedestrians clustered, waiting for the light change. He wormed through the impatient crowd, pressed the button on the switchblade held along his thigh. The flawlessly honed Solingen blade would cut tissue paper.

As the light changed, only the lower part of his arm moved, like the strike of a fer-de-lance and as deadly. The blade sliced through the sleek man's coat and shirt, sank into the soft abdomen just below the rib cage, jabbed upward to paralyze the diaphragm, then downward to sever the iliac artery.

The clot of people moved into the trafficway. When he was halfway across the hot pavement, he heard a woman's shriek behind him.

Reifsnyder woke in sweaty horror. He snapped on his bedside lamp. Only after he was able to fix his attention on familiar objects—the circassian walnut paneling, his wallet, keys, and pocket change on the hand-rubbed oak bureau— did the thudding in his chest begin to subside.

With a corner of the tangled sheet, he wiped the sweat off his face. God Almighty! Only a dream, sure, but another dream so consistent with all the others. Every night. Every night since he'd returned from that damned Horger Clinic.

His work was inevitably affected, not only by the haunting depression of the nightmares. The flashbacks also occurred with increasing rapidity. He felt like a stricken Vietnam vet who found himself catapulted without warning back to the battlefield. But Riefsnyder had never been in the places his flashbacks took him.

One midafternoon, the benign carpeted CIAS downstairs hallway became the forbidding whitewashed corridor of a prison. Just for an instant before it snapped back into focus. His own office transformed one sunny morning into a jungle shack where he crouched in wait for . . . What? Then he was back behind his desk again.

The worst of these sudden and momentary snaps out of reality occurred during a brief encounter with Lieutenant Horn just outside his security office.

"Good morning, Doctor," Horn had said pleasantly enough, stirring his coffee with a plastic spoon. Then in an eye-blink, Reinfsnyder found himself facing a green-uniformed police *capitán*—Samos, his name was. A hard man he'd met before, here in the secret detention cells in the sub-basement of the old *cabildo*, which the public was led to believe housed only a museum.

Samos held an enameled cup of water. Reifsnyder's mouth was parched, but he couldn't be bought for cups of water, and Samos knew it. He glared into the officer's feral features. Then he realized he was staring at Marty Horn who stood before him in CIAS navy blue.

"Sorry," he muttered. "I'm a little preoccupied this morning." He hurried into his office, conscious of Horn's following gaze.

Was he going insane? Reifsnyder shut his door and crumpled into his desk chair. Thank God for the seclusion CIAS residents were offered without question. He picked up his pen. Should he make some sort of notes? How do you make coherent observations when your mind is disintegrating?

The pen seemed to move by itself. The first letter was a *K.* Then his fingers formed two loops. Double *O.* Next a *V.* Then it seemed logical to add *E* and *N.* KOOVEN. A word he'd never heard of. What in hell did "KOOVEN" mean? A name? Yes, a name. But meaningless.

Then he felt it did have significance. It meant he shouldn't tell anyone what was happening to him.

Abner Dortman set his bag of donuts on the desk in front of the TV monitor console, shucked off his navy poplin jacket and shook away the snow.

"It's a bitch out there, Marty. Started around three. Supposed to go on most the night. Have a nice evening, Chief."

Marty lingered in the doorway.

"You ain't got snow tires or something?" It wasn't usual for Marty to hang around.

He came back in and shut the security room door behind him. That wasn't usual, either. He could read the interest in Dortman's bony face.

Marty perched on the corner of the desk, arms folded. He wasn't at all sure about this.

"You noticed anything about Reifsnyder since he came back from that place that fixed him up?"

Dortman, sunk in the chair with his knees braced against the desk edge, twisted his face around to peer up at Marty. "Like what?"

"You tell me."

"What's to tell? How's a man supposed to act after he's slammed his head into the steering wheel or windshield or whatever bunged him?"

"That bothers me, too. If he'd hit the top of his head on

the windshield or even the side of it against the door, you could figure it. But that bandage behind his left ear?"

"Probably turned his head to the left when he smacked whatever he smacked."

"Yeah, probably." Marty was unconvinced. "I wonder if Carlisle has noticed any 'Documentable Personality Change'?"

"You sound like the book."

"I'm quoting the book, Abner."

"You won't get any report out of her about him."

Marty studied Dortman's angular profile. "Why not?"

"I'm telling you, you just won't get anything out of her." Dortman was ducking the question.

"You know something I don't?"

"Just a feeling, Marty. Let's get off it."

Marty shrugged, but Dortman's evasion bothered him. The guy was usually gabby about anything you brought up.

"Merry Christmas," Dortman offered. "Look out for sleds out there."

Christmas was still a week away. Marty didn't like to be reminded. He was never sure of Celia's reactions to the gifts he had so much difficulty selecting.

"Good night, Abner." He buttoned his storm coat, walked down the hall, nodded at Whimple and pushed through the front door into a swirl of flakes. The stuff was already ankle-deep. Dortman had been right; he didn't have snow tires, not on the front-wheel-drive K-car. So far, it had never failed him.

With a gloved hand, he brushed the powdery fall off the windshield and back window. The car started promptly. He pulled out the headlight knob. The beams laid bright paths across the snow. Two hundred feet distant, the security fencing gleamed through the milky swirl.

He backed out of his space in a long arc that brought him close to the front of the residence building. Someone stood in the broad bay window of the library. The face was in shadow, but the bulky silhouette was unmistakable. Reif-snyder.

For several seconds, they stared at each other through the twilight-thickened screen of dancing snow. Then Marty put the car in drive and pulled away. The disturbing impact of Reifsnyder's stare didn't lessen until he turned into the main road past Joe Blanchard's "information" booth, now with its winter glass in place, heated, and brightly lighted, an obvious anachronism in the touristless Catoctin winter.

CHAPTER
10

THE *FOTOGRAFÍA* HAD to be in the office. He'd seen Colonel Careras enter with it in his gloved hand and emerge almost immediately without it. The colonel would return from regimental HQ in probably no more than twelve minutes, his morning pattern.

Where in hell could he have placed the picture in such a short time? The desk was neatly stacked with the *Morning Report,* a small clutch of mail, the fiberboard-bound Duty Roster awaiting signature.

He opened and shut the desk drawers in frantic succession. Two were crammed with mimeo'd military verbiage. Had Careras slid the *foto* somewhere in these piles? No time to check. The center drawer held only the material of a desk-bound man: paper clips, rubber bands, a ruler, scissors. . . . The two drawers on the right: a half-full bottle of imported Cuban rum and two glasses. In the remaining drawer, nothing at all.

Where? Then he noticed the slightly dislodged cushion on the chair behind the desk. He flipped it up. Ah! How obvious, after all, for a man in a hurry.

He pulled the glossy black-and-white eight-by-ten from the manila envelope. The aerial oblique had clearly picked up the five SAM sites despite their hedgelike living camouflage. You can do better than that, Fidel. You're getting overconfident.

He snapped open, then telescoped the Minox three times, bracketing the estimated f-stop. Then, before he had time even to return the photograph to its envelope, he heard the footfall. Just outside the door. His body jerked.

Reifsnyder jolted awake. Good God! Not a dream. A memory! He knew what happened next. The office door swung open and there stood a lunkhead of a private in baggy chinos who muttered that he had been sent for something Careras forgot.

By now the Minox was in Kooven's . . . Kooven? Here was that name again. Reifsnyder stared into the bedroom's darkness, sweat beading his forehead. The Minox was in his pocket, the photo back beneath the cushion. He reached down beside the desk, grabbed the wastebasket and carried it past the private, slack-faced, playing the trashman. Outside, he set down the metal basket and climbed straight up the sun-yellowed sod berm behind the row of low, green-painted military offices. In forty seconds, he was through the rent he'd cut in the chain link.

The memory faded.

What was happening to his mind? Beneath his clammy pajamas, his body leaked icy perspiration despite the room's mid-December chill. During the day, he increasingly experienced the eerie sensation that he was someone else watching himself from outside his own body. He'd read about cases of multiple personalities in which a subject (A subject? Was he becoming a medical "subject"?) developed several or even many distinct personalities. Could this be happening to him? Was this how it began? Sudden, out-of-context flashes during the day and pervasive dream sequences at night?

He sat up and huddled, arms locked around trembling knees, in the room's blackness. The multiple personality cases had consistently been just one personality at a time, even the women whom psychiatrists determined had developed almost a hundred distinct characters within herself. No, his flashes were different. He seemed to be two people at once, each conscious of the other.

If the dreams had credence, and certainly they did seem related to his sudden slippages into Spanish and the quick visions so totally alien to reality, then he could almost describe the alter ego that seemed to be forcing itself into his brain.

A man. Short, sinewy. Quick reflexes. Spanish-speaking and apparently South American. A man with a chaotic past. Espionage at the least. A man who fomented terrorism. Revolution? And who . . . murdered. God Almighty, a man called Kooven!

Reifsnyder stared into the blackness. Horn, the security chief, suspected that something was wrong. That was obvious in the man's eyes and the tone of his voice. But what could be done about Horn? *Should* he do anything? Horn no doubt linked his erratic behavior to the accident. To the effects of concussion. He may be right, Reifsnyder thought. Hadn't Dr. Horger pointed out that concussion could produce strange effects? In fact, Horger hadn't wanted to release him as soon as he did. Reifsnyder had pressed that issue. Now it may be that Horger, quack though he seemed, had been right.

Reifsnyder touched the bandage behind his ear. Should he have Doc Thayer take a look at him after all? He lay back slowly, arms at his sides, rigid and frightened. *No estoy bien*, he told himself. *No estoy—* What kind of hell *was* this?

He failed to consult Dr. Thayer for two reasons. One, a Reifsnyder realization, was that any sign of certifiable mental aberration or a DPC—Documentable Personality Change— was grounds for a hearing by a Pentagon-appointed board of three psychiatrists. Object: PCD—Potential Cause for Derecruitment from CIAS resident status. The procedure was detailed in the CIAS Resident's Information Manual.

Even if the poor, suspected sucker managed to talk himself out of the star chamber proceedings, he would thenceforth be a marked man, Reifsnyder knew. Like Horn, come to think of it, that pathetic son of a bitch.

The other reason to avoid Thayer, or any doctor, was a—God save him—a Kooven necessity. The fear of discovery. He could feel it along his spine, an icy crawl. Trying to concentrate on his work was pure hell, an argument with himself. With two selves. He fought panic and forced himself to stare at Key's "Media Sexploitation." Some minutes later, he realized he had automatically read and turned a half-dozen pages without being able to recall a single point of the text.

Gerta Heissen, copper hair seeming to flame with her anger, tensed on stiff arms across Lefroid's desk. Her white knuckles smudged the polished teak.

"Stupid! Incredibly stupid!" she shouted, though Lefroid's parchment face was only inches from her jutting jaw.

"The jury," Lefroid said evenly, "is still out."

"You had that idiot Horger release him before anybody observed anything at all conclusive! That was stupid. How do you know he isn't laying out a lovely story for the FBI this minute?"

Lefroid was maddeningly calm. "The FBI?"

"CIAS is a Pentagon subagency. FBI Intelligence Division CI-3 is the logical section."

"You are leaping at a conclusion."

"You already have," she railed. She could hold her own with Lefroid. She was possibly the only person who really knew him who wasn't petrified of him. She was as intelligent as he, and she knew he knew it. He needed her computer wizardry. And most important, she had intimately diaried and updated her Rapier connection from day one; had entered it in the New York Public Library's mainframe computer storage. No one save Lefroid and she, herself, knew it was there. She had secured it with an access code cryptogram that she had recorded only once: at the end of a paragraph of instruction that she had sealed and placed in the hands of one of Manhattan's most conservative legal firms. If she failed to make a coded call to that firm for a period exceeding thirty-two days, the legal firm was empowered to open the instruction and access the stored data.

The outcome of that, she had informed Lefroid, would not be to his advantage. To which he had only murmured, "It's reassuring to be trusted." She had never been certain that he believed the threat, but she was not a bluffer. When she'd first detailed its existence, the pupils of his cold eyes betrayed an emotional reaction. Now that same frigid stare refused to react. He had better control after three years of confronting her flaring temper, a flaw she despaired of mastering. But she was certain she was justified in defying him now.

"You are a fool, André." She pulled back and stood rigid, arms tight at her sides, fingers flexing. "I say he should be eliminated, the project scrapped."

"And I say we haven't given it sufficient time."

"Time enough to destroy Rapier."

Lefroid stood to look straight across the desk into her fuming glare. "You are an incredibly intelligent woman," he said analytically, "but you suffer from the typical female frailty of impatience."

Words calculated to infuriate her, to underline his disdain of her anger. She fought back a surge of fury that threatened to choke her.

"Think, Gerta. CIAS was becoming more and more concerned about Reifsnyder. Their security head was on the verge of appearing at the clinic. Horger certainly wasn't up to a face-to-face interrogation by a federal security professional. There was no choice involved. And now who would believe what Reifsnyder would tell him, were he able to reveal anything other than what we let him perceive? He was unconscious from a moment after a disorienting impact until the operation was completed. He regained his senses, such as they were at that point, only in his recovery room."

"So you assume."

"So I have been assured by Elmo Horger."

"That ass."

"He does follow orders," Lefroid pointed out. "Explicitly."

"Nevertheless I believe we are at serious risk. Undue risk. And I insist that we need a contingency plan."

"A contingency plan," Lefroid echoed. The corners of his near-lipless mouth twitched upward almost imperceptibly. "All right, Gerta, if it will make you feel more comfortable. After all, if the procedure fails to produce a useful result, the termination of even what I consider a small risk will represent no additional loss to Rapier."

"Then we agree?"

"To eliminate Reifsnyder, yes. But I want to give him more time."

"How much more?"

"Two weeks."

She shook her head.

"But we are dealing with an imponderable."

"That's precisely my point." She knew she was winning now. Her fingers stopped their unconscious flexing and she smoothed her skirt before placing her hands in an aggressive hands-on-hips stance.

"A week, then."

"It has already been three. I believe twenty-five days should be ample."

"Based on precisely what?"

"Based on my gut feeling, André."

He gazed at her, his face showing nothing. Then he said, "Seven more days, Gerta. If we have no indication by—" He consulted a desk calendar. "By the twenty-seventh—"

"Send Stark."

"Yes, it should appear an accident."

"Precisely." She turned and strode toward the door. Then

she paused, almost attractive in her Black Watch plaid skirt and soft knit black blouse. "Merry Christmas, André." There was no softening of her brittle voice.

He awoke to gray daylight insinuating its flatness around the bedroom's drapes. He moved cumbersome legs. His arms in light blue pajama sleeves felt outsized. His body was too big. His brain at first refused to accept it.

He lay still and concentrated. He knew this was Reifsnyder's bedroom. Reifsnyder's bed. Reifsnyder's body.

He could think and feel as Reifsnyder, but it was as if he were someone else controlling arms and legs and brain. He forced his mind backwards, before this incredible mental dichotomy—to use a Reifsnyder word, to the time prior to this confusion of . . . Where had he been?

A *clinica* of some sort.

Begin before that, back to his earliest memory. A frame house without paint. A gritty road where mongrel dogs lifted their legs against the sagging gate, all that remained of a once-respectable fence in the decaying suburb of . . . He grimaced with the effort. Then it came. Buenos Aires.

A woman, graying at not more than thirty, her once pleasantly alive face already seamed by the challenge of survival. His mother, deserted by her transient Dutch man-friend the day he learned she was with child—his child.

Then came the terrible days of school; derision from his classmates for being a bastard. He learned to fight, to pay back harder than he was hurt. And he learned that the world may belong to a chosen few by inheritance, but a lot of it can be taken back by those who have the craft to steal it. What he lacked in size, he compensated for through guile, stealth, and sublimation of the Catholic conscience his fading mother sought to instill, an admirable but futile effort for an underpaid, overworked souvenir store clerk.

He lived in her house, but he was brought up in the streets. From an eighteen-year-old *carcelero*, an ex-con, he learned how to shoplift. From a twenty-seven-year-old *puta*, he learned the raw basics of life. And from a less-than-honest police officer, he learned the financial worth of selling information. He wormed his way into the confidence of street cops and sold their off-duty sins to *Sargento* Jimenez. When Jimenez trusted him enough to become careless, he sold Jimenez to *Tenente* Ramiro.

Then he skulked after bigger money. A week's wandering of the Islas Malvinas gave him enough to sell to Argentine Naval Intelligence. A lot of good that did his customer some years later, but by then, he had allegiance only to himself. The theft of a Chilean *Departmento Estado* briefcase culminated in his first killing when the courier, handcuffed to the heavy leather case, swung it like a club. For his efforts, he was strangled, his self-defense inhibited by the same briefcase. After that, the killing in Linay Mahuida's town square was easy. The theft of the Cuban SAM site *foto* for a Venezuelan client was child's play.

He had come to the United States on an Ecuadorian passport. The NSA was not above purchasing purloined intelligence, either, particularly if it concerned San Salvador. Which his report on rebel matériel stores did. Both he, on behalf of a shadowy NSA subdepartment, and an inept freelancer were courting the same Washington-based Honduran Embassy employee. The freelancer, a striking brunette with the face of a seductive angel, not surprisingly scored first.

He stalked her to a small apartment hotel on K Street NW, and gained access to her room by posing as a panicked Honduran Embassy servant. He then applied the most excruciating of intimate tortures, hand over her mouth all the while, to drain her of information including her employment by an organization he'd never heard of: Rapier. Her fee from Rapier was far larger than his NSA agreement. Killing her was a simple matter of closing off nose and mouth, then he contacted Rapier himself and consummated the sale. Lefroid was not distressed to replace an inefficient independent with a contractor of obviously greater skill.

There had been the Listox assignment, successfully carried out at the U.S. Army's Alabama chemical warfare storage depot. Then came the curious report out of Maryland that a CIAS researcher had developed an entirely new offensive-defensive tactical concept. Forcing Reifsnyder's still disoriented brain to function more precisely, he suddenly recalled the excruciating chest pain, his collapse in Lefroid's New York office. The . . . He pressed heavy fingers to his temple.

. . . Horger had come to his room, a torture chamber of chirping electronic consoles, obscene dual IV bladders, and an intestinelike tube leaking chemicals through the insistent needle taped into the primary vein of his right arm. Horger had turned a valve, and the room had faded to echoing black.

Now it was as if no time had passed. He had returned to consciousness in a different body, his memory apparently intact. Born again, as the *Norte Americanos* say. He knew he was in the body of a man named Reifsnyder. That was shocking enough, yet acceptable because here, indeed, he was. In a different body, yet with a degree of concentration that generated near-physical pain, he could shift his thought sequence into Reifsnyder's.

The focus was becoming sharper. The current assignment was here. At CIAS. The Strakhan research. A *perra* . . . a bitch of a challenge, but he could meet it. He could meet it because he was Kooven.

He lay inert and experimented with shifting from his own conciousness to that of Reifsnyder and back again. Incredible! An exhilarating ability. With practice, he knew he could perfect it to a skill.

He switched again to Reifsnyder's thought stream and attempted to run a memory scan. Middle . . . something. Think like Reifsnyder, *bufon*. Midwest, that was it. Like—what did they call them?—Like "quick shots" on the television. A girl, *muy linda*. Pretty. Marriage, then long days alone in an automobile on lonely, arrow-straight roadways.

Selling, or trying to sell. The marriage broke apart. A move to . . . Washington? Then the CIAS arrangement.

The fragmented image cleared. That was good. He would need the details of recent memory. There was another woman. Here. *Isabel?* Elizabeth. Elizabeth Carlisle. More than a working relationship, he realized. What was it? He forced the rebelling brain to function. *Dios!* An arrangement of intimacy. And she was the CIAS *directore*. This could be dangerous.

Then his lips pulled back in a smile. It could also be useful.

He had tired rapidly. The thought process reverted to Kooven's. He was Kooven now. He threw aside the sheet and blankets and stood on unexpectedly weak legs. Big legs, but without strength. He opened a paneled door that he was aware led to the bathroom and stared into the full-length mirror he knew was affixed to the door's reverse side. It was then that the full impact of this bizarre awakening hit him, sang through his disoriented brain like the whine of a power saw, slid down his heavy body in a spasm of incredulity.

He seized the door jamb to steady his shuddering bulk. Then the seizurelike trembling drained away, left him numb and uncoordinated. He fought back a threat of panic and stared into the mirror.

He faced a shambling, rumpled image; a big man with thinning hair. On impulse, he shucked the pajama top and dropped the bottom. A big soft man. Once powerful, perhaps, but now beginning to sag to deskbound flab. Fleshy shoulders, a thickening waist, heavy thighs nesting large genitalia. Kooven was impressed by that, an unexpected benefit to this overpowering metamorphosis that had taken place without his conscious participation, or even awareness.

Then he noticed the bandage behind his right ear. A floodgate of memory broke open. The *clinica*. The enforced stay. An accident? Of course not. He knew Rapier. But how this had been done, he could not imagine. Why it was done, though, was becoming quite clear.

The risk, Greta Heissen determined, was close to unjustifiable. She had disagreed with Lefroid in the past, but never on an issue as substantive as a Rapier MO. Now it was precisely the MO itself that she felt was the risk. She had engineered Lefroid's agreement to terminate Reifsnyder if no confirmation of conversion had been filed by the twenty-seventh. But now she feared his agreement was not sufficient. For one thing, it had come too easily.

She felt trapped in her little office, a victim of the administrative assistant role she had agreed to maintain. She was as intelligent as Lefroid—five points above him, in fact, in IQ scoring; fully as motivated and just as ruthless, though in a less direct manner. Lefroid enjoyed reactions, relished the immediate effects of face-to-face castration of an adversary. She was fulfilled more by working quietly, even unobserved, with equally devastating results. She could castrate just as effectively, but her victims often did not realize what was missing until they tried to screw someone else.

Greta took a long pull at her Virginia Slim and tapped off the ash. The worst of this was the season. She could very well do without Christmas, the most empty of holidays. She did not look forward to any holiday, but Christmas in her upper sixties highrise was the bleakest of all. And it threw critical scheduling right out the window. God knew what Lefroid needed Christmas for, but he seemed to acknowledge its season in his own reclusive way. That realization was her current problem.

She had forced him into agreeing on the twenty-seventh as the termination date for what was obviously an ill-conceived and highly dangerous project, but she was afraid the slackness of the holiday season would cause that determination to slip. Fatally. Perhaps such an awareness on Lefroid's part had been at the root of his not-so-stubborn agreement with her to set a deadline.

133

Worrisome. And she hated worry. She had $262,000 American in a numbered Zurich account. A solid base, but not yet quite enough to underpin a new life. Not yet quite enough to establish her beyond extradition in a developing country that was sufficiently stable and progressive to welcome a white female computer genius into its government at cabinet rank. She needed time and low-risk projects. Lefroid's attempt to penetrate CIAS was anything but low-risk. Its failure could cost her a lot more than time. Reifsnyder's experimental treatment could very well produce the antithesis of Lefroid's intention. It could provide CIAS with a walking blueprint of Rapier's plan.

She took a final drag at her cigarette and noted that her fingers trembled as she stubbed out the butt. This was intolerable. She would rather face Lefroid's after-the-fact wrath than this pervasive fear. And, after all, they *had* agreed on the twenty-seventh.

She tapped the phone buttons. Stark used an answering device. "Code Ninety-nine," she said. "Albert Reifsnyder, CIAS, Thurmont, Maryland. After twenty-four hundred, December Twenty Six. Priority: Prompt. Open end unless cancelled by direct notification only. Have a nice day."

His response came three hours and twenty minutes later. Toneless. "Ten four" was all he said. He was consistently unimaginative, she thought. A plodder. But so was a pit viper. A chill shot through her and left her shaking. This was for the good of Rapier, damn it! But could she really face Lefroid afterwards?

Her body was congealing with anxiety. She needed release. God, how she needed it. At seven P.M., she lay on her back on her bed, naked. She had turned up the apartment's heat to the prescribed eighty-three degrees. Only the bedside lamp was on, just one light in the shadowed room because she needed light for the precision placements.

She opened the little tan leather kit. The three needles glittered in their plum-tinted plush depressions. Her meticulous research had revealed nine hundred acupuncture points on twelve meridians, based on the four-thousand-year-old *Nei Ching* text, modified by Fu Hsi's *I Ching*. This basic medical philosophy she had herself further enhanced with later findings of practitioners in India and Burma. In an obscure translation of a sixteenth-century text published in Rangoon, she had found the key to reducing the twelve meridian paths to just two. Then she had learned how to focus those two concentrations to just one central locus of all sensation. And finally how to activate that excrutiatingly sensitive focus.

Just three needles were required. She selected one of the three-inch-long pair, held its short octagonal hilt delicately between thumb and forefinger and wiped its slender steel shaft with a bit of alcohol-soaked cotton.

She dabbed the swell of her lower abdomen with the cotton, savoring the bite of its cool wetness. The needle picked at first. She twirled it expertly, seeking the exact blocking point as she forced it deeper. Then her left leg ceased to exist. The numbness drove upward. It engulfed her shoulder, her entire left arm. Then the blocked nerves began to transmit their sensitivity to the concentration point, a delicious build of erotic anticipation.

She placed the second long needle with equal care and precision. The redirected flow of nerve response from her left side was complemented by the right side cluster of blocked meridians. She stopped the rising numbness at her right shoulder. She needed the use of the arm for placement of the final needle.

It was shorter that the other two, its shaft hair-thin, no more than a metallic gleam in the glow of the bedside lamp; less than an inch of thready steel protruding from the tiny octagonal grip. She drew a long breath, held it.

The importance of totally accurate placement could not be overestimated. The ancient texts warned of undefined but drastic consequences should the placement be inexpert or should it extend beyond the rigidly prescribed "breadth of a sesame seed." In practice, she had never been able to withstand the incredible reaction long enough to penetrate even to that seemingly innocuous depth.

She reached out slowly with the cotton dab, then lifted the final needle from its tiny recess, slid her arm into position, and held the little steel probe vertical. Then she deftly placed the thread-thin point.

The explosion of erotic sensation had nowhere to dissipate its shattering potency, not with every energy flow meridian blocked. Her mouth shaped soundless cries. Behind her twitching eyelids pulsed wave after wave of brilliant multi-colored fire. Perspiration soaked the sheet beneath her. The muscles of her right arm began to jitter. Now it was essential that she release the concentrated complex of sensations or brutally lose control.

She forced her rapidly shattering concentration to focus on the fingers of her right hand and inched the hand to the large needle protruding from her quivering right side. As she drew it out, the dammed-up nerve energy bathed her side in convulsive surges. She plucked out the opposite meridian blocker quickly, found the small needle where it had fallen on her thigh and luxuriated in the yin and yang forces equilibrizing through her body in delicious ebbs and flows of gradually receding intensity. She lay there two hours, two full hours of physical involvement in herself and her needs. Two hours of total isolation from Rapier and Lefroid.

That this was a critically dangerous practice, Greta Heissen knew full well. All her research had warned her. But without release, she would go mad. And what man, other woman, or drug could give her release like this?

He knew, using the Reifsnyder range of his memory, that all phone calls, outgoing and incoming, were recorded—not to inhibit the residents but to make available to them any requested transcript. The practice, though, now inhibited Kooven. He was aware that he should notify Rapier of his remarkable presence here. But use of the phone was effectively blocked. The outgoing mail was picked up at a central hallway mail drop. His obvious need was to get to a safe phone.

Yet he hesitated. Between Lieutenant Horn and Elizabeth Carlisle herself, Kooven knew for a certainty that he was being watched. Horn because of his damned police dog instinct. Carlisle for a far different reason. And she was potentially the larger threat. How long could he pass as her lover?

Fortunately, the approaching holidays had already thinned the ranks of the residents. Only Natali appeared at lunch the day Kooven had awakened to find himself in another body. Natali, the dapper space propulsion wizard. A fool with all the perception of an errand clerk. Kooven had put Reifsnyder's physical presence, voice, and memory to work by joining Natali at his table, and even enjoyed the ruse.

Elizabeth Carlisle was another matter. She had come to his room the following Sunday. "You can't just hole up here most of the day, Albert. You've been through a trauma, but isolation is not the most effective therapy."

Her kittenish tone unnerved him. She thrust out her hand. "Come. Come with me."

Dios! Like a mother, but with a salacious undertone. He followed her through the utility closet. Two grown people playing at bedroom intrigue. Then he realized they were playing at more than that. He had not quite mastered the simultaneous two-track conversation he knew he would need when Dr. Strakhan returned. Some of Reifsnyder's practices, mind-sets, and peculiarities startled him when he forced them into focus.

Such as Reifsnyder's relish at watching Dr. Carlisle's preparation ritual. "Remember, it's your turn," she reminded him in an oddly feline growl.

Kooven dredged Reifsnyder's memory cells. Some sort of game. Ah, *naturalmente!* The game. "My turn, indeed," he agreed in Reifsnyder's voice.

From the bed, he watched her deft work at the dressing table—the dusting of cheek rouge, the precise brush application of lipstick. His mind knew the sequence, yet each step was a revelation to his consciousness, like seeing a long-forgotten movie that he remembered only as each scene unfolded.

She released her brassiere. Only now did he recall the breasts' fascinating firmness, a young girl's texture supporting the fullness of maturity. Her white briefs pooled at her feet. She thrust them aside with a little kick.

"Come to me, Albert. It has been much too long." She stood statuelike in the center of the shadowed room, arms at her sides, head lowered, eyes fixed on him.

Kooven set his glass on the bedside table. The liquor had disturbed his concentration. He wasn't certain what was expected in this erotic sequence. He stood and moved toward her.

"Your clothes, Albert."

"Ah, of course."

He unbuttoned Reifsnyder's shirt, pulled off the T-shirt, stepped out of loafers and trousers, pulled off the nylon over-the-calf socks. Then he stripped off the boxer shorts. Naked, he felt his unaccustomed size far more than he had felt it fully clothed. A big man! She had already affected him, and he was startled at his own impressiveness.

He towered over her, touched her shoulder tentatively.

"No, no, Albert. The rules! Only with the lips, darling."

Now he knew. She awaited his ingenuity. He lowered his head, kissed the angle of her neck. She smiled but remained immobile. He faced her, clasped his hands behind his back and touched her with a flurry of lightly brushed kisses.

Elizabeth Carlisle trembled, then set her teeth against it. "Tonight," she announced, "you are up against monumental control. Mind over matter, Albert, dear."

Bitch. He'd show her something about control. His lips trailed down the slight protrusion of her belly, paused at the dimpled navel. She shuddered against him, again suppressed it. Some tigress, Kooven scoffed to himself with satisfaction. She's already purring.

He dropped to his knees, kissed her thighs unhurriedly. "Damn!" she murmured. Kooven smirked. She wanted games? He would show her games.

She gasped happily, almost a giggle. "You fiend! You absolute fiend!"

Her fingers clenched and unclenched at her sides. "Forget the damned game," she breathed. Her arms locked around his neck.

"No!" He'd show this overeducated *puta* who was master. He pulled her arms away. "Behave, Elizabeth," he said in Reifsnyder's rumble. "You lose too easily."

"I do, do I!" She grinned wickedly, slapped her arms back to her sides. "Ice maiden. I defy you to thaw me out!"

He had to give her grudged credit. It took fifteen minutes, with her denying to succumb to the intimacies he sensed her body now screamed for, before Kooven lowered Elizabeth to the rug. Then he learned that the infernal game had taken its toll on him, as well.

Her delighted laugh shot a flash of anger through him. He subdued it. Let her think she'd had that moment of mastery over him.

The carpet's pile was harsh against his sweating back. This body he inhabited may be *grando,* Kooven reflected, but it is also *blando.* He would have to be constantly aware of its limitations.

Nestled beside him, she began to giggle. "So, Albert dear, you had thought for a moment you had won? Such a short moment."

He hid his irritation and began to get up.

"No, wait." A wildness flashed in her violet eyes. She stared down at him. Her lips drew back.

Then with no warning at all, she flung herself upon him. Her puppy teeth nipped his ears, his neck. Her mouth fastened on his. She broke free and threw her head back. "Albert," she hissed, "you're like a different person!"

Kooven froze. Then he said smoothly, "It's the accident. It made me realize how much you mean to me."

Her face was close to his. He watched her eyes fill. She took his head in both hands. "Settle back, you wonderful big man," she whispered fiercely. "We have just begun."

CHAPTER
11

ROLLO STARK LAY belly down in the snow at the edge of the brush line a half mile south of the CIAS compound. Here was where the security clearing of the rising slope had stopped. The stone residence, incongruous brick laboratory building, and the surrounding fences lay in a shallow bowl with the ascending slopes cleared of brush, rocks—any sort of cover in a half-mile radius. A lousy position against artillery, Stark thought, his infantry training still an instinct. But effective as hell against infiltration. No doubt the cleared area was swept with electronic surveillance, and he assumed the triple fencing was a lethal dandy.

He focused his binoculars. The compound leaped toward him. One access road, guarded by an entrance gatehouse. And TV security, of course. The place appeared casually guarded, but its exposed isolation was effective. What were his options?

Were he somehow to work within sniper range, he would have to wait until Reifsnyder became available as a target, and Stark had no knowledge of the man's movements about the compound. The bulky .45 caliber single shot Lisle silent

141

carbine concealed in his Ford was accurate up to a hundred yards. But even if that application were cleared, the risk was unthinkable. Stark worked for money. Such a risk wasn't worth what he would be paid for this contract. The danger to him was already above the level of comfort. His car with its New York plate was pulled well into the abandoned logging trail in the woods behind him. But it had left tracks in the snow. A particularly perceptive county cop or sheriff, if there were such in this forsaken part of Maryland, could wonder why tire tracks led off the county road into the woods. His cover story of scouting land for an Albany real estate developer might or might not hold up.

Another way to go at Reifsnyder? Through the gate, of course, in the guise of a delivery man. He discarded that old ruse as quickly as he had thought of it. They undoubtedly had checklists, passes, or some other means of intercepting inappropriate arrivals.

A gust eddied snow across the lenses. He brushed them clear on his jacket sleeve. Cold up here. Cold and, aside from the wind, as silent as Kae Song where he had trained his army issue binoculars across the 38th Parallel day after silent day until the night he had focused all his frustration, boredom, and rage into a single knife thrust.

Praszka had called him "Chink." It should have been a simple NCOs' club brawl with fists, but Praszka had to bring up the hated nickname. Stark had battered it out of his high school peers after three years of pumping iron to give him the mustard to flatten Arch Moxley's pimply nose. Now here it came again, and from a guy with a name like Praszka, for God's sake! Stark knew he was no beauty. His little close-set eyes, slitted above bunched cheeks in his pie-plate face did look oriental. But that was his business, nobody else's. When Praszka started on him in the club, Stark had warned him once. The Pollack kept up his boozy jibes, so Stark had sunk the jackknife in his thigh.

The court-martial ended his army career, though mitigating circumstances were cited in granting him a discharge for convenience rather than a full DD or even a stretch in the Seoul stockade. Then, barely out of the Los Angeles airport, he was mugged on Inglewood. An arm snaked out of the night, collared him from the rear. He thrust backwards three steps to throw his invisible assailant off balance, reached behind his head to grab two handfuls of long hair, then doubled at the waist. The inept attacker flew over Stark's head, landed flat on his back, which cut off the startled howl. His switchblade skittered across the dark sidewalk. Stark kicked him hard in the right temple. That not only caused a hairline fracture, the LA coroner's office discovered. It also broke the mugger's neck. And killed him.

In his Monza across the street, one P.V. Salito had watched this entire episode. He finally realized that the rough son of a bitch who had just tossed Mitch Morris and kicked him in the head was wearing a dark jacket and light trousers almost like P.V.'s own, was the same height and build, and—hey, man! The sucker had just saved P.V.'s life. Mitch had been laying for P.V., who had arrived at the meet late enough to see Rollo Stark wander into the trap intended for P.V. Salito.

He should just thank whatever perverse angel happened to be watching over him and drive away, P.V. knew. But he stayed, fascinated, as Stark looted Mitch's pockets. No saint, this guy. P.V. got out of his car, cat-footed across the deserted street and held up his hands as Stark pirouetted into a defensive crouch.

"No sweat, brother," P.V. called softly. "Saw your action. Good stuff. You employed?"

"You kidding?"

"You are now."

After that, it was an easy escalation from the fist-and-knee of petty collections to carefully choreographed hits, though P.V.'s coke business didn't involve anyone high enough to guarantee Stark a major income. He ran across Rapier, or rather Rapier ran across Rollo Stark in a computer search. Gerta at the console. She was leisurely penetrating the Intrastate Police Data File in an executive search for contract staff potentials.

He could play a role. Flunky at Horger's clinic, for one. Reifsnyder knew him as an orderly. He was playing a role now. Even if he were invisible and could walk right up to the CIAS fences, even if Reifsnyder were to stand facing him on the other side of the triple barrier, Stark couldn't have done a damned thing about it. Rapier's code Ninety-Nine on his answering unit called for an accident, and a sniper shot would be anything but. So Stark was playing a role again, though his recon of CIAS did confirm his assumption that he had to hit Reifsnyder elsewhere. That had been obvious as soon as he'd seen the place, of course, but Stark had a day to kill. This was the twenty-sixth, and the contract wasn't good until midnight. The problem was to get Reifsnyder out of there.

Blowing snow had almost filled in the footprints he retraced through the woods to his car. It had filled in the tire tracks, too. As he backed carefully down the logging trail, he suddenly thought of a way to maneuver Reifsnyder out of the fortress down there. Imperfect, but certainly low risk.

Stark's face broke into what might have passed for a smile. No sweat, man. No sweat.

Kooven took the call in Reifsnyder's office at 4:20 P.M.

"Dr. Reifsnyder, this is Dr. Ira Agajanian at the Horger Clinic. I don't think we met, but I was on your case when they first brought you in."

"No," Kooven said uncertainly, "we didn't meet." What was this?

"Dr. Horger asked me to call you. He's attending a medical seminar in Gettysburg tomorrow, the twenty-seventh. He realized you were close by, and he'd very much like to take a quick look at you. How are you feeling?"

Did Agajanian realize the incoming calls were taped? Was this some sort of code to . . . to what?

"I'm feeling quite well, thank you," Kooven said in Reif-

144

snyder's baritone. Unconsciously he passed his free hand across the smooth V-shaped scar, now partially hidden by newly sprouting hair. "Is it important that Dr. Horger see me?"

"Yes, it is. At 10:00 A.M. at the Sheraton Inn, Business Route 15. Will that be convenient?"

"Certainly," Kooven said. It would be most convenient. Meeting Horger meant nothing, but he would take advantage of the opportunity to use a safe phone.

Marty Horn had signed out a whole case of audiocassettes—all the incoming and outgoing phone calls for the past thirty days. No one except Celia knew he had them because he was the custodian of the cassettes and of the inventory book in which they were meticulously logged, day after day. Celia knew he had them because he had been listening to the damned things since he'd arrived home.

"If you're going to spend all night plugged into that tape player," she had said, "at least let me hear them too."

"Sorry, they're classified." They were, but as long as he had been at CIAS, no one had ever expressed the slightest interest in the stacks of cassetted phone calls. Still, it may have been illegal for him to have taken this batch out of the building, and it certainly would be illegal to treat Celia to them.

He reinserted the earplug and tried to stay awake. Some treat. It was all business, and only the dullest side of business since the CIAS residents were frequently briefed in security precautions.

He caught his own conversations with the New York police and the Horger Clinic. But there was a lot of chaff on either side of that date. And on through December. The daily call frequency began to drop off noticeably around midmonth as the residents drifted away for holiday breaks. By yesterday, Christmas Day, phone traffic was about nil. He had been on duty but had taken a short day himself, thanked Dr. Carlisle for the gift-wrapped fifth of Chivas Regal she had placed on his desk the day before, then left after lunch. Abner Dortman had come on early to cover for him. Dortman wasn't married and was glad to build points.

Marty changed cassettes again. About a day's normal traffic was carried on each one, with simultaneous calls recorded on any of four additional machines, then automatically transferred to the master during slow traffic load periods.

No doubt today's calls would be just as few. He had taken this cassette directly out of the master recorder at 5:00 P.M.

Agajanian? Who the hell was that? He'd talked with Horger and a nurse, but nobody had mentioned a Dr. Agajanian. Then he sank back against the sofa cushions. For God's sake, Horn, stop trying to find a spider under every rock. You think they should have read you the clinic's staff list?

". . . *Gettysburg tomorrow, the twenty-seventh,*" the voice named Agajanian said. Peculiar? Not really. If Dr. Horger was to be in Gettysburg, what was more natural than his interest in checking up on a patient whom he had possibly released too soon? Marty felt a pang of guilt. Hadn't he, himself, pressured Horger into doing just that?

". . . *At 10:00* A.M., *at the Sheraton Inn,*" Agajanian's recorded voice said.

That was the last call on the tape. Marty pulled out the soft plastic plug and rubbed his aching ear. Had he gained anything at all through this dumb exercise? He glanced at his watch. Lord Almighty, 2:35 A.M!

Celia was asleep with the light on. He undressed, brushed his teeth and slid into bed without waking her. He lay in the dark with his head cradled in laced fingers. To hell with it. Reifsnyder's going to meet Horger in Gettysburg was innocent enough. There wasn't a rabbit's pellet worth of real evidence that anything out of the ordinary was going on at CIAS. He was succeeding in just one thing: making a horse's ass of himself. He'd already refined that to an art.

* * *

But when Reifsnyder's silver Jetta pulled away from the CIAS gatehouse, Marty was already in the ornate vestibule.

"I want you to handle the security room for a couple hours," he told Lydia Whimple.

"But I'm supposed to be here."

No imagination at all, he lamented. "That's right. You can do both. I'll program the security room phone to your desk here. Hell, that's about all there is to do back there, take phone calls. Crawford'll call in when the gate isn't opened from the security room. You pick it up here, go to the room, hit the buttons, then come back here."

Her hard gray eyes narrowed. "That means I'll be in charge of overall security."

"Until I get back, yes."

She couldn't hide the effect of that. The corners of her little mouth twitched up.

That's as close to a "hot damn" as she'll ever come, Marty thought. Through the entrance door's leaded glass, he saw Reifsnyder's car dwindle down the snow-crusted macadam approach road. Marty shoved through the door and trotted to his Reliant.

He hung on Reifsnyder's tail a good mile back. That wasn't difficult. Traffic was light, and he knew where Reifsnyder was going. The silver Jetta turned south on 550, then on the north edge of Thurmont swung onto U.S. 15, Gettysburg bound. Three miles later, the highway divided. Tailing was even easier now. In a few minutes they passed the Emmitsburg interchange and crossed the Pennsylvania line. The long stretches of open highway let Marty drop well behind, though he was sure that Reifsnyder, if he was his usual preoccupied self, was unaware he had company.

The Jetta swung off the divided highway at the first interchange on the Pennsylvania side, climbed the long exit ramp that crossed over the highway, then descended onto the narrow blacktop of PA Business 15, a straight pull into Gettysburg six miles northeast. A beeline for the Sheraton. This was too easy.

Just short of the national military park, the Jetta slowed, then turned sharply right into the entrance drive of the Sheraton Inn. Marty hung back until he was sure Reifsnyder's attention was fully occupied with finding a parking space, then he too turned into the long drive to the low, pseudo-Tudor style inn. The big communications man strode to the entrance and disappeared inside as Marty neared the parking area. He backed the Reliant into a space ten cars distant from the Jetta in a lot seventy-five yards north of the lobby entrance.

Now what? He hadn't thought beyond this point. He wasn't even sure why he was here. How long could he play hunches before he made an obvious jerk of himself? He felt like one now, hunched here in the rapidly cooling Reliant between a massive Olds and a Cadillac. The stubby K-car could hide in a parking lot as well as any import shortie.

The Sheraton seemed asleep, but that wasn't surprising on this doldrum day between Christmas and New Year's. He glanced beyond the row of cars in another lot southwest of the inn to a cluster of buildings that was apparently a deserted amusement park or one of the strangest pieces of apartment architecture he'd even seen.

One guy over there in a brown Ford, facing out. Front plate obscured by snow, but it looked orange. Marty wondered what he was waiting for? His wife to come out? Maybe for someone not his wife to come in. Then from the front entrance came Reifsnyder. He looked puzzled. He'd been in there just under seven minutes.

Before he'd driven three miles out of Thurmont on U.S. 15, Kooven realized he was being followed. A light green Reliant rode a mile behind him like it was connected to him by an invisible wire. When Kooven eased Reifsnyder's Jetta back to fifty, the green car fell back too. When he inched up to sixty-five, the Reliant obliged.

Kooven pondered. Then he mentally kicked himself and concentrated on Reifsnyder's thought track. Of course! He was being tailed by CIAS's own chief of security, Marty Horn. He almost laughed aloud. No threat from *El Teniente Estupido*. Kooven made no attempt to lose him. Let him play.

When Kooven reached the Sheraton and parked, he pulled up the collar of his storm coat against the sharp wind, walked straight to the porticoed main entrance and turned slightly as he opened the big door. Yes, there was Horn's car, just now drifting along the entrance drive.

He checked his watch as he entered the broad low-ceilinged lobby. Ten o'clock exactly.

And no Horger.

The blonde at the registration desk was unhelpful. "Medical conference? We have a crafts wholesalers meeting coming in tomorrow, but no medical group."

He frowned at the heavy-set girl. "Maybe I misunderstood. Have you a Dr. Horger registered? An Elmo Horger?"

She checked the registrations file and shrugged. "Sorry, sir."

He was perplexed. Why would Dr. Agajanian have asked—insisted, in fact—that he come here? Yet this confusion of plans should not affect his chance to use a safe phone. She showed him where the pay phones were.

He recalled Rapier's 212 area code number easily. Fascinating. Born again with two operational memory banks.

He recognized the voice of the attractive but granite-hard woman who guarded Lefroid's office.

"I'm sorry, Mr. Lefroid is not available at the moment. Would you care to leave a message?"

Stock Rapier response.

He debated only briefly. He'd shock the cold son of a bitch. "Tell Mr. Lefroid that Mr. Kooven called."

He distinctly heard a sudden intake of breath. Now her computer-bland voice trembled, just slightly, but he picked it up. "Would you repeat that?"

"Tell Mr. Lefroid," he said, enunciating every syllable, "that Mr. Kooven—that is K-O-O-V-E-N—called."

149

"Mr. Kooven," she repeated, apparently in an effort to control her suddenly ragged breathing. Interesting. "Where can he reach you, Mr. Kooven?"

"I'll reach him." He didn't think Lefroid would be stupid enough to call him at CIAS, but there was no need to tell this secretary any more than she had to know.

He turned from the public phone so that his eyes ranged the lobby in an unobtrusive sweep. Still deserted, except for the desk clerk. He felt no threat from her. He realized now that he'd been set up, but by whom and for what?

He pushed through the entrance door slowly, downcast eyes darting left then right, seeking the shoes and legs of a crude ambush. The entrance portico was empty. He could feel tension in the icy wind. There was danger here, but he was ready for it.

For more than an hour, Stark had hunched in his suede jacket behind the wheel of the Ford in the Sheraton's south-west parking lot. He was cold, bored, and he suspected he might have already blown this assignment. Reifsnyder could have called the Horger Clinic to verify the call from "Dr. Agajanian." Something else—any number of possibilities—could have stopped the CIAS man from driving to Gettys-burg this morning. Stark compressed his thin lips and began to plan his cover story for the inevitable showdown with that ice-blooded, red-haired bitch at Rapier.

Then the Jetta, which he didn't recognize, pulled in, parked, and Reifsnyder, whom he certainly did recognize, walked from the northeast parking area to the hotel en-trance. The doc didn't even look around. Eyes straight ahead and down, watching his footing on the ice patches. He did swing his head around at the lobby entrance, but that could have been the action of anyone opening a big door then moving past it.

Stark's gaze shifted to the parking areas and entrance road. A light green car—what was it? One of those stubby K-cars. A Reliant. It rolled into the hotel grounds, passed a hundred feet in front of Stark's Ford, then pulled into the lot on the far side of the open area adjacent to the main entrance.

One guy aboard. Stark waited for him to get out. He didn't. What the hell was *he* waiting for?

Five minutes. Six . . . seven. Then the Sheraton entrance door swung open. Reifsnyder stepped out, head down. He reached up to raise his collar against the chilly wind. Stark turned his ignition key. This had to be done with split-second precision. The guy in the green Reliant, whoever he was, would have to be part of the risk. By the time he got over the shock enough to make it to the lobby and call the locals, then calmed down enough to make sense, Stark would be long gone. The roads were full of brown Fords. He had carefully applied slush to both license plates to obscure their numbers. With a potential witness, the risk was higher, but it was still acceptable.

Reifsnyder was a third of the way across the open area between the two parking lots when the Ford rolled out of its slot and accelerated. The big communications man grew in the Ford's windshield, but he seemed not even to be aware of the car bearing down on him.

Then Stark floored the gas pedal. He cut hard left. The rear tires screamed across the icy macadam. Stark saw Reifsnyder's bulk flash past on the right, waited for the thud of the big body against the rear fender.

Failed to hear it!

He fought the wheel to straighten the wildly yawing Ford, managed to skid it into the exit drive, then glanced into the rearview mirror.

How had he missed? Reifsnyder had sprawled flat, but he was getting up. The son of a bitch sure had fast reflexes for a big man. Or had he somehow expected something like this?

Now what? Stark had to make good. Rapier permitted no mistakes. He'd have to work out another MO. Fast. But first he had to get out of here, that was for sure.

He skidded northeastward onto business Route 15. In the

other direction lay only the long straight stretch of U.S. 15. A potential trap. Northeast was Gettysburg and a lot more options were he somehow pursued.

That was a laugh. The nerd in the Reliant probably was still sitting there with his mouth hanging open. If he did get it together enough to get to a lobby phone, he wouldn't even remember the make or color of the car. Relax, Rollo boy. No sense risking the attention of a speed cop. He slowed to a normal speed. Piece of cake. What's to worry?

He checked the side mirror. One car back there. A half mile behind. He squinted against the snow glare. Was it green? Light green?

When Marty had seen the Ford pull out suddenly, he'd sat up so fast he'd bumped his head against the Reliant's padded roof. Then he stared in helpless horror.

The Ford had raced after Reifsnyder, skidded leftward— God, had he clipped him? No accident, this; not with the Ford racing now for the main road. The guy behind the wheel had to be an expert. He used his vehicle as a weapon, then cut out before Marty had time to do a damned thing. The most chilling part of it was that he had to know Marty was watching, but he went ahead anyway.

Marty yanked the door release and slammed one foot to the parking lot ice. Then he hesitated. How in hell was he going to explain his presence here?

And while he sat, half in and half out of the car, Reifsnyder suddenly scrambled to his feet and trotted to his Jetta. He didn't appear hurt at all. Then, like a slow-motion replay, Marty realized what he'd really seen: not an unsuspecting man struck from behind by an out-of-control car, but a man leaping back from the oncoming fender a fraction of a second before it would have crashed into him. A man who had known what was coming and timed his escape precisely. The Ford had never touched him. Marty wouldn't have bet a nickel that Reifsnyder had reflexes like that.

He slid back into his car and jerked the door shut. The

Jetta swung into the exit drive. Marty started the Reliant and nosed out cautiously. Reifsnyder turned left, back toward the highway to Thurmont. Marty could gain nothing by following the Jetta home. When he reached the main road, he turned right and gunned the little four-cylinder car toward Gettysburg.

He spotted the Ford on the near-empty road before he'd rolled a mile and a half. The bastard certainly was sure of himself, cruising along like a tourist.

Then Marty tried to close the gap between them. The Ford increased its speed. He'd been made, Marty realized, but he sure could use the plate number.

He knew he was going to catch the guy because far ahead he saw a tour bus lumbering toward Gettysburg at no more than thirty on the treacherous packed snow of the roadway. An oncoming truck was about to trap the Ford neatly behind the bus. Marty grinned in satisfaction. He had the guy.

Then his grin faded. The Ford had swung right—into the military park. Marty slacked off speed and followed, the light rear of the front-wheel-drive Reliant yawing wildly. A sign flashed by. The Peach Orchard, the south flank of the Union line on the second day of the battle. Marty and Celia had toured the battlefield last summer. Took a whole day to do it. Marty had been fascinated, but Celia had taken her recipe cards with her and mostly stayed in the car to work on them.

The Ford was only a quarter mile ahead now, flashing through the Wheatfield where De Trobriand's brigade had been pushed back by Anderson's rebel infantry. They rushed down a slight grade between snow-capped monuments and statuary commemorating the men of various units who had fought and died here.

Now he could almost make out the rear license plate, its obscuring snow cracking off at the jolts in the macadam road. Then the Ford spun right again, its rear skidding wide to slam a marker post before the driver straightened for the steep run up Little Round Top.

The road twisted upward among winter-stripped trees, topped the rocky promontory for which so many men of the 20th Maine and 140th New York and 15th Alabama had died in the hand-to-hand struggle for command of the valley to the west.

The K-car's front-wheel drive took the hill efficiently. Now Marty was only a hundred yards from the fleeing Ford. Then it cut hard right again, plunged down the steep slope, and they wound through the surrealistic boulderscape of the Devil's Den. The narrow roadway snaked through this tumble of huge rocks where Ward's Union bluecoats had been pushed back by General Hood's division. And in the maze of boulders, Marty lost the Ford.

He didn't know he had until he emerged on the level road south of the Wheatfield and was able to scan the battlefield to the north. Empty. A deserted expanse of snow dotted with monuments, reconstructed cannons and historic markers of a long-past struggle between two mighty armies.

He stopped the car where the loop around the Devil's Den rejoined the arrow-straight Peach Orchard-Wheatfield Road. Then he spotted the Ford, tiny in the distance, speeding north on Taneytown Road. Too late he realized its driver had taken one of the obscure lanes through the Devil's Den to double back south of the Wheatfield, then had sped east on the tour road to Taneytown Road on the far side of the battlefield.

Marty would never catch him now. The license plate had been orange, front and back. That ruled out Pennsylvania, which used only a rear plate. Orange plates were what? New York, maybe a couple others. New York State was where Reifsnyder had had his accident. Where he had been treated at the Horger Clinic.

Fear curled upward from Greta's stomach, left a trail of ice between her breasts and speared a frigid tentacle along her throat to explode into pain behind her forehead. She

154

thought she would be sick. But she took a deep breath and forced her throbbing brain into sharp focus.

She had to stop Stark. She'd already placed a recall order on his apartment answering device. But he was in Maryland. Unless he called his machine, that recall was useless.

She had also placed two unanswered calls to the mobile phone in his car; one yesterday afternoon, the other early this morning. Possibly too early. Then Lefroid had arrived. She found herself paralyzed by the fear that he would burst out of his office at the precise moment she was placing another call through the mobile operator. That reaction was so unlike her that for ten minutes she closed her mind to everything but a searching self-analysis to determine the reason for such a pervasive dread.

She found it. Never before had she experienced failure. But she faced it now. She had assumed that the experiment had collapsed, but incredible as it was, now she knew that Kooven lived in Reifsnyder's body. If Stark were to succeed in carrying out her order to terminate Reifsnyder/Kooven, God only knew what Lefroid's reaction would invoke. Because of her fail-safe backup in the New York library computer bank, he couldn't kill her. Or had he found a way to short-stop the access code? Was there a way? She worried about that too.

She had to take the chance of calling while Lefroid was not thirty feet beyond the paneled partition of her office. Had he planted a bug since the last security sweep she had authorized? Still another worry. She was choking on apprehension.

Then Stark's car came from behind a mountain, or he got in it for the first time today or something else had happened that let him hear the buzz of an incoming call.

Mindful that mobile phone conversations were open broadcast, she held herself in remarkable restraint, particularly in view of the fact that her heart thundered in her head and her bladder suddenly felt about to burst.

155

"Have you . . ." Her mouth dried. She didn't want to ask the question or hear the answer. "Have you made delivery?"

The delay in his response was unbearable. Then his handset cut back in. She could hear the background noise of a racing engine. He was driving the Ford hard.

"Not yet."

Relief swept over her. The background noise cut out. "Then call home," she ordered. "Now!"

She had intercepted him in time. Thank God! She slumped back to let the hard tension fall away. At that moment, Lefroid's office door swung wide.

The pale eyes glared down at her. Her stomach muscles stiffened. Then the thin-lipped mouth split in a cold smile that showed the oddly pointed teeth.

"You look like you've had a fairly disastrous day so far." This was as close to humor as he had ever come. She pulled herself together fast.

"He's alive, André. Kooven is alive!"

"He reported in." Not a question; a statement. How confident this bastard was! She had sweat ice crystals for nearly two hours and he accepted a resolving miracle as if it were inevitable.

What in hell had he accomplished, Marty asked himself? He had followed Reifsnyder to Gettysburg, but he still had no inkling what the man was doing there. He had been an eyewitness to an apparent attempt to run down the big communications expert, but he hadn't been able to do a damned thing about it except try to chase the fleeing Ford in an ineffective pursuit through the battlefield until the guy lost him with the simplest of all evasion tactics. Marty drove back to CIAS feeling ineffective, even stupid.

Yet he had seen the Ford skid into Reifsnyder as if the driver had precisely planned it. And he had seen Reifsnyder just as precisely escape contact with the Ford's onrushing quarter panel as if he'd expected something like that to happen. No mistake about it, not after Reifsnyder had scrambled back to his feet and gotten his Jetta the hell out of there.

Sorely missing was conclusive evidence . . . of what? Marty thought Reifsnyder was behaving oddly, but that could be the lingering result of severe concussion, couldn't it? Reifsnyder's cold stares? The inexplicable feeling of unease Marty experienced whenever he encountered the man? Was all that evidence? No, it was a cop's hunch. And cop's hunches didn't count anymore, not in a time when you could stop a car full of just-stolen merchandise, then have the case thrown out because the car was stopped on a cop's hunch.

He needed something a lot more solid than gut feelings. He knew he'd get it if he kept his eyes open. What he didn't know was that when he finally did get his hard evidence, there would come a time when he would wish he'd stayed out of it altogether.

Stark had ripped through Gettysburg's east side, broken quickly into open country and continued eastward. He doubted that the clown in the K-car had been able to make out the Ford's plate, but he couldn't be sure. At eleven forty-two, he swung around a tight bend on State Route 116 near Bonneauville and there, bigger than hell, sat a blue-and-white Pennsylvania State Police unit. Parked on the shoulder of the inside of the curve. Tubular radar eye staring.

Stark checked his speed. A conservative forty-five. He cruised past, shoulder muscles tensing. In the rearview, he saw the blond trooper slap on his campaign hat.

Stark's right foot clamped down. The Ford leaped. Then he fought instinct. The cop could be going to lunch or changing location. The Ford slowed to forty.

Then the big central roof light flashed crimson. Stark stiffened. His mouth went dry. The damned Reliant driver had read his plate after all. He should have taken the chance to stop on a Gettysburg side street, rip off a Pennsy

157

plate from a parked car and slap it in place of his New York set. Too late to think about that now.

Outrun the guy? An off-chance of that, but he sure couldn't outrun the guy's radio. Take him out? Kill a cop over some eyewitness report on what would be a hit-and-run rap at the worst? No way. Stark hit the brakes and pulled over. As he did, though, another thought hit him. Would Rapier pull him out of this or let him take a fall?

The cop was big, dressed in hard dark gray, hat brim low over his eyes like a Marine DI. No rube. A Pennsylvania trooper, all business. Stark got out, sweat breaking across his chest. The hell of it was that this was going to tangle him up in God-knew-what, and he hadn't yet gotten to a phone to do what the Rapier bitch had told him to do: call his answering machine. He couldn't do that from the car because whatever she had put on the machine would come down to him on open broadcast.

"License and registration, please." The cop stood a good three inches taller than Stark. He checked the cards Stark handed him. Routinely, Stark suddenly realized. What was this?

"Your rear plate's obscured," the cop announced. "Like you to clean it off right now."

Stark almost laughed. "Yes, sir!" He trotted around the rear fender. The wild flight through the battlefield hadn't dislodged all of the frozen gray slush after all. He was free and clear! He kicked off the grimy crust. The cop nodded and walked back to his unit.

Fourteen minutes later, Stark stopped at an outdoor booth in Hanover, punched his own phone number and hit the playback code.

"Cancel code Ninety-Nine. New information: remain in area. Check daily for revised assignment."

What the hell went on here?

He slid back in his car and drove aimlessly out of Hanover. This was crazy. What was going on? He'd been instructed to terminate the guy, had blown that, and now he was supposed to hole up in the vicinity and call in periodically for instructions? Stark liked simple, direct assignments that he could plan in logical one, two, three sequences. This was a one, two, then turn it around thing. He didn't understand it at all.

But if that hard-voiced broad said go back there and wait for new orders, then there was no choice about it. He pulled into a farm road, reversed, and headed the Ford back to Maryland.

CHAPTER
12

AN ACCIDENT OR an attempt to eliminate him? Kooven couldn't decide. The incident in Gettysburg had shaken him, but he'd had close ones before. The assignment was important, not some *imbecil* driver in a Sheraton parking lot. But he would certainly be more alert than ever as he proceeded.

Of the four current CIAS residents, Roland Strakhan, Reifsnyder's memory told Kooven, was the loner. He worked alone, ate alone, relaxed in a corner of the library alone. And this was the man Kooven had to cultivate to the point of confidence. Perhaps an impossible assignment, but he had no choice.

He began by stumbling into the small corner table to which Strakhan customarily retreated from the cafeteria-style breakfast serving line. As he had planned, the collision slopped most of Strakhan's coffee into his saucer.

"Oh, hell! That was clumsy of me," Kooven said in Reifsnyder's rumble. "Let me get you another cup."

Without waiting for a response, he put his tray on Strakhan's table and hurried back to the serving line.

Strakhan was obviously taken aback by the solicitude. Kooven moved in.

"Mind if I join you?" He sat down before Strakhan could answer. "I guess we're all pretty much loners around here. Nature of the work."

"Obviously."

Kooven buttered his toast. "Too bad. Isolated physically out here, then further isolated by our projects." He was intrigued at how smoothly he could manipulate Reifsnyder's voice and couple it with both thought processes.

But Strakhan seemed singularly unapproachable, the customary cockiness of a small man apparently replaced by defensive coldness. Yet every man had his access.

"MIT, I understand."

Strakhan's sharp little eyes flicked up from his plate of scrambled eggs. "You know MIT?"

"I know of MIT, of course. Worldwide reputation."

Strakhan nodded. "And ECAT? You know of that too?"

A jab of vindictive humor here? "ECAT?"

"Eastern Center for Advanced Technology. Providence, Rhode Island. You need the proper doctorate to apply." The bastard was playing a game of educational institution chess.

"I'm afraid my schooling was limited to Chicago Northwestern." Let him win it.

Strakhan sniffed. Eloquently. That was that. Another tack, Kooven determined. He'd already explored Reifsnyder's memory in this area and knew where he wanted to go with it.

"That was a fascinating experience you put us through some weeks back."

Strakhan stirred his coffee. "We're not to discuss our work." Kooven discerned a degree of self-satisfaction behind the curt response. Was this arid little man susceptible to flattery?

"I realize that, but it occurred to me that our projects may be parallel in a way."

"Indeed? What way is that?"

161

"Affecting behavior by teletransmission. My approach is the use of subliminal symbology in standard video and audio broadcast formats. Yours, though, appears to be far more direct."

How am I doing so far, Kooven wondered in Reifsnyder's vernacular. Then he noticed that Strakhan's piercing Dresden blue eyes had swung his way. Got him.

"There is a parallel," the bioelectronics engineer mused aloud.

"One that may eliminate my work as obsolete?" Kooven fished in earnest now.

Strakhan's eyes met his. Kooven sensed self-debate behind their unblinking stare. Then the frowsy little scientist glanced around the dining room—needlessly, as Natali and Moyle had already left—and hitched his chair closer. Kooven noticed the gray ring lining the open collar of his rumpled white shirt. Now the aroma of fresh coffee failed to mask the musty smell of the man.

"It could make your work valueless at short ranges," Strakhan said with unconcealed satisfaction. "Longer ranges when it is perfected, of course."

"Ah, you have problems? In that case I can go right on with my snake, skull, and sword embeds?"

"If the management is willing to pay you for that."

"They're paying you, and you admit you have problems."

Strakhan went for the challenge. "What I have done to date is light years ahead of your damned snakes, skulls, and swords. My limitations aren't those of concept. They are temporary difficulties of transmission range and focus. Effective reach. And beam width."

Strakhan stopped abruptly. Kooven was elated, but he sensed the value of an apparently unimpressed response.

"Interesting," he offered in a tone of near dismissal, "but I'm afraid I don't exactly feel the scientific ground quaking beneath my feet." He shoved back his chair to stand and glanced at the bioelectronics expert.

Strakhan's wizened face had colored. He shot another

look around the empty dining room. "If you were sincerely interested, I could . . . No. No, it's best not to involve other—" He checked his watch and rose abruptly, the top of his head barely reaching Kooven's shoulder. "Excuse me," he muttered and hurried from the room.

In Reifsnyder's office, Kooven sank into the comfortable swivel chair with satisfaction. Through Reifsnyder's memory, he had corroborated Lefroid's information that Strakhan was developing, or had developed, a weapon (was it a weapon?) . . . a device, at any rate, with the unique ability to influence or even control human emotion. Now his breakfast with Strakhan had revealed that the thing had propagation limitations that Strakhan was working to overcome. And focus problems. What had he meant by that?

What Kooven had to do now was stay here long enough for the little *pulga* to work out those problems. In the meantime, it was essential that he see what Strakhan was working on. Was it the size of a television set or big enough to fill a truck? Was it nicely contained in a single unit or was it a sprawl of modules across a series of cluttered laboratory benches?

When he had the answers, he would know whether to attempt to somehow duplicate the blueprints and wiring diagrams, steal them, or attempt to remove the device itself. And somehow transport it past security cameras, through the gate in the triple fencing and down the long entrance road to Route 550.

But before all that, he knew he would have to neutralize Lieutenant Marty Horn.

The hill behind the A-frame rose steeply ahead of them. Celia climbed well, her boots instinctively testing footholds before she shifted her weight. The snow-clad rocks were treacherous. Marty slipped, fell to one knee, and swore. It had been her idea to take this late Sunday afternoon climb up the hill behind their house. He'd welcomed it. He was tired of sitting and brooding and listening to her

163

endless tap-tapping on her portable typewriter. She was finished with compiling the recipes she'd received from her classified ads (a miracle she got any response at all, he'd thought), and now she was typing what seemed to be endless pages of manuscript. "MS," she called it, trying hard to sound professional.

She reached the crest of the hill first, lithe even in her bulky tan jacket and blue snow pants, fine platinum hair streaming in the breeze. He admired her competitiveness, but at the same time he resented it as he clumped up the last few feet and stood panting beside her. His frosting breath shredded in the wind.

"Look!" She pointed. "You can see CIAS from here."

He'd forgotten the straight line distance was so short, only a few miles. Through the leafless maple and pin oak branches, the fenced residence and lab building were starkly visible in the snow-covered valley. He hadn't expected this reminder of the installation's proximity, and it visibly depressed him. Surely there were worse places to work, but the circumstances of his assignment here, the monotony of his job, and now his impotency with the Reifsnyder thing combined to make the complex in the valley an unpleasant vista, even a forbidding one.

"All right," Celia said beside him. "What is it?"

He scuffed snow with the toe of his boot. She was too damned perceptive when she was away from her various manias.

So he told her. Threw security regs to the wind and filled her in on his calls to the Horger Clinic, Reifsnyder's subsequent odd behavior, the confusing Gettysburg incident, and finally—it came out hard—Marty tried to defend his gut feeling.

"That he's still suffering from concussion?"

"More than that. Can't pin it down, but he just doesn't seem to be the same man."

"Everybody changes."

"Not like him."

164

"You changed, Marty." She said it so quietly that the impact didn't hit him for some seconds.

"That was different."

"How do you know? How do you know what went on up there in New York State?" Somehow they'd shifted sides.

He stared into the distant valley, colorless as a black-and-white photograph in the overcast afternoon. How had it all grown so complicated? Or was it the damned snake in his brain taking nothing much and twisting it into complex but useless suspicion?

". . . smoking gun," she was saying.

"What?"

Her nose had reddened in the wind. "I said, what you need is a smoking gun. The Watergate thing."

"Yeah. That's what I need."

He broke his stare into the valley. They started back down the treacherous hill, Celia in the lead. Then she turned, looked up at him, and he wasn't sure whether she reached out to him or was trying to keep her balance. Her foot slipped and her outstretched mitten grabbed a sapling. So typical of what their marriage had become. Tentative gestures interrupted by more urgent necessities.

A smoking gun? How in hell was he going to find that when all he could do was watch?

Kooven's carefully cultivated friendship with Roland Strakhan progressed well. Now they often had breakfast together before going off to their separate tasks. Kooven retired to Reifsnyder's office in the residence building where he compiled notes in Reifsnyder's handwriting. Strakhan would struggle into his heavy black overcoat for the hundred-foot stroll through the door in the rear of the hall, along the rock salt-crusted flagstone walk to the brick laboratory building.

It moved as rapidly as Kooven could expect, but at this rate he'd have Reifsnyder's thick loose-leaf notebook filled with useless, time-killing reference book and scientific paper excerpts before he got near the lab. Though he had extracted a surprising amount of information during their initial breakfasts, Kooven realized later that he had gone too far. Strakhan hadn't appeared alarmed at the time, but Kooven suspected he had subsequently gone through post-prattle anguish, a Reifsnyderism for that hollow apprehension that loquacious conversationalists, unorganized speakers, and certain interviewees are assailed with after they have said more than they intended. He had made a serious error in their first meeting, Kooven soon realized. So he hadn't referred to Strakhan's project since. Not only had he sensed that Strakhan suspected he may have told Kooven too much, Kooven also knew that in this security-tuned environment, it might even be possible for a mismanaged Strakhan to destroy him.

Yet during this, their seventh breakfast together, Kooven knew that he must accelerate progress. He had, he was sure, successfully biased Elizabeth Carlisle against Horn during their weekend assignations, but the security chief's omnipresence unnerved Kooven. He'd encountered the type before. An unimaginative plodder, but remorselessly persistent. It would not pay to linger here longer than absolutely necessary.

He set down his coffee and sighed. "Ah, it's discouraging, Roland. Damned discouraging."

Strakhan's ratty gray eyebrows climbed. Kooven had learned that the little scientist didn't say a lot. Kooven had to read his facial expressions and body language.

"I mean, to be working my balls off on this subliminal stuff when it's possible you're onto something that will supercede it before I really get underway. That's what's discouraging."

Strakhan only nodded. This was like trying to hook a fish with no mouth. Then he said, "What I have developed is limited at present. But you do bring up a valid point. It might be useful for you to see it."

Blood thundered in Kooven's ears. Had he heard Strakhan correctly? After six excruciatingly nonproductive breakfasts, was this somber mid-January day actually to be the one of breakthrough?

"Can you get me cleared into the lab?" His voice almost betrayed his excitement.

"By recommending you for temporary associate assistant status, yes. Now and again CIAS residents have found their work in apparent parallel and have used the TAA status to compare notes, so to speak."

Strakhan was talking down to a member of an inferior scientific discipline, Kooven realized. He made an effort to appear deferentially impressed. "That would be most helpful." Then he let his face fall. "Of course, it could . . . Well, I suppose in the interest of what we're all trying to do here, I shouldn't let that worry me too much."

"What?"

"The possibility that your work will make mine quite useless. If that turns out to be the case, I'd have to be honest enough to notify Dr. Carlisle to that effect. And that would terminate my assignment here."

He could see Strakhan's close-set eyes dance at the thought. "That would be unfortunate for you."

But Kooven could sense that the little *pija* was chortling inside. Hard science over the soft communication discipline. He'd given Strakhan an emotional motivation.

"I'll see to the paper work," Strakhan promised. "You'll be cleared into the lab on a TAA by this afternoon."

Kooven hadn't known what to expect—anything from a giant conglomeration of electronic modules with lightning dancing along their poles to a cannonlike barrel with a big black box as its breech. What he saw when Strakhan threw back the green vinyl dust cover in his little research lab was closer to a large metal suitcase than had been any of Kooven's far more elaborate imaginings.

"It's—" He had almost blurted "transportable," but stopped himself in time. "It's quite compact."

167

"Yes, Albert." Strakhan's tone was mocking. "This is the age of the microchip."

The housing was sheet steel, gray-painted. "I've used the basic components of a standard M60 LDNB—Long Distance Narrow Beam—transmitter."

"So that's what an M60 looks like." Kooven's Reifsnyder thought track was intrigued. He'd heard about them often enough: microwave CIA transmitters that had overcome inherent distance limitations and were capable of beaming their signals in a narrow angle propagation field.

"It must have taken a hell of a modification." Strakhan seemed particularly susceptible to flattery. Kooven laid it on. "To take a standard continuous wave transmitter and adapt it to such a specialized application. I marvel at it, s—Strakhan." He had almost said *"señor."*

The bioelectronics expert didn't suppress a self-satisfied smile. "What I've accomplished is quite simple in theory. I've managed to focus the microwave beam component much as light beams are focused and highly concentrated by a laser. This has considerably increased the magnitude of the transmission along with the beam amplification."

"Sounds fairly understandable." Kooven could barely suppress the elation in his voice. Here it was, almost in his grasp.

Strakhan supported his elbow in his left hand and cupped his chin in his right. "The theory is quite elementary. Its application has proven to be another matter."

"But the test you conducted with us was—"

"A failure."

"A failure!" Kooven concentrated in Reifsnyder's memory. "But the three of us went through a range of emotions. Anger, humor, self-pity . . ."

"That was the failure." Strakhan dropped his arms disconsolately, then reached out to flip open a set of clips on the device and withdraw a briefcase-sized module.

"The problem is here, in the disc drive. Three flexible discs run in tandem. One projects a pulse rate actuation fre-

168

quency, thirty-five percent variable above and below norm. The central disc produces a highly amplified microwave in sync with the human brain's cortex and reticular formation for depressant effect, variable to synchronization with the hypothalmus, again in combination with the reticular formation for stimulant reaction. And the third disc produces a deep-penetration lower frequency that influences breathing rate."

Kooven had trouble submerging the great rush of elation that swept through him. *Virgen Santa!* Here it was, imperfect, but in working order.

"It seems compact enough for field use," he probed.

"One hundred fifty-seven pounds."

And transportable, indeed.

"Power supply?"

"Obviously, it's one hundred ten volt here in the laboratory, but eventually convertible to generator current for field use."

"And the problem you mentioned?" Was he pushing too hard?

No, Strakhan was wrapped up in the electronic cleverness of it all. "The problem is in the central disc."

"The brain effect transmission."

The little scientist looked as if he were surprised that Kooven had paid attention to his condescending explanation. "Yes, you could put it that way."

"But our reactions when you tested—"

Strakhan waved him silent. "Your reactions were erratic. Consistent with each other, I discerned, but certainly not in synchronization with what I assumed the device was transmitting. The brain component control monitor circuit is not in stable lock. Not stable at all. Since that test, I have enhanced the power output and broadened the beam width, but the basic problem of stability remains, unfortunately."

"You're saying you set it to transmit a specific emotional trigger and it may not do precisely that."

"That's precisely what I thought I said." Strakhan

169

hunched over the control panel mounted high on the rear of the boxy device. "It has to be the central disc." He replaced the activation module, snapped its retaining fasteners closed and stood back to regard his incredible creation as if it were no more than a troublesome TV set.

Kooven had difficulty in maintaining the interested-but-obtuse pose he was certain Reifsnyder would have fallen into by now. He had actually progressed to the halfway point in this initially impossible assignment: from the nonproductive guise of a victimized displaced Cuban to this deep penetration into the CIAS laboratory, complete with an explanation of the device by its naive developer.

"Have you a name for it?" That was the kind of question Reifsnyder would be sure to ask.

"A name? I'm not concerned with names. I'm certain the Department of Defense will convene a panel of experts to devise a suitably ludicrous code name."

Not even a name for this erratic but miraculous perversion of electronics. Its perfection could mean, at the very least, control of the emotion of key individuals in a variety of useful situations. A delegate suddenly going insane at a crucial conference. An undesired candidate for high political office destroying his own campaign with emotional instability.

Extension of Strakhan's principle to battlefield applications could have devastating results. A tank assault run amok by its disoriented commander. A fighter strike deflected by its pilots' sudden incomprehensible fear. The possibilities were without limit! Small wonder Rapier had gone to such extremes.

But that was for the future, perhaps only theory. Present fact offered present problems. The first was whether to wait for Strakhan to master his intended technical refinements. The second, and there were only two, was the matter of getting the device out of CIAS.

Then he had a better thought. How obvious. He needn't concern himself with the bulky machine at all, of course. "Perhaps," he suggested in what he hoped was an off-hand tone, "you could simply recheck the circuits against your wiring diagrams. Who knows, the problem may be just—"

Strakhan stared at him as if he were a hopeless subspecies. Had Kooven gone too far this time? His question had been intended to lead to disclosure of the location of the plans. They certainly should be easier to copy or even steal outright than lugging one hundred fifty-seven pounds of dead weight.

"Diagrams?" Strakhan echoed. "The plans are here." He tapped his forehead. "All up here. Plans are for those who cannot think without paper to refer to. I don't need such a crutch. The plans will come after the prototype is perfected."

So much for that. To steal the plans, he would have to steal Strakhan. Possible? Perhaps, but there was no guarantee that the unpredictable scientist would cooperate in Rapier custody. If Rapier were to seize someone close to Strakhan—hadn't he told Kooven he had a sister somewhere in the Pacific Northwest?

Too conjectural. And there was the possibility that Strakhan, quirky as he was, would not react favorably even were his sister detained. No, appropriating the device itself for Rapier's delivery to the client was the procedure he was forced to follow.

But how?

Lefroid strode along the red carpeting of Baltimore-Washington International's U.S. Air dock toward the terminal. He didn't like this; detested going into the field. His place was at Rapier's Avenue of the Americas office, secluded behind the wholesaler facade. Safe, not exposed as he felt this fog-blurred morning in the low hills southwest of Baltimore.

But Kooven had insisted. The operation was nearing fruition and now there was a problem. He had detected desperation in Kooven's telephone voice. And there was another factor. Raw curiosity. He wanted to see the man, observe him come to life in another man's body.

Lefroid had been outwardly cold-blooded and objective about the acquisition of Reifsnyder, the use of a dying Kooven's brain, the transplanted embeds procedure. Only to himself would he admit that he expected failure. His aloofness had been self-protective. He hated emotional involvement, particularly in high-risk projects. Now here he was in Central Maryland responding to a plea from a field operative. Involved.

He took the escalator to the lower level, caught a shuttle bus and debarked moments later still on airport grounds at the International Inn. The dining room was nearly empty. He asked the hostess for a seat in a remote corner, ordered coffee, and watched the entrance.

Lefroid was jolted when the big man in brown twill came straight to his table. He realized he'd never seen Reifsnyder, but subconsciously he couldn't shake an image of Kooven the last time they'd met—a skinny little man hunched against the pain of his faltering heart, his skin ashen beneath its normal ivory pigmentation.

This man, though, was a good six feet two, soft but nonetheless impressive in his direct approach.

"Ah, Lefroid, we meet again."

Lefroid half rose in spite of himself and took the pillowy hand. He saw a stranger, but sensed Kooven's cunning behind the facade. He'd never felt so unsettled.

"Relax, for God's sake. Don't believe what you see, *amigo*. Believe what I tell you." Reifsnyder's voice, Kooven's attitude. Lefroid suppressed a sudden chill. "And sit back down." This incredible manufactured man had taken control. Lefroid had to get it back.

"What precisely is the problem?" Lefroid made his tone hard. Kooven deserved it. Lefroid was increasingly discomfited by this demanded meeting. "I don't like phoned ultimatums. And I don't like this meeting. It's too close to the project. Far too risky."

Kooven ignored his steely outburst. "The problem," he said in a dead-flat voice, "is precisely this: there are no blueprints, no plans, not even sketches. It is all in the head of the man who developed the . . . machine. It doesn't even have a name."

"But it exists. It's there at CIAS, and it works."

"And it weighs almost a hundred sixty pounds."

"You look as if you could handle that."

A waitress approached, and Kooven started to wave her away.

"Order something." Lefroid found he needed the security of the appearance of two businessmen breakfasting together.

"Scrambled eggs, bacon, coffee." Kooven turned back to him as the chunky blonde trotted off. "I could handle one hundred fifty-seven inert pounds if—" He ticked off the points on his fingers. "—If there were no security people wandering around the area. If I didn't have to manhandle it from the lab building through the main building to the parking area. If— Well, I'm sure you get the idea."

"What do you need?"

"A pickup truck and a hole in the fence. Snow and a dog sled. I need a way to get that damned machine out of a TV-monitored, guard-patrolled, triple-fenced, isolated compound. You originated this project. You tell me what I need."

Lefroid finally sensed that he could gain control. "First you need to calm down. Is this you or Reifsnyder talking?" The strangeness of the question jarred him as he asked it. He still hadn't recovered from the shock of talking to one man in the body of another.

"All right, all right. It's not so easy thinking on two levels simultaneously. Sorry." He took a long breath, held it, exhaled slowly. "You're right. Let's look at this with *logica*. With logic. We must take a one hundred fifty-seven pound object out of a guarded, fenced compound, down a two-mile access road, past an outlying guard station—"

"Outlying?"

"Where the access road meets Route 550. It's passed off as

173

a tourist information booth, but everyone at CIAS knows it's a guard post."

"It would be helpful—" Lefroid stopped talking as the waitress returned with Kooven's order.

"More coffee, sir?"

Lefroid shook his head, and she left them alone again.

"What would be helpful?"

"A drawing of the place would be helpful."

Kooven took out a ballpoint pen and with surprising dexterity, made a rapid sketch on his paper napkin. He slid it across the table.

"Lab building, main building, fence gate." The ballpoint tapped each in turn. "Access road. The fence is triple with the center run electrified."

"Lethally?"

"There's a legend about a raccoon being fried in midair."

"How many guards?"

"A force of ten. Day shift of four and two night shifts of three each."

"How would you rate them?"

Kooven picked up a strip of bacon in his fingers, chewed, swallowed. "They're not the Eighty-second Airborne. Political appointees, but with some qualifications. Military or police backgrounds. The lieutenant in charge is an ex-Chicago cop. Left there under a cloud."

Lefroid glanced up from the sketch. "Such as?"

"Psychological disturbance of some sort. Killed people in a shootout, then couldn't remember it. They got him the CIAS job to get rid of him without a messy hearing or trial. That's the rumor."

"No threat there."

"Don't underestimate him. He's the only one who suspects me."

Lefroid riveted his pale eyes on Kooven's. "Did I hear you correctly? He suspects you of what?"

"Of being different from the Reifsnyder he knew."

"My God! That jeopardizes everything. How could you possibly—"

"It was at the beginning. Like running a complicated new machine. I made some slips."

"But certainly not now."

"No, no slips now."

He was a magnificent accomplishment, Lefroid marveled. A creation of endless possibilities. A weapon as important—perhaps more important—than the CIAS development he'd been created to acquire. And now Lefroid realized he'd made a tragic error when he'd had Csorna eliminated by the Montreal contract team. Intent on the obvious, he'd overlooked an immense potential.

He reached for his coffee to break his futile thought sequence and bring himself back to the current problem.

"Lieutenant Horn. His name is Horn."

Lefroid set down the cup with a hard clink. "He's the one Horger reported had called the clinic."

Kooven's expression congealed. "Horger. That *pija* let me die in the operating room."

"You were dying whatever he did."

". . . Took me off oxygen. Cut off the support systems."

"And worked with Csorna to bring you back, Kooven." It was surprisingly difficult to say his name while staring into the face of a stranger.

"Life after life. There was nothing out there, by the way."

"I never had expectations there would be." He checked his watch reflexively. The longer he remained here, the more exposed he felt. "The options, Kooven. Surely you have worked on that."

"I already told you. We have to get that damned machine out of there. It's the only option. Blueprints do not exist."

"The inventor exists."

"You want to speculate on how he would react to an attempt at enforced cooperation? And if you're thinking of 'peer pressure'—" Kooven smiled wryly—"Forget it. He's

175

got only a sister he hasn't seen in years. And he's a son of a bitch at heart, so don't depend on that kind of plan."

"It has to be the machine then. But it's your problem."

"It's *our* problem."

Lefroid rested an elbow on his chair arm and leaned forward. "You understand brainstorming? Let's see how it works with our three brains. Frontal assault?"

"What kind of strength can you put together?"

Lefroid kept his eyes on Kooven's. "Armored truck with six men. Armed with Kalashnikov AKMs."

"They might get in, but it would be messy and obvious. I doubt they'd get very far if they managed to get clear of CIAS after the pick-up. You see this?" He tapped the sketch with his ballpoint. "Take out this 'tourist booth' on the way in, and you can be sure an automatic alarm will be tripped at CIAS. Leave the booth until the team is on its way out, and it will be there waiting."

"With what? A .45? A couple of dents in the truck as it goes past. Or we could have a second team to take out the booth simultaneously with the assault on the main installation."

"This is a federal installation we're talking about, Lefroid. Telephone and no doubt emergency radio contact with local police, probably Washington as well."

"You're guessing."

"I think these are guesses accurate enough to rely on. This thing's got to be done not with a sledgehammer, but with a scalpel. And done well enough so they don't know it has been done until we've had a chance to be away from there. A diversion, a feint. Enough time unobserved to let me transport that thing at least a short distance."

Lefroid was silent. While Kooven had been rambling, he had matched a succession of fragmentary ideas with their probabilities of execution, logistics required, personnel needs, and cost factors. Finally a possibility survived his mental testing. There were, in fact, several—but this partic-

176

ular approach seemed to Lefroid to have the highest probability of success.

"—yet another problem," Kooven was saying in that damned meaty baritone of Reifsnyder's, "is that elimination of the outer sentry position would—"

Lefroid waved him silent. "I want you to listen closely, Kooven." He couldn't get over how strange it was to call this hulking stranger by that name. "Then I want you to tell me how you would evaluate this proposal."

When Lefroid had finished, Kooven sat back and smiled for the first time since he'd entered the dining room. "A flash of inspiration," he said. "If you'll pardon the pun."

Lefroid nodded at the paper napkin between them. "Don't leave that lying there." He regretted the obvious admonition when he noted the hardening of Kooven's adopted green eyes. Through the lengthy meeting, Lefroid had been unable to shake his uneasiness with the incredible hybrid man across the table.

Kooven stood, crumpled the napkin in his hand and, Lefroid thought, made a mocking little nod of the head. The kind of non-bow that would have been considered a formal insult by an oriental. The man was full of unexpected nuances.

"I'll confirm the date by phone," Lefroid said.

"Remember, they're monitored."

"What do you expect, 'Tora, Tora, Tora'?" Sarcasm was as close as Lefroid allowed himself to approach humor.

"The phrase we agreed on will suffice," Kooven said coldly. At the restaurant's coat rack, he pulled on his voluminous overcoat and stuffed the napkin in its pocket while Lefroid settled the check. He drove Lefroid back to the terminal. "Until *der tag,*" he said as Lefroid closed the Jetta's door. Insufferable bastard, Lefroid thought. Even more so in jumbo size.

He had an hour to kill, bought a *Wall Street Journal* and fidgeted in the multicolored plastic lounge off the main cor-

177

ridor. He needed about twelve days to pull together the manpower and support. The beauty of the operation was that most of it would be accomplished by people who would have no idea what they were really involved in.

CHAPTER
13

MARTY SMOOTHED THE bit of paper across his thigh, picked up his coffee cup and stared at the sketch. From the fireside chair in the A-frame's living room, Celia peered at him. The typing, he noted, seemed to be finished. He wondered what she would throw herself into next.

"Is that why you've been so quiet ever since you got home?" she asked. "What is it?"

Marty said it slowly, his elation tempered by an unexpected blank at what to do now. "It doesn't look like a hell of a lot, but I think what I've got here just might be that smoking gun."

She looked oddly childlike as she rose and walked across the living room to his side, pink puff slippers bouncing the hem of her pastel blue housecoat. She liked pastels. She was pastels herself. Cornsilk hair, pale gray eyes, Guernsey cream skin.

"Looks like a napkin. A drawing in an International Inn napkin."

"A sketch of CIAS."

179

She bent down, hair framing her face. "The main build-ing here, right. The lab. What's this?"

"The booth on Route 550." He'd never told her what the booth really was.

She sat beside him on the sofa. "I'm not sure I see why— Where did you get this?"

"On the hallway floor at CIAS. It got there in the dumbest way possible."

"Fell out of someone's pocket?"

He glanced sideways at her. She could be pretty sharp sometimes.

"That's right. Reifsnyder's overcoat. Around four, I went to the front entrance to tell Lydia about a shift change. Reif-snyder was putting on his coat. Nothing on the hall floor then. When I went back to the security room, there it was. In a little ball. I figure it came out of his pocket when he pulled out his gloves."

She took it from his knee and held it up. "He's got little *X*'s on it. Here at the front door. At the gate in the fence. At the information booth, too. What do they mean?"

"Security points."

"The information booth? That's a security point?"

He nodded. Telling her was a breech of security in itself, but he had begun to feel more and more alone in this, and he couldn't face being totally alone.

She handed back the crumpled bit of soft paper. "You think that this, added to the other things you told me about Reifsnyder, is enough to . . . what?"

"I don't know. But it all adds up to something. Why is one of our residents walking around with a drawing of CIAS se-curity checkpoints on an airport hotel napkin? The same res-ident who's done a couple of other odd things. Or am I going nuts?" He looked her straight in the eye. "Again."

She surprised him. Her eyes suddenly misted. "Don't, Marty. What happened to you was a reaction to something too awful to remember. The psychiatrist said it was not so unusual in cases of extreme stress."

"They thought I went crazy, Celia. That's what they decided, that's why I'm out of Chicago, that's why I'm here."

She studied her hands folded limply in her lap. "And now you're afraid that if you go on with this thing, CIAS will decide you're . . ." She couldn't say it. "But you're afraid that if you don't, you're not doing what they pay you to do."

He stared across the living room seeing not the black rectangle of window set in the pine-paneled slope of the wall, but seeing Reifsnyder hunched in his cubbyhole of an office; Reifsnyder striding across the icy parking lot in Gettysburg; Reifsnyder staring at him through the CIAS front window. Nothing definitive, but even here in his own house, Marty felt an aura of evil about the man. There had been a change in him since the accident in New York State. Of that, Marty had no doubt. But try to convince someone else of that. This was the worst kind of police work. It wasn't police work. It was hunch work, and hunches were illegal now. Either it was an open and shut case, or it wasn't a case.

"This could cost me my job," Marty said softly. "I've already lost one. What do we do if I lose this one?"

She lay her hand on his arm, a feather touch. Then she squeezed a little. Just a little. "I go where you go," she whispered.

He took it to Elizabeth Carlisle despite his misgivings. And he realized he'd made a mistake the instant she said in a resigned voice, "Oh, Lieutenant Horn. What can I do for you?" But he went ahead anyway.

Her office was the last room on the right down the long hallway that ran the length of the main building and ended in a doorway with a wire glass window that opened onto the walkway to the lab. It was a corner office with deep-set windows offering views of the west lawn, the triple security fencing beyond, and the incongruous brick facia of the lab to the south. A no-nonsense executive's office of polished walnut paneling and earthtone upholstery. Her high-backed chair was butternut, maybe not designed to intimidate, but it did.

"Can I shut the door?"

She was still concentrating on the papers that had preoccupied her when he had entered, but now she stared up at him again. This time her wide-set violet eyes held his.

"Yes, you may shut the door if you feel it is necessary. I haven't a whole lot of time, Lieutenant."

Wanted to be rid of him when she didn't even know why he was here.

"It's necessary."

"Then close the door and sit down."

He took the knobbly weave brown chair in front of her desk, a low chair without arms, obviously chosen to be uncomfortable and unsettling. It worked fine. He'd forgotten how he wanted to begin and sat hunched forward, tapping his fingers on the manila file folder he'd brought.

"Well?"

"This is a sort of delicate—" Delicate, for God's sake? "A difficult matter."

"Lieutenant," she said with the exaggerated kind of patience she might have offered a stumbling fifth grader, "please make an effort to come to the point. If there is one."

She didn't have to throw that in. "It's a problem with one of the residents."

"A problem?"

"Well, a situation."

She toyed with an ornate letter opener, a miniature sterling silver replica of a Spanish sword with an inlaid enamel hilt. Tapped its point on the polished walnut. Interminably. When she at last met his eyes again, he saw sour displeasure there.

"You'd better have something concrete, Lieutenant."

He fought back the flare of heat that threatened to rise above his uniform collar. Let it go and cold sweat would surely follow. He didn't want to sweat in front of her.

"Might I have the name?" she prompted.

He cleared his throat. "Dr. Reifsnyder."

She seemed jolted by a tiny invisible slap. But her voice was unchanged—low, and affecting disinterest.

"You said you had something to back up this remarkable impression of yours?"

"Since the accident . . . Since he came back here from that New York State clinic, there have been several things—"

"Precisely what 'things'?" She sure wasn't making this easy.

"His general attitude. A feeling I get." The damned hunch again. He wished he weren't so tongue-tied in front of this woman.

"Really, Lieutenant. An 'attitude'?"

"Before he went to New York, he was the most open and easygoing of all the residents. Now he's . . . well, like he's hiding something."

Her eyes never left his, and her voice was lethal. "What you've told me certainly doesn't impel me to file a Documentable Personality Change. If that's what you're after, I trust you've got more than an 'attitude'—" She gave the word a nasty inflection—"to bring you in here."

"I followed him to Gettysburg on the twenty-seventh."

"You followed him? Why on earth did you do that?"

He was all the way in now. "A phone call. Incoming. On the record tapes."

"You've been listening to the phone record tapes?"

He couldn't suppress a flare of anger. "The calls are recorded for security purposes, and I am the chief of security. The manual says—"

She nodded, a dip of the chin that shot a glint of hard light across her tightly coiled black hair. "Spare me your interpretation of the manual."

"At the Sheraton up there, he was supposed to meet one of the doctors from the clinic where he was taken after the accident. Only the guy apparently didn't show. When Dr.

Reifsnyder came out of the place, I swear somebody in a brown Ford tried to kill him."

For the first time, he could see that she was interested. "You're certain of that?"

"It sure looked that way to me." He detailed the incident in the ice-sheathed parking area, but now he could see her interest revert to annoyance.

"Really, Lieutenant Horn. You realize that could have been nothing more than someone driving carelessly. You'll have to do better than that."

"I followed the Ford. And he went to a lot of trouble to lose me."

"Is that surprising? Suppose you'd had a near-accident and someone chased you from the scene. Might you not panic and try to evade him? You of all people," she threw in.

"No, ma'am." He met her gaze.

"Perhaps not you, then," she relented. "But a lot of people would. Is that all you have to offer?"

"No. There's the matter of his TAA clearance, which gives him access to the lab building with Dr. Strakhan."

"Obviously I know about that since I signed it at Dr. Strakhan's request. A TAA clearance is routine when one of our residents is of apparent value to the work of another." She gestured impatiently. "Is that it?"

He pulled the napkin, now carefully folded, from the file folder. "There's this." He leaned forward to lay it on her desk pad.

The silence seemed endless.

"It's a drawing of CIAS," she said tonelessly.

"Yes, it is."

"With security points marked."

"That's correct."

Without looking up, she said, "Where did you get this?"

"On the floor in the hall. Near the coat rack. Yesterday."

"You didn't see who dropped it?"

"Not precisely."

"What does that mean, 'not precisely'?"

"I walked past the rack about noon to tell Officer Whimple about a shift change. Dr. Reifsnyder was putting on his coat. The napkin wasn't on the floor at that time. When I came back, he'd left, and there it was. I figure that when he pulled out his gloves, it came out with them."

"That's what you 'figure'."

"Yes, ma'am."

"Not very conclusive, is it?"

"I beg your pardon? Here's the napkin. Not there when he was putting on the coat. But there after he left."

"How long were you at the front entrance with Officer Whimple?"

"Not more than three or four minutes."

"And you assume no one else could have visited the coat rack area after Dr. Reifsnyder? I don't believe you can see the coat rack from the front entrance."

"That's correct, but no one went out the front door during that time but him."

"Did anyone go out the rear door to the lab?"

"I don't think so."

"You don't think so, but you don't know for certain."

"I'm reasonably sure."

"Would you swear to it, Lieutenant?" Her eyes reflected the desk lamp's glare in hard pinpoints.

"Swear to it?" He'd had his back to the hallway while he'd talked with Lydia. "No, ma'am."

"Then this could have been dropped—or even placed purposely—by a number of people. By a staff member, for instance, as a misguided joke on you."

He hadn't thought of that possibility, but he suddenly felt that she was protecting Reifsnyder.

"You're on very thin ice, Lieutenant. Think of your background and record. Isn't it conceivable that even one of your own men might see himself in your place if you were to leave—or be asked to leave?"

Was she threatening him?

"I asked you a question, Lieutenant Horn."

"I can't think of anybody," he faltered. But he could think of several.

She stood abruptly, seeming to tower over him. "I'm going to do you a favor. I'm going to forget we had this conversation. You return to your work, and I'll return to mine. And CIAS will do very nicely without the kind of misguided suspicions you appear to be obsessed with."

She had rounded the desk and stood almost touching his knees, her hands clasped behind her. He'd felt as defeated as this only twice before: when he'd been sent before the principal at Marquette Elementary for putting a clot of bubble gum in Sally Flanherty's red hair and when the board in Chicago had given him their decision. All at once, it got to him. Really got to him.

He shoved back his chair and shot to his feet. "What the hell good is a security force if you won't pay attention to it! I think we are faced with a definite threat of some kind, and I want to go on record as formally stating that to you."

"Duly noted. And I want to go on record as pointing out that if I thought you had grounds for Potential Cause for Derecruitment of any of our residents, I would be willing to tape this conversation for a subsequent hearing. But you don't even have a DPC, let alone a PCD. Go back to your work." Her words had a steel edge.

He whirled, yanked open her office door and barged into the hall, barely restraining his urge to slam the door in her face behind him.

The afternoon light had faded, and Dortman had come on duty. "Chocolate donuts tonight, Chief. I'll leave you a couple." He never changed. Put in his hours, took his pay, waited out the years. Did he give a real damn about anything?

"I think we've got something coming down, Abner." He had to talk, had to burn off some of the anger.

"Like what?"

So he told Abner Dortman, told him about Reifsnyder's personality change. Told him about Gettysburg, and the

186

napkin in the hall. And, after a long silence, even told him about the infuriating conversation with Elizabeth Carlisle just moments before.

When he had drained himself of it all, Marty slumped in his chair and stared blankly at the console of TV monitors. Behind him, Dortman stirred a cup of coffee.

"I'll tell you one thing, Chief," Dortman said into the silence. "I'll tell you why she don't want to hear what you told her."

Marty swiveled his chair around. "Yeah? Why would that be?"

"Because . . ." Dortman paused an ungodly long time to take a pull at his coffee. "Because just about every weekend, your boy, Reifsnyder, is screwing her cross-eyed."

"Alfred," she said dreamily, her eyes still not in sharp focus, "you wouldn't believe what Lieutenant Horn told me Friday."

A splinter of ice shot through him. But Kooven managed to keep his voice steady, even light.

"What on earth could that pathetic fool have said that would be of interest to you?"

She giggled and threw her arm behind her head on the pillow. "He thinks you're in some sort of plot. He had a paper napkin—" She couldn't restrain her laughter. "A paper napkin with a sketch of CIAS on it. A paper napkin, Alfred, to try to hang you with!"

He forced a laugh of his own. That damned napkin! He propped his head on an elbow and looked down at her.

"Where did this idiot say he found the . . . what was it? A napkin?"

"In the downstairs hallway. What's the difference? He could even have drawn it himself. What does he have against you?"

"Who knows with a psychotic? What did you tell him?"

"I told him to go on about his business. I wasn't listening to his nonsense."

187

"You should have fired him on the spot."

She sat up holding the sheet across her breasts defensively. "No, I don't think that would be advisable. People like him can be awfully unpredictable."

Her face was shadowed in the bed lamp's glow, framed by the untidy fall of her hair. "Maybe I should have humored him. Just thanked him and told him I'd look into the matter."

"You did keep the napkin?"

"In my desk."

"It's obviously a joke. Somebody's playing a joke on him—or on you."

"I thought of that."

But she had kept the napkin. Was she altogether unconvinced that Horn had something? Only seven more days, and now this stupidity. In grim silence, he cursed Horn and her and most of all himself. All this planning, all the problems nearly surmounted, all the incredible accomplishment, then a paper napkin he had stupidly dropped in the hall—it had come out with his gloves, of course, and Horn had made a one-hundred-percent correct deduction—all this, then a paper napkin threatened to destroy the entire effort. The stupidest part of it was that he thought he had thrown the thing away days ago.

He had to divert her so completely that she would think of nothing else for the next seven days. Lefroid's code phrase had reached him Friday. "We have the book you ordered, Doctor. Seventeen dollars plus shipping." Set for the seventeenth. Next Sunday. Between eleven and midnight, the time frame they had already agreed on at the airport meeting. Seven days. He had to keep her off guard that long.

He leaned close, tipped her chin up. Kissed her softly. "Elizabeth, darling. I want you to be my wife."

Her breath caught. Then she reached out with both arms, pulled him down, and he crushed his mouth to hers.

"Oh, God!" she gasped in his ear. "If only I were a free woman. But there's Henry. We're separated, not divorced."

"Surely you have grounds for desertion by now. It's just a matter of filing the proper papers." He drew back, held her by the shoulders, stared unblinking into her suddenly misted eyes.

"Do it, Elizabeth. This week. Tomorrow. The sooner you begin legal proceedings, the sooner you're free of him. And the sooner we can begin to spend the rest of our lives together. Not just these furtive weekends, but the rest of our lives."

"Albert, dearest, I . . . I will! Tomorrow I'll call Tom Squier—"

"Tom Squier?"

"My lawyer in Washington. And I'll have him start the legal process. Darling—" She reached out to take his head in both her hands. "Thank you. Thank you so much for making me make the decision."

Her fingers locked behind his neck. With remarkable strength, she pulled him down again, engulfed his mouth in hers, lips mobile, tongue insisting.

CHAPTER
14

"OFFICE OF FEDERAL SECURITY FORCES. May I help you?" The woman's voice was computerlike.

"This is Lieutenant Martin Horn, CIAS Facility, Thurmont, Maryland. Is Captain Jarelsky available?"

After a couple of muffled clicks, Jarelsky came on the line with his customary load of hearty crap.

"Hey, Horn! How's things out there in mountain country? Getting enough snow for you? You doing okay these days? Ought to call in more often, or we'll forget you're out there."

Marty cut into Jarelsky's mechanical chuckle. "I got a problem, Captain."

"Yeah, Carlisle told me. The napkin caper."

Marty felt frigid sweat break across his shoulders. "She called you?" His mouth had dried.

"First thing this morning. Said you told her you thought something might be coming down out there. You got any more on it, or is that napkin thing all you got?"

The bastard was humoring him. What could Marty say now? Elizabeth Carlisle made an end run to head me off because I might have something on the guy she's been sleeping with?

"Marty, you still there?"

"Yeah."

"Look, you got anything solid, I'll back you up. But hunches don't fly, know what I mean?"

"I know what you mean. Thanks." He hung up with numb fingers. One more possibility, though he already suspected the futility of this. Still, all he had to lose was more of what he'd lost already. He dialed again.

"Agent Busch."

"Marty Horn at CIAS, Walt. You answering your own phone these days?"

"Horn? Oh, how you doing, Marty? You been to see Roy lately?" When Marty had been assigned to CIAS, he made courtesy calls on the local constabulary and to the FBI Field Office in Hagerstown. Walt Busch had offered him lunch, then an unexpected call had forced them to cut lunchtime short. The nearest and quickest restaurant was a Roy Rogers.

"I got—I think I got a problem here, Walt." Why had he qualified it? That had weakened his case, and he could sense Walt Busch's reservation as he detailed the incidents leading up to his finding the crumpled napkin.

Walt took too long to respond. Then he said, "Let me assume everything you've told me is accurate, Marty."

What did he mean by that?

"Let me assume that, and I still can't intervene at this point in time."

"Intervene? I'm asking you for some kind of guidance, Walt. Some kind of help. I don't know if I'm sitting on a powder keg up here, or if somebody's having a good pull at my shaky leg."

"You said that; I didn't."

"That's what you think?"

"Come on, Marty. You know how people are. You know what some people think about a guy with a problem like yours. Sorry to put it that way, but let's face it. You're not the most convincing guy in the world when it comes to—"

"Rational analysis."

"Say again?"

"A little chunk of jargon I picked up along the line, Walt."

Silence. Then Walt said, "Let's go at this another way. You know how damned restricted the Bureau is. Even for an obvious kidnapping, we got to wait for a note or a ransom call before we can step in. I can't just come barging into a federal installation on the kind of 'evidence' you think you've got."

Marty said nothing. From the narrow viewpoint of a federal officer protecting his flanks against his own bureaucracy, Walt was right. That was how the country seemed to be run these days. And I'm doing the same damned thing, Marty realized.

"You get yourself a smoking gun, Marty, and I'll be there before it has a chance to cool off."

The damned smoking gun again. "All I can offer is a smoking napkin."

"It's not enough. Could be no more than a crude gag."

"That's not the way this place operates, Walt."

"Tell you what. You want to have the thing run through our DC lab, bring it on up here. We can tell you what day it was made, who made it, and what kind of a love life they have."

"Thanks, but that's not what I'm after."

"What are you after, Marty?"

"That's the hell of it. I'm not sure."

"Take that pretty wife of yours off to Deep Creek Lake for a week, Marty. She'll do you a hell of a lot more good than I can. Gotta run, buddy."

Marty hung up feeling more alone than he had before he called. The locals? Holmes was a pleasant and accommodating fellow, but this was no clear-cut stolen vehicle or vandalized property case. It might not be a case at all. The

192

Maryland State Police would tell him the same thing. Probably send him right back to the feds.

Dead end.

He reached in his pocket and unfolded something Elizabeth Carlisle didn't know he had, a Xerox copy of the napkin drawing. The quickly sketched lines and marked security points leaped up at him. This was no plant to make his life miserable, no misguided Abner Dortman prank. Dortman didn't have the imagination. The others were too serious about their work to try this kind of gag.

He could feel the threat right here on the Xerox paper. Hunches don't fly anymore? What do you do when that's all you've got?

He drove home, unsuccessfully fighting the beginnings of a headache, and sprawled at the little kitchen table pinching the bridge of his nose with forefinger and thumb.

"It's sinus," Celia offered over her shoulder from the stove.

"It's not sinus. It's frustration. Nobody, nobody at all will listen to me. I *know* something's going on out there. Something big's going to happen, and nobody will listen to me."

"Maybe you haven't talked to the right people."

He sloshed the dregs of a beer back and forth across the bottom of his glass. "That's the damned truth."

She put down her wooden spoon, turned the burner to low and sat across from him. "I'll listen, Marty. I really will."

She was so naively earnest that he almost laughed. He reached out in an unusual gesture for him and took her hand. She was trying to help, by God. That was more than anyone else had done this dismal Monday.

"I thought we could go to the mall down in Frederick after supper," she suggested, "but maybe it would be better if we . . ." She lay her free hand over his. ". . . If we went to bed early."

Her eyes were misty, and he knew he couldn't turn her down. But tonight of all nights, he would have to keep con-

193

trol, pin his sanity to the pale plank in the ceiling and hold back the serpent. Hold back the coiled snake of insanity that would surely destroy him if he let it squirm free.

The device was a simple one: a cigarette and a book of paper matches. Kooven's self-imposed assignment was to set it in place late Sunday evening. Fortunately that dolt Dortman was on duty. No problem there, though Kooven was certain that Horn had warned his security group to be particularly alert following Horn's stumbling upon Kooven's stupidity of the napkin.

Kooven had pleaded work load with a surprised Elizabeth Carlisle. "But darling, it would be so special." A whispered conversation in the hallway at the foot of the ornate staircase. She had talked with Tom Squier as promised, had written Henry to go on record with the formal request that their separation be permanent. Now she was understandably baffled by Kooven's insistence on working on Sunday and even working late.

"It can't be helped. The report's already overdue."

He returned to his office to wait. At 10:55, he asked Dortman to open the lab for him.

"Open the lab?" The slender security sergeant reminded Kooven of a Doberman. A Doberman with half a brain.

"I need some notes I left in there yesterday." And he had made sure he had done so, placing a small notebook on the lab bench as Strakhan had jabbered away with his self-impressing jargon.

"You're aware that I do have a TAA clearance," Kooven reminded the hesitant guard.

"Yes, sir." Dortman swung out of his chair and jangled his keys. "Make it fast, will you, Doc? I'm not supposed to leave this console area unmanned for more than six minutes."

Neither of them bothered to put on coats for the brief walk between the buildings. In the frigid night, the overcast seemed to press down on the floodlit compound. Dortman unlocked the lab entrance door, found the corridor light switch and stood by the door while Kooven scurried into Strakhan's work room.

Shortly, Dortman's voice came from the hall. "Hurry it up, will you, Doc?"

"There's something I have to check on here, Sergeant. I'll just be a minute or two more. Go on back. The door has a spring lock. I'll close up."

A more experienced officer might not have accepted that, but Kooven knew his man.

"Okay. Just make sure everything's secure when you leave."

Absurdly easy. When he heard the faint slam of the main building's rear door, Kooven trotted to the far end of the laboratory building's long hallway, thankful that all the security cameras were external. During his visits here this week with Strakhan, he had ambled through the other lab rooms and noted what would be essential to execute the next step of Lefroid's plan.

He had found it in the laboratory work room assigned to Ed Moyle. For two reasons: Moyle's work area was at the other end of the building and possible damage to the Strakhan device had to be minimal. And Moyle was a messy housekeeper. His area was strewn with the debris of fluid force research. Wadded notepaper and discarded publications overflowed his trash basket, not due to be emptied until the Tuesday maintenance rounds. Canisters, jars, and flasks of random sizes and shapes crowded the shelves over the broad lab sink and encroached on the drainboards of the sink itself.

Moyle appeared to be engrossed in hydraulics at the moment. Two gallon jugs of what looked to be a lightweight oil stood on his cluttered work table with some sort of complex piston-and-pressure scale arrangement.

Kooven hadn't much time. He uncapped one of the jugs and turned it on its side. The oil spewed across the work table in gurgling spurts and began to puddle on the floor.

Kooven nudged the metal trashbasket beneath the dripping fluid.

It didn't smell particularly volatile. He lit a king-sized cigarette, puffed once, then inserted an inch and a half of the cigarette's butt end in the matchbook, clamping it in place across the matchheads when he closed the cover. He lay the matchbook among the oily crumpled papers in the trash with the glowing coal away from direct contact.

He knew that unlike a cigar that would go out if it weren't drawn on occasionally, a cigarette has a chemical additive to keep it burning. Kooven's test in his room had established the length of cigarette needed for the required delay until the coal reached the matchheads.

He left Moyle's lab door open, hurried back to Strakhan's area and grabbed the notebook. He held it in obvious sight when he stepped out of the lab building's entrance into security camera range, made a show of checking the lock after he'd pulled the lab's entrance door shut. Then he strode through the chilly areaway between the buildings, his breath vapor riding raggedly in the glare of the security floods.

"Your trouble, Marty, is that you're nuts," Walt Busch said. "Nobody'll tell you that right out, but I will." He stood an inch taller than Marty, dressed in FBI blue pinstripe with a white shirt, dark red tie, in front of the big blue and gold FBI seal on the paneled wall.

"I say it out loud, but these other guys are afraid too."

Marty swung around slowly. Elizabeth Carlisle stood behind him. And Chief Ott from Chicago. It was then that Marty realized he wasn't wearing any clothes. Then the phone on Busch's desk rang. It rang again. It kept on ringing.

"Marty!" Busch was shaking his shoulder but calling his name in a woman's voice. Celia's voice. The dream was so real he couldn't pull out of it.

"Marty! The phone."

He snapped on the night table lamp and grabbed the receiver. "Yeah?" He must have sounded like he was strangling.

"We got a fire, Marty!" Abner Dortman's squawk was way up there in the high register of near-panic.

"Where?"

"In the lab. I saw smoke on the monitor, went out there, and when I opened the door, the fireball like to knock me ass over tin cups. I just turned in the alarm. What do—"

"I'm on my way!" He was already out of bed, shucking off pajamas with his free hand. "Do what you can with extinguishers."

"In all that smoke, they ain't worth a damn, Marty. I—"

"Do what the hell you can till the trucks get there, Abner! Keep people away. Who knows what the hell's in that place. Keep them away from the doors and windows."

He slammed the phone down and saw that Celia had caught some of the fear.

"It's a fire. In the lab building. I've got to get down there."

"Fire! How bad?"

"Don't know. At least nobody's hurt. Yet."

He was on the road in just under five minutes, cursing the K-car's slow pickup. He could see only the glow of CIAS security floods against the dark overcast until he reached the booth on Route 550. Then he saw rolls of smoke clouding the two-mile distant halo of the floods.

To his surprise, Joe Blanchard's Chevy screeched up to the booth as Marty began to make the turn. Marty jammed his brakes. Blanchard, white stubble making his face haggard, ducked into Marty's open window.

"Thought I'd better get out here, give Stan a hand."

Marty was aware that Blanchard considered Stanley Prohaska a green kid, but not this green. "It's a fire, Joe, not an attack."

"So Dortman told me." Blanchard's sunken eyes glittered in the glow from the dash lights. "How do we know what it really is, Marty?" So Joe, too, had the built-in suspicion of an old trooper.

To the south, toward Thurmont, sirens screamed, distantly at first, then as they rounded a hillside, startlingly nearer.

"Keep your eyes open, Joe." Marty gunned the Reliant.

"Watch yourself, too, buddy." Blanchard dashed toward the booth's rear door. Prohaska held it open for him, silhouetted against the pale interior light. Some secret outpost, Marty thought. The dumbest citizen must wonder why a tourist info booth was open all night, even in winter.

Marty hit his brakes again as the Thurmont pumper roared around the tight turn into the CIAS access road, its horn blares mingling with the siren's shrieks. Ungodly ear-shattering howls and blasts hit Marty physically, thudded into the pit of his stomach.

More lights flashed beyond the trees that lined Route 550. A second fire truck, smaller but with an even shriller siren, blared around the turn and drummed down the straight access road.

Marty began to pull out a second time, then jammed his brakes to let a third emergency vehicle pass, this one a Jeep mounted with a chemical tank and hose reel.

He nosed out more cautiously, then followed the parade. Halfway along the two-mile stretch, yet another vehicle pulled close behind him, its red-and-white emergency blinkers flashing frantically. He pulled over to let a yellow rescue truck rush past. This one was from Gettysburg. Gettysburg? Everybody was getting into the act.

Chubby-faced Leon Fedderson was on the gate shift. He hopped from one foot to the other like an overexcited, blue-uniformed leprechaun. "G'wan in, Chief! Might's well drive right over the lawn to the lab. Everybody else has." Fedderson seemed to be having a ball.

Marty bumped the Reliant over the low curb at the south end of the parking area and skittered along the fresh truck tracks in the snow. The fence-mounted floods bathed the compound in dazzling brilliance. Everything stood out in too-sharp focus. The rescue truck had pulled between the two buildings, but the real activity was around the far end of the shedlike lab structure. Smoke billowed from two windows down there, boiled upward for a hundred feet, then was shredded on the night wind.

He slewed the Reliant to a stop near the lab's southwest corner. The packed snow was turning to ice. Abner Dortman ran out of the crowd at the lab's rear entrance, his uniform cap slapped on the back of his head.

"Don't know what started it, Chief. Nobody in here all day."

"Nobody?" They shouted over the roar of the pumper's engine.

" 'Cept Reifsnyder. Had to pick up a notebook he forgot."

Reifsnyder! "When?"

"Maybe half an hour before the fire started."

"Where is he now?"

Dortman swung his head around, searching the clump of people near the trucks. "Dunno. Haven't seen him since."

"How about Carlisle?"

Dortman jabbed a thumb at the crowd. Marty plowed through it until he found her. She clutched a moss green housecoat unevenly around her shivering nightgowned body. He'd never seen her with her black hair down, and he was startled that it fell below her shoulders. She looked like a confused little girl.

"Doctor!"

She was absorbed in the confusion of entering and exiting firemen. He gripped her surprisingly soft shoulder. "Dr. Carlisle, have you seen Dr. Reifsnyder?"

"Albert? No, not since supper." She turned uncertainly toward Marty, eyes wide and red-rimmed from the acrid smoke that drifted from the lab's rear entrance. "Oh, Lieutenant Horn. But you're not on duty tonight."

"I'm always on call, Doctor."

A burly firefighter clumped out of the lab, boots slithering

199

on the crusty lawn, chief's badge gleaming on his helmet. At his emergence, the truck's howl subsided to a mutter.

"It's out, ma'am. Seems to have started in that corner room there." He nodded his blunt face toward Moyle's area. "In the trashbasket. Then it spread to the chemicals. One of the jugs was on its side, top unscrewed. Some kind of oily residue in it. Had to fill the place with foam. Hell of a mess, but it's out." He turned away to shout something to his men.

"What's in there?"

She stared up at Marty, trying to pull herself together.

"Damn it, what's in the lab that somebody would want to steal?"

"Steal?"

"A wastebasket fire, a container of oil tipped over with the top off. It's got to be a diversion. What the hell is in there that's worth this kind of thing?" He fought his impulse to grab her by the arms and shake her.

"Look around you, Doctor!" He swung a frantic arm around the garishly lighted scene. Only a faint drift of smoke escaped the rear door now, but the smell of burnt substances soured the air. There were hoses, firemen, and dirty ice everywhere.

The chief returned, picking his footing carefully. "We'll be out of here in another half hour. Understand you're the security chief?"

Marty nodded.

"Suspicious origin fire."

"You're certain?" Elizabeth Carlisle's face was chalky in the floodlights' wash.

"Yes, ma'am. I'll have to send in an inspector tomorrow morning," he said to Marty.

"This is a classified government installation," Elizabeth Carlisle bristled. Her indignation seemed incongruous with her teenager's hair and askew housecoat. "And I am the person in charge!"

"It's a security matter now," Marty shot back, "and I'm responsible for that." He turned to the firefighter. "You and your boys did a fine job, Chief. Thank them for us. And the guys from the rescue squad in Gettysburg."

"From Gettysburg? Hell, man, we never called them. Even if we had, they couldn't have gotten here this quick."

"You sure?"

"Sure I'm sure."

"Well, they're parked back there between the two buildings right now." Then Marty's stomach constricted. He whirled back to face Dr. Carlisle. "I need to know right now: *What's in there that's worth all this?*"

She bristled at his anger, then her eyes darted to the big fire chief.

"Tomorrow," he said hastily, touched his helmet and was gone.

"Dr. Strakhan's development," she said so low he almost missed it.

"Is it portable?"

"Yes. About one hundred sixty pounds, I understand."

"What's it do?"

"You don't have a need to know, Lieutenant."

"*What's it do?*"

Her voice seemed to come from a distance. "Projects emotions. It's not perfected. He tried it just once. In late October. His preliminary report said he couldn't accurately focus—"

"Abner!" Marty shouted. Near the lab door, Dortman turned. "That truck between the buildings. We've got to—"

He heard the engine's howl before he saw the vehicle. Then it shot into the open lawn, slewed wildly as the driver fought for control. The rear swung wide. The driver spun the wheel to straighten the skid, but he didn't let up on the gas.

The truck's tight northward swing became a skidding sweep that erupted a fan of tire-chewed ice. The rear bumper smashed into the triple fencing hard enough to crumple the inside run into the electrified center fence.

The night exploded in a blue-white crackle, momentarily

blinding Marty and Dortman and everyone else who stared at the fleeing truck. Then the overloaded circuit failed. The floodlights faded to black. The compound plunged into darkness, save for the cluster of firetruck floods at the end of the lab building.

The fleeing rescue truck bounced over the curb into the parking area.

"Fedderson'll stop him." Dortman's words were already behind him as Marty scrambled for his car.

Fedderson apparently assumed that the power failure was part of the fire problem. From his gate position, he did not have a view of the fenced area the truck had rammed. To him, Marty realized, the truck was an emergency vehicle, an ambulance presumably rushing an injured party to the medical center in Thurmont.

Not only did Corporal Leon Fedderson not try to stop the truck. He stepped clear and waved it through.

CHAPTER
15

"DAMN!" THE CHUNKY gate guard wore an expression of anguish. "I just let 'em tear on through, Chief."

"Call the security booth," Marty rapped. "Tell Joe to *stop that truck!*"

"Blanchard's on duty?" Fedderson's words were lost in the Reliant's acceleration. Joe Blanchard wouldn't let them get past him. Korea, Nam—Blanchard was a pro.

Fedderson's panicky call took less than a minute but far longer than it should have because he couldn't get his tumbling words organized until Blanchard yelled at him to shut up, then tell it right. In that time, the truck raced nearly a mile. When Fedderson finally made sense and Blanchard grabbed the awkward MBA Gyrojet pistol, the truck was no more than sixty yards distant, already decelerating a shade to enter the turn into Route 550.

Blanchard crouched in the middle of the access road pavement, legs spread wide, the pistol steadied in both hands. He squinted against the onrushing headlights. He knew damned well the truck was not going to stop. He aimed between the blinding high beams and pulled the broad trigger.

The pistol flared in his hands as the propellant ignited and flashed through the four venturi vents just above his knuckles. The rocket-boosted projectile zinged down the roadway like an oversized tracer bullet, straight for the onrushing truck. Then it dipped, struck the icy pavement, deflected sharply upward and burned out three hundred feet over the valley.

"Son of a bitch!" Blanchard muttered. No wonder the damned weapon had been turned down by the armed services. What penny-bending politician had saddled federal security with it!

The headlights were on top of him. He dove to his left. The right front tire scrabbled past, kicked up ice spray and loose gravel inches from his feet. Joe Blanchard rolled, fired again from his prone position. The second missile streaked beneath the truck to detonate with a sharp crack in the snow-clad bank across the state road.

The truck fishtailed north. Blanchard scrambled to his feet, ran into the main road, leveled the clumsy Gyrojet, and fired the remaining three missiles in quick succession.

The cluster of bright light points streaked after the fleeing vehicle. Then they diverged. One struck a small tree and blasted its trunk in two. The sapling fell across the pavement as the truck passed, a fraction of a second too late to impede its escape. The second missile burned itself out in the snow on the right side of the highway and failed to explode.

The third missile of the cluster bored straight in on the truck's running lights. Then it began to wobble, painting a zig-zag flame trail against the night. It tumbled, hit the back of the truck sideways, fell to the road and blew up in a blinding flash.

The truck's lights dwindled. "Hell!" Blanchard cried.

A car skidded to a stop close behind him, its headlight beams angled across the highway. Marty Horn stuck his head out. Across the road, Stan Prohaska peered out of the security booth, looking distraught.

"Damn Gyrojet's not worth a—"

"I saw, Joe. Get on the phone fast. Give the state cops a description. Notify Walt Busch in Hagerstown." Damn right, notify Walt.

"About what, for God's sake?" Joe's breath came in frantic vapor gusts.

"Check with Carlisle. She'll tell you enough. I'm going after them."

Prohaska finally trotted across the road toward them. Great reflexes there. Marty tramped on the accelerator. Whatever Joe shouted was lost in the scream of his tires on ice. Then the front-wheel drive took hold, hauled the Reliant around the corner, and he raced up 550, leaning forward to urge the low-powered car to its limit.

He trailed them with his lights out, not an easy trick but one made practical by the near-luminous snow edging the road. He could take a chance on cars coming the other way. But if one caught up to him from the rear, he wasn't sure what he'd do about that.

He needn't have worried. The truck, which he had in sight after the first mile, was making time, rolling as fast as it could under far from perfect road conditions: pavement scraped by plows to a thin coating of packed snow with ice glaze where it had melted then refrozen.

Marty was totally familiar with the first few miles; it was his route home. They passed his house seven miles out. The downstairs lights were on. Celia probably wondered what the hell had happened to him.

Then the road climbed more steeply to wind along the eastern edge of the Catoctins. The truck's lights were visible only intermittently now, glimpsed on infrequent tangents between swooping curves.

They whipped past the sleeping crossroads at Lantz. The countryside began to open into occasional fields among the decreasing patches of woods. Farming country. People went to bed early out here. There wasn't a light for miles.

Marty let the Reliant fall further back. He could keep the truck in sight at greater distances in this open country. Eight minutes later, it slowed then turned into what in the gray distance looked like—had to be—a farm.

He slowed to a crawl, thankful now for the small quiet engine. A quarter mile short of where he judged the truck had turned in, he pulled off the road into an area that had been cleared beneath a grove of white pines for access to a cluster of RFD mail boxes.

He stepped out and closed the car door noiselessly. Sound traveled too well in the dense air of a cold night. He felt totally alone out here. How long would it take thinly dispersed state police units to converge on the Thurmont area, even if CIAS security were able to get them right on it? Whatever was to happen in the next few minutes was all his. No doubt about that. It was all up to a written-off cop who'd been sent to professional Siberia.

To muffle his footsteps, he eased along the powdery snow of the roadside shoulder. He wished he'd had the foresight to pull on his boots, but he'd rushed out of the house wearing only his thin black uniform shoes. His toes were already beginning to numb.

The night was dull gray beneath the low overcast. And dead silent. He placed his feet carefully, moving now in the cover of a stand of winter-stripped roadside brush, ears set for the slightest sound. He had almost reached the farm. The silence was unnerving. Had he somehow misjudged the point where the truck had turned off?

Then he heard a door open. Men's voices, too low for him to make out the words, drifted to him on the light breeze.

He heard a vehicle door slam. The truck?

He reached the end of the brush line. A driveway. From the cover of a big juniper, he made out the bulk of a small barn. Apparently they'd parked the truck in there. As he squinted into the darkness, stock-still behind his unreliable cover, two men emerged. Judging from their gusty breathing, they carried an object of some weight. Was one of them Reifsnyder? And did they carry the Strakhan device?

Damn the Federal Security Forces and its bare-bones

budget! He'd asked for vehicle radios, but the request had been denied—twice. With a radio in his Reliant, he could have hurried back to where it was parked, called the state cops and had this place covered in short order. If it then turned out to be a false alarm, he would take a fall, but he was willing to chance that. Yes, on a hunch—and some pretty good circumstantial evidence.

But without a radio, the troopers could be wandering around God knew how long trying to find the truck and him. So here he was, isolated somewhere near the Maryland-Pennsylvania line, with no other house visible, in the dead of a winter night, wildly scratching for a way to stop obviously professional thieves and recover a scientific device about which he knew nearly nothing.

Nice, Horn. And your own doing. You could have stayed at CIAS and diddled around watching the fire troops roll their hoses.

Whatever this was, it was all his now. The two men lugged their bulky load across the driveway and up the front steps of the farmhouse. The front door showed a brief rectangle of dim yellow then closed behind them.

Marty decided to move closer to the two-story frame structure. Two ground-floor windows on the near side showed light. Several possibilities here. The house was owned by somebody in on the heist. Or it was deserted until these two guys took it over. Or the owner was away—or had already been disposed of. Marty was willing to make book on the last possibility.

He realized all this deliberation was killing time because killing time was easier than doing something. He felt instinctively that he couldn't long afford not to do something.

When he heard the distant chopper and realized that its stacatto *thock-thock-thock* was growing louder, the whole thing fell into place. Now he knew he didn't have any time left at all.

He felt obvious as hell, hunched in his dark blue alpaca-collared jacket and fur-lined trooper's storm hat. But the

two guys should be in the rear of the house, obviously waiting for the helicopter to spot this place in the gray-and-black
patchwork of fields and woods. Surely one of them was
hanging out the back door signaling by flashlight by now.
That would leave only one inside. And with luck, his attention would be concentrated toward the approaching copter.

The aircraft was no more than three miles distant now,
from the sound of it, no doubt flying low under the radar
sweeps from Camp David to the southwest. No more time to
shuffle around in the ankle-deep snow, wishing to hell somebody else would suddenly appear to take sensible charge of
this; wishing he were more of a macho cop and less of a
washed-up psycho on what was supposed to have been old
man's retirement duty. No time left to figure out a better
plan.

He pulled his .44 from its frost-stiffened holster and went
in.

On the topmost of the three steps, his foot slipped. So did
his brain. Back a cog to an eon ago. Another time, another
house. Chicago. A rotting slum house like so many neglected
single-family structures in Chicago's southward sprawl.

He fell to one knee, caught himself with an outflung
hand. Was this Chicago or Maryland farmland? For an instant he wasn't sure. But in that frozen sliver of time, he was
sure what was going to happen behind that door. The man
was big, in a dirty T-shirt and tattered jeans. He slammed
the four-foot one-by-six flat into Marty's belly. Marty fell
backwards, fighting to hold a bare thread of consciousness.
The big bastard scooped up his gun, swung it with both
hands, centered its muzzle on Marty's forehead.

As he grabbed the rickety banister and pulled himself up,
Marty heard footsteps on the stairs behind him. The big
guy's glare flicked away—for just a fraction of a second.
That had to be enough.

Marty threw himself sideways. At that instant, his Police
Special bucked in the big ape's hands, blasted the hallway in
a thunderclap of searing fire. Plaster chips whizzed. A pall

208

of dust and cordite reek filled the narrow space. Marty whirled toward a gasped *"Oh!"* Then her body tumbled down the rest of the stairs and thudded into his knees.

"God, no!" the big man screamed. "No! Oh, *God!*"And he shoved the revolver's muzzle up under his chin and blew his brains into the ceiling.

With only reflex left, Marty bent down, took the gun from the twitching fingers, then just stood there. That's how they found him.

All this time he had lived in the hideous fear that what he had done in Chicago would destroy him. But the serpent lurking in his brain had been a fraud. A fake!

The paneled door of the farmhouse snapped into focus. He felt strength surge through him. He knew what he had to do, and there was no hesitation in him now. He raised his foot and slammed it just below the knob.

The door flew inward.

"Freeze!" he roared and crouched low with both hands locked around the searching .44.

The shattered door exposed a large sparsely furnished living room, dimly illuminated by the light from the kitchen beyond. An empty living room. From the kitchen came ominous silence. The light back there went out. Outside, the copter's rotor thud moved in.

Then from the kitchen shadows came a flash but no sound. Something snapped just below Marty's left ear, blew a chunk of alpaca into a little cloud and thudded into the door jamb.

Marty dived for the floor. He'd been shot at before with a silencer, but not one as silent as this.

From the bottom of the dark rectangle of the kitchen entrance came the flash and bark of a small caliber automatic. That Marty cound understand. He returned fire twice as he back-pedaled on knees and elbows for the front door. He heard the back door open, rising the chopper's blat to a roar. The thing was landing.

All right, you bastards! Change of tactics. He whirled,

leaped down the front steps and skirted the house on the driveway side, keeping close to the clapboard siding.

At the corner, he eased his head around. The two of them had started to lug the thing down the three steps of the small back stoop. He could have gone through the house if he'd waited a few seconds. They must have figured they'd gotten him with the automatic. As best he could make out in the fuzzy luminescence from the snow, they were occupied with their clumsy burden from the truck in the barn, though the smaller man also carried a bulky-looking rifle in his left hand while he scrabbled for a better handhold with his right. The bigger man—Reifsnyder, Marty could see now—wrestled with the machine with both arms.

The helicopter chuffed impatiently on the nearest level area, seventy yards from the porch.

Now or never. Marty gripped the revolver with both hands and jumped from the corner into a straddle-crouch.

"Hold it right there!"

To his amazement, the night exploded above him. He felt a blow to his left arm. There were three of them! They'd set him up, and the guy still in the house had read him like a book. Marty pitched backward, his arm numbed by shock.

"Got him!" the man in the kitchen window yelled. "I got—"

His shout was swallowed in the roar of the .44. Marty fired flat on his back. Twice—the two shots so close together they sounded like one.

The ambusher lunged half out of the window and hung by his belly over the sill, arms dangling. His pistol dropped into the snow beneath the window.

Now only the bulky Strakhan device was on the porch. Reifsnyder and the other guy had ducked back into the kitchen.

Above Marty's head, the body half out of the window dripped black down the siding. Now what?

* * *

"We're going out there." Rollo Stark whispered hoarsely in Kooven's ear. "You're my hostage, understand?"

"He'll never swallow that."

Jeez, this clown was dense. "He'll have to swallow it," Stark pointed out. "You think he's going to let a CIAS resident get knocked off? You just said he's the chief of the people assigned to protect you. You pick up that thing and we'll get our asses out to that chopper while he does nothing but watch."

"That 'thing' weighs one hundred fifty-seven pounds. And it has no lifting handles."

Stark hesitated only a moment. "Then leave it."

"Leave it! It's the reason we're here. It's the reason for all of this!"

"The contract is blown." All but the final part, but he sure wasn't going to tell Reifsnyder that. No sense warning the guy about what was going to happen to him when they reached the chopper. "Look, either you carry that thing out of here, or it stays here."

He prodded the big bastard's side with the fat-barreled Lisle.

"You know damned well I can't carry it alone."

Stark sensed in his tone that the big mushy scientist had begun to realize he really was a hostage.

"What did you say that clown's name is?"

"Horn. It's Horn out there."

Stark moved nearer the open door. "Horn! You hear me, Horn? I've got your man in here, and I've got a gun on him. Him and me are going to walk on out of here, and you're not going to do a damned thing about it, you hear me? One move outta you, and he gets it right in the kidneys. You got that?"

Silence. Then low in the night, Horn's voice: "I got it."

"Use your brain, Horn. You're getting the damned machine back—"

"No!" Reifsnyder sounded like he was strangling. "There's got to be—"

211

"There isn't." Stark prodded him again with the Lisle's big muzzle. If Horn realized the thing was a specialized single-shot sniper's carbine . . . "Move your ass out there."

The scientist stepped out on the little open porch. "Hold it there," Stark ordered. "Horn, he gets it if you so much as twitch, you hear me?"

The guy's voice was low and lethal. "I hear you."

Reifsnyder looked down at the thing they had lugged this far, the thing all this had been planned for, worked for, and now blown.

"You want to strain your balls lifting that damned box, be my guest, Reifsnyder."

In the dull light from the snow blanket, he saw Reifsnyder's mouth set in a thin line. Then the big man started down the steps. All that was left to do now, Stark told himself, was to get out to the chopper, no problem with that, then complete at least half of this contract. He was going to put a bullet through this clown's head with an unusual degree of pleasure.

Marty stood in the open now, his .44 hanging impotently at his side, a taste of bile in his throat. The bitter taste of futility. He'd often wondered how he would react in a "hostage situation," as the Federal Security Forces Operational Manual so cutely called it. Now he knew.

He wasn't about to do a damned thing. What were the choices? Blast them both? He had the machine back. And everything he had against Reifsnyder was circumstantial. That was a degree up from hunch but still not conclusive.

Great, Horn. He had to stand here and watch. And that's what he did. Stood and watched. Watched as the smaller man climbed aboard, watched as he raised the strange fat rifle. And watched the silent stab of blue-white fire snake out at Reifsnyder. Then watched Reifsnyder fall.

God!

The helicopter's *chuff-chuff-chuff* blended into a roar.

The chopper rose, swung around, pointed its nose his way and came on.

The rotor howl was deafening. The chopper turned, hovered a hundred feet above him. A streak of white fire reached out. The bullet thudded into the porch flooring beside him.

He grabbed the rickety wooden rail and swung up the steps fast. The skin on his back quivered, waited for the second shot. A third. None came, but the copter hovered up there, a floating sniper's platform out of pistol range.

Marty dived through the open kitchen door, whirled. Out in the field, the crumpled dark figure that had to be Reifsnyder sat up. They saw that from the chopper, too. It turned and slid back over the open field.

Marty steadied his two-handed grip against the door jamb. In range or not, he pumped off three. Like firing at the wind. The chopper began a tight circuit of the field, came in low over the struggling man in the snow.

They're going to finish the job, Marty realized. If he'd been wrong about Reifsnyder—He was sworn to protect CIAS people and property. He had the property here on the porch, but a CIAS resident was at risk out there. Damned high risk.

He had the property. Right here in front of him.

Another stab of flame from the helicopter. But Reifsnyder still moved. The copter drifted off again. Turned back. As if the odd rifle needed reloading time.

If he only had a weapon that could reach out there. All he had was a now empty .44, whatever was left in the weapon the kitchen ambusher had dropped in the snow. And the Strakhan machine.

Ice rippled down his spine. Was it possible?

It looked like a big metal box, the size of a two-drawer filing cabinet. Electrical. It had a three-prong plug. And some sort of lensed opening at one end.

What had Elizabeth Carlisle told him out there in the

213

wind and ice and burnt smell? It projects emotions? Strak-han had tested it once . . . in October?

October.

The helicopter's engine picked up revs. There was another gunfire flash, but again he heard no sound of the shot. The distant form that was Reifsnyder seemed to jump sideways. In the near darkness, from a moving platform, they were killing him by inches.

October! The realization hit him all at once. That crazy afternoon when he'd gone into a rage, then a giggling fit all by himself in the security office. A string of inexplicable emotions. From this damned thing?

He stared at it then at the chopper. Its engine accelerated for another pass at the lonely figure in the snow. Do I have one last hope here, Marty wondered. Or one last dumb ef-fort by a cop who'd already blown it?

He manhandled the thing through the kitchen door, searched frantically for an electrical outlet, found one over the sink. Two-prong. Damn! No opening for the ground prong.

To hell with the ground prong. He mashed it sideways against the sharp edge of the sink and jabbed the plug home. He pointed the lens end of the clumsy unit out the open door, realizing for the first time that the flesh wound on his left arm hurt and he was leaking blood down his sleeve. He ignored that and flipped up every switch he could find along the sides of the device.

It hummed. A tiny tongue of magenta light pulsed from the lens aperture toward the hovering aircraft. Marty jumped back, the hairs on his neck rising. He could feel the power of the thing in his gut.

He looked past the open door into the field. Out there, as the helicopter came around again much lower, the man in the snow struggled into a defensive crouch.

The first pulses from Strakhan's projector lanced into Koo-ven's brain like whizzing shards of molten metal. He felt a

214

burst of uncontrollable fear, rose suddenly to his knees then felt fear dissolve in a hot wash of anger. Next he had an overpowering urge to weep.

And with it all came a tidal sweep of pain. Fiery billows of it darted through his skull and vibrated cruelly through every tissue of his brain.

Was this a deserved punishment for his failure? The moon-faced man had panicked when Horn had incredibly crashed out of the night. He had left the third man behind as a sacrificial rear guard then had even abandoned the device for which all of this had been so carefully planned and executed.

But the moon-faced man was trying to carry out what Kooven now realized was the final part of his assignment: he was intent on killing Kooven.

He couldn't even do that well. The flame from his infernal silent rifle had seared Kooven's cheek when the helicopter unexpectedly rose as Kooven was about to climb aboard. The bullet had lodged in his thigh. He had fallen back, the helicopter had made several passes, and the rifle had flamed again, pocking the snow close to him. Then the awesome brain pulsations had begun.

The aircraft was close above him now, its blue exhaust flaring against the overcast.

Suddenly it veered hard left, then yawed right. As if . . . as if the pilot were experiencing the same repeated jolts of fear, anger, then confusing depression that swept over Kooven.

The copter slanted down in a long, shallow dive, pulled up abruptly. Its blunt nose rose steeply, then vertically upward. Then past vertical.

The helicopter flopped over on its back. The nose plunged. The engine roar wound into a banshee howl. The copter bulleted downward, a huge deadweight dart spitting blue exhaust flame.

It slammed into the field a hundred yards from Kooven and exploded into a blinding gout of red-orange fire. The fireball rolled upward, a twisting donut of flame that pulled a trail of black smoke behind it.

But Kooven was barely aware of the impact. He had clapped his hands around his searing skull. His brain was aflame, a broiling mass of pain. He was dying.

Damn the moon-faced man and Elizabeth Carlisle and Horn—all of them! The pain was incredible. His head was bursting open. *"Damn you, Lefroid!"* he shouted.

He twisted in final agony. Someone ran toward him.

The pain stopped.

He looked up in confusion. "Lieutenant Horn? Is that you? What are—" Then he looked down. He was on his knees. In snow. "What I am doing here?"

Marty Horn crouched beside him. "You've been hit. Let me take a look at that leg."

He could see that Horn had been hit, too. A glistening stain spread down his sleeve.

"Flesh wound. We're both lucky." Horn stood and reached down to help him up. "What was that you were yelling?"

"Yelling?" This all was impossibly confusing.

"Sounded like 'Freud.' "

" 'Freud'? I have no idea."

"Do you know who you are?" Horn asked suddenly. He seemed serious.

"What an absurd question. I'm Dr. Reifsnyder. Albert Reifsnyder. You know me."

For what seemed an endless moment, the security officer stared into Reifsnyder's eyes.

"I think I do, Doctor," he said. "I think I do now."

Greta Heissen had never felt more in need of therapeutic escape, as she called it, than at this moment. Lefroid had been impossible since the very first obscure news report that announced the western Maryland helicopter crash. He had spoken to her as no man should ever speak to a woman. She was humiliated, then infuriated.

There was no way she could retaliate without inexorably involving herself. Her only recourse was the centuries-old physical release of *Nei Ching* and its painfully learned modifications.

She lay relaxed in the tepid bath, the meridian blockers in place. The numbness they produced glided through her like exquisite balm. All physical sensitivity was channeled by the meridian blockers to the excruciatingly sensitive focus center.

She positioned the delicate third needle precisely, inching it against the encroaching numbness of her arm. *Lefroid,* she thought suddenly. A burst of fury made her react without judgment for the first time in her life. The hair-thin thread of tempered steel glinted in the bathroom light as it plunged—far deeper than the breadth of a sesame seed, far beyond that limit set so long ago by the wisest of ancient practitioners.

Her body convulsed in a spasm of consuming agony. Her spine arched. Her head flew back, struck the edge of the tub as her upper body accelerated under the tension of lightning-fast muscle contraction. She died of a fractured skull without knowing she was fatally hurt.

Seven days later, Merrill Hunnicutt of Pitcher, Wilsen and Hunnicutt, checked his "tickler file." Could he have missed the never-before-omitted call from Ms. Heissen? He checked one more time with his secretary. There was no mistake. No call had come through.

He removed his horn-rimmed glasses and rubbed the bridge of his nose. He hated these arrangements. Book clubs might build fortunes on negative response, but to a lawyer, it was a hazardous way to do things. Nevertheless, he had accepted a fat fee to do exactly as the odd Ms. Heissen had directed.

He rose from his desk, a young-old man with white hair framing a pink-cheeked face, and withdrew the typed instructions from his files, broke the seal, read slowly. Then, on his desk terminal, he tapped in the access code and typed in

217

those instructions. He made a tent of his fingers, sat back, then was aghast at the amber-tinted revelations that began to spurt across his CRT.

When he realized Gerta was missing, Lefroid could not escape the hot wave of near panic that broke over him. Then he forced himself to think.

She had warned him about her self-protection arrangement. In general terms. Was it credible that she would put herself at such risk in the event that she somehow simply missed one of the periodic contacts necessary to keep the recorded revelations in check? Would anyone, particularly a woman as intelligent as Gerta, place herself in such personal jeopardy?

On the other hand, she was indeed smart enough to bluff him. And that put her at no complex risk, only the risk that he might see through her.

André Lefroid, master of complex dealings, shrewd judge and ruthless manipulator of people, was in his office when the three FBI agents arrived. He was still trying to decide whether Gerta had been bluffing.

Marty Horn found himself singing in the shower, something he hadn't done for years. Then he was aware of Celia outside the stall shouting at him.

"Hey! Turn off the water. Open up. I've got something to show you."

He came out dripping. "What the hell?"

She held it up shyly. "Look, just came in the mail. It's out."

"Your cookbook? I'll be damned! *One Hundred Ways to Serve the Lowly Potato.* That's what it's about? Potatoes?"

"Careful, you'll get it wet. It goes on sale this week in Hagerstown and twelve Baltimore bookstores are going to take it. A couple in Washington, too."

He took her by the shoulders. "That's really something,

lady. Why didn't you tell me what a big thing you were up to?"

She held his eyes. "I didn't think you—that you were ready to accept . . ." She set the book on the sink counter and slid her arms around his neck. "You were so . . . troubled."

"Gutless. I'll say it for you."

"No, not that." Her housecoat-clad body was warm against his naked skin. "More like no confidence."

"That was up to nine days ago. I left it all back there. Everything's new for us from now on. New and good."

"I want to keep working, Marty. On books like this." She leaned back to watch his face.

"I wouldn't dare get in the way."

"But what about you?"

"I might stay at CIAS. I might not. Carlisle shipped Reif-snyder off to Walter Reed, then asked me to stay. If I do, it's up a whole GS grade. That's what I call remorse. But you can do books anywhere, right?"

"Anywhere. Anywhere you want."

"Before we decide, woman," he said gruffly, "get out of those damp clothes."

She giggled. "Marty, you don't mean—"

"Sure do."

She came back to him softly nude. "Lover, you know I can't make it any way except—"

He pulled her into the stall and turned on the warm water, and they clung to each other shouting with laughter as the torrent seemed to melt away the coldness that had grown between them.

"Yes, you can. Now you can." He could feel his strength flowing to her. He knew she could feel it too.

She looked up, her curious white-lashed eyes more vulnerable than he had ever remembered them. Her arms tightened around him.

"Yes, I can," she said.